D1125528

PRAISE FOR
Dressed to Keel

"Wow! This is the cruise you don't want to miss. Twisted, wicked, and outrageously funny, it's a great read for a lazy summer afternoon. With a story like this, Candy Calvert is the perfect cruise director!"

—Dianne Drake, author of Playing Games

"Dressed to Keel is an accomplishment not to be ignored. Ms. Calvert is one of the newer murder-mystery authors to watch."

—Alan Paul Curtis, reviewer, Who-Dunnit.com

FORTHCOMING BY CANDY CALVERT

Aye Do or Die

Dressed

to

Keel

DEDICATION

For Mom, a strongly independent woman with a sassy wit, a green thumb, sunshine on her face, and—always—a book in her hands. I'm so very honored to hand you my book. And for Dad, the supreme storyteller. Your dauntless energy inspires me.

ACKNOWLEDGMENTS

My heartfelt thanks to:

Literary agent Natasha Kern—for launching this dream and for your passionate encouragement of future dreams. Acquiring editor Barbara Moore—for loving this story and its crazy crew of characters enough to invite us to sail under the Midnight Ink flag. My editor Karl—for his expertise and his patience with a rookie author so full of questions. Alison, Kelly, Kevin, Jennifer, Eric, and the entire Midnight Ink and Llewellyn team—for the dedicated work and talent required in getting this book on its voyage.

Ruth Widener (formerly of the Kern Agency)—for unwavering support and for calling yourself my very first fan. Writing coach Gloria Kempton and my talented online critique partners—this book would never be possible without you folks. My heroic co-workers in the medical professions—this dose of love and laughter is to honor you.

My children—nothing compares with hearing you say, "We knew you'd do it, Mom." And especially to Andy, my husband and real-life hero—for countless laughs, twirls on the dance floor, cruises into foreign sunsets . . . and for never doubting that this dream would launch.

Candy Calvert

Dressed

to

Keel

MIDNIGHT INK
WOODBURY, MINNESOTA

Dressed to Keel © 2006 by Candy Calvert. All rights reserved. No part of this book may be used or reproduced in any manner whatsoever, including Internet usage, without written permission from Midnight Ink except in the case of brief quotations embodied in critical articles and reviews.

First Edition
First Printing, 2006

Book design by Donna Burch
Book format by Steffani Chambers
Cover design by Kevin Brown
Cover Illustration© by Kun-Sung Chung

Midnight Ink, an imprint of Llewellyn Publications

Library of Congress Cataloging-in-Publication Data
Calvert, Candy, 1950–
  Dressed to keel / Candy Calvert.—1st ed.
      p. cm.
  ISBN-13: 978-0-7387-0879-9
  ISBN-10: 0-7387-0879-8
  1. Cruise ships—Fiction 2. Nurses—Fiction. 3. Vacations—Fiction.
  I. Title.
  PS3603.A4463D74 2006
  813'.6—dc22

                                                              2006041884

This is a work of fiction. Names, characters, places, and incidents are either the product of the author's imagination or are used fictitiously, and any resemblance to actual persons, living or dead, business establishments, events, or locales is entirely coincidental.

Midnight Ink
Llewellyn Publications
2143 Wooddale Drive, Dept. 0-7387-0879-8
Woodbury, MN 55125-2989, U.S.A.
www.midnightinkbooks.com

Printed in the United States of America

ONE

THE CRUISE BROCHURE PROMISED confetti, melting wedges of Brie, well-stuffed tuxedos, and silver buckets of Dom Pérignon. Glamorous, right? You bet. The Fall Foliage Tour would be a quiet time to mull things over and re-think my muddled life while sailing from New York to Canada and back. Boston, Bar Harbor, Halifax, and Quebec City, it all sounded wonderful. But the fact was that right then, right that minute, I was basically fighting to stay upright on a treadmill surrounded by miles of ominous ocean. More than weird. Like planting my pink Nikes on some sweaty, revolving techno island. And damned dangerous, too. Champagne was the last thing on my mind. *Jeez*—was that a whale?

I let go of one handgrip to push a sopping strand of my reddish hair back toward a ponytail that was starting to frizz like a Chia Pet. My fingers trembled as I glanced toward the huge window again. I was used to dodging doggy doo and spiky-haired skateboarders when I jogged—no biggie—but a rubber-lipped, blowhole-topped, Pinocchio-eating whale? Unbelievable. God's truth, I should've fallen flat on my face and been catapulted across the ship's gym when the thing surfaced near the window in front of me. But I kept running, with the relentless rhythm of my nurse's clogs across the ER floors back home. I was sweating and puffing and getting absolutely nowhere. Nowhere—career and treadmill both. And if that wasn't enough, now there was a teeny woman in a zebra-print leotard calling my name and peppering me with questions. That bingo champion, Edie Greenbaum, was about my grandma's age, I'd guess. I'd been trying to avoid her since before Monstro surfaced, but it wasn't working. Her zebra stripes shimmered in my peripheral vision like I was wearing 3-D glasses. I was getting queasy. Maybe if I pretended that I was engrossed in the TV, she'd go away.

"Miss Cavanaugh . . . Darcy? Yoo hoo?"

No. I'd been trying to be polite but there was a limit. This cruise was supposed to be about hanging out with my best friend, eating great food . . . okay, and maybe making an ass of myself doing that chicken dance in the Lobster Disco last night. I should never, under any circumstances, drink rum. But I was still entitled to some shred of dignity, right?

"Well, dear?" Edie squinted at me through rhinestone-trimmed bifocals and smiled, tipping her pinkish blonde head backward in order to see my face. At five-eight I would tower over her by at least a foot, even if I were standing on the floor beside her. There was a lipstick speckle on her front tooth. Or maybe some of that incredible cherry tart from the lunch buffet.

"Mmm." I ran my tongue over my teeth, smiled, and then glanced back up at the TV like I hadn't really heard her. The ship's channel was running the infomercial about protecting your valuables, a throaty Elizabeth Taylor impersonator loading jewels into a cabin safe. *"Ladies, give him the key to your heart, but never ever the combination to your safe.*" It was the third time they'd run it since I arrived in the gym. A bit much. But still, there had been all that buzz about some shipboard purse snatchings, and I'd bet that was what Edie wanted to gossip about.

I raised my fingers to my neck and counted my heartbeat for six seconds, multiplied by ten, and compared it to the treadmill's digital display. One hundred sixty? Could that be true?

"Excuse me, Darcy, but I was asking what brings a pretty young lady like you onto a cruise ship full of old folks?"

"What? Oh, pardon me—*whoops.*" I grabbed for the handgrips as the ship rolled and dropped beneath me like a watery earthquake. My gaze darted to the expanse of Plexiglas and the dark ocean beyond. A whale couldn't tip a ship over, could it?

Edie Greenbaum patted her cotton candy hair and grinned up at me; wiry little legs splaying wide as she hunkered down and swayed with the wave motion like a salty merchant marine. Her perfectly lined eyes twinkled behind her glasses and she batted blue-tipped lashes.

"First cruise? You'll get used to it, sweetie. Same with that awful roar of the cabin toilets. Won't really suck your tushie in. Relax. It takes time," she patted her zebra-striped thighs, "to develop your sea legs."

I tried to smile. "Of course. No problem. I'm sorry, but did you . . . ask me . . . something, before?" My words came out in short puffs even though I'd slowed my jog to half-pace. I was barely thirty years old and, except for some therapeutic macaroni and cheese binges, I was far too fit to be winded like this. What was wrong?

The woman cackled and tapped a jewel-studded fingernail against my hipbone. "My husband, Bernie—you know, he works in the show? Well, we have a bet going with a few of the other passengers about why a lovely young thing like you would be traveling with a crowd of Florida retirees." She clucked and tugged at my waistband. "I mean, look at you, dear. What is that little waist of yours, all of twenty-five inches?" Her gaze climbed, eyes squinting like she was checking the odds on a racetrack tote board, until her eyes fixed on my neon-striped Lycra tank. She was checking out my breasts. "Genuine articles?"

Oh my God. I coughed and stepped sideways on the treadmill to avoid the woman's probing fingers. The waistband stretched wide and my brows rose in disbelief. I was being felt up by a Munchkin! Where was my best friend when I needed her?

"Hey, Edie. *Easy there.*" My voice climbed as her grip tightened.

"And those coppery curls, peachy skin, and green eyes," she oozed. "Like a wild Irish rose, I told my Bernie." She sighed and winked up at me, lowering her voice like a conspirator. "I'm betting on love, a broken heart. You've gone to sea to forget some scrumptious man?" She belched, exuding a waft of garlic. "Excuse me, dear, midnight buffet. Absolutely delicious. So, why are you here?"

I pressed a fingertip to the digital controls and felt the treadmill begin to slow. Enough was enough. Time to tell my cover story again. About why I'd grabbed the chance to take this cruise, go *anywhere* for that matter. The treadmill slowed to a halt as the ship rolled once more and my stomach lurched. I'd probably get eaten by a whale for what I was about to do. But what the hell? I was feeling more than a little reckless lately.

"It was pretty much the peanut butter and jelly sandwich," I said with a slow smile. Loving it.

Edie raised her precisely drawn brows. "What?"

"Why I came on the cruise. It was the peanut butter and jelly sandwich. White bread, trimmed crust . . ." I paused, enjoying the moment, "and that penis, of course."

I watched Edie Greenbaum's grin dissolve and her mouth form a tight little "O." The woman tilted her head like a cat with ear mites and tapped her fingernail against a tiny plastic hearing aid. She let go of my Danskins and staggered a few steps backward, yanking the appliance out to blow on it.

"*Excu-uuse* me?" She shouted, whining through her nose. Her eyes were wide and her hand was over her heart like she'd just heard the whispered confession of Lorena Bobbitt.

I closed my eyes, shook my head, and sighed. Great. Now I felt guilty. It was the truth though. Well, part of it.

Maybe only another nurse could understand, but there comes a day of reckoning, of self-evaluation. When, after seven years of living in Gumby-green scrubs and feeling a stethoscope smack you in the boobs every time you move, that you start to wonder if there isn't something more—Ann Taylor suits, Prada pumps, a buttery leather attaché case, and a notebook—doing paperwork on a real desk instead of the top of a biohazard waste bin. For me the catalyst had been a peanut butter and jelly sandwich.

It had been like any other day in the emergency department triage office—fevers, kidney stones, and lawn mower injuries, the usual. And really, psychiatric patients were only too common. It must have been my frame of mind that day. The last straw piled onto a growing haystack of career doubts.

I'd read the patient's chief complaint on the sign-in sheet: "Rash."

Suitable for the clinic, I'd thought as I called his name through the microphone. It took forever for the kinky-haired man to walk across the crowded waiting room, maybe because he ambled like a pigeon, bobbing his head with each knock-kneed step. So slow. I'd smiled and waved my hand to encourage him when I noticed that he was clutching a handful of his khakis. At the crotch. *Oh jeez.*

"Got a rash. And bugs, maybe. Green ones," he mumbled, his face solemn and his fist as tight as an outfielder with a last-inning-last-out fly ball.

"Where?" I asked, wishing I didn't have to, knowing I did, and wondering for the very first time what it felt like to be a bank teller.

"Here," he answered.

I was fully prepared to see a penis. That wasn't the problem. In my career as a nurse I'd probably seen hundreds of them, all shapes and sizes and colors, and for that matter had heard all the ridiculous euphemisms.

"I've probably seen more tallywhackers than a hooker," I'd announced after nervously downing two dirty martinis on a blind date last year. The sweaty-palmed little CPA, too short and with no sense of humor, never called me back, of course. My track record with men is pretty pathetic.

Anyway, it wasn't that I was unprepared to see a penis that day. It was just that I wasn't ready to see the half-eaten peanut butter and jelly sandwich in the hand that covered the khaki-clad organ. White bread, no crust, and molded by proximity to the shape of the painful part. And worse—what still made me shudder—was to watch my patient raise the warm, crumpled sandwich to his lips and take a bite. *Ughhh.*

I was fairly sure that as a bank teller—or even an orthotic sales representative, which was my only real alternative—I would never have to witness that phenomenon again.

I looked over at the composite horror and confusion on Edie Greenbaum's face and sighed. Peanut butter and demented flashers? Total lie. Sure, it happened, but nurses didn't leave the profession because of that kind of stuff. Not in a heartbeat. Those tales were the war stories, badges of courage, and hands down the finest topping for any greasy pizza devoured on a holiday night shift. Those things didn't make nurses leave the profession. The truth was so much worse. And it was exactly why I was here in the middle of the Atlantic, and at the mercy of whales, re-thinking my future.

The truth. I ran my tongue across my lip and tasted salt, then shook my head. Pick up a newspaper. The nursing shortage was getting some press, but would people ever really get it? What did they see? Long waits in emergency rooms, re-routing of ambulances, and an alarming rise in insurance costs? Tip of the iceberg. You had to walk in a nurse's shoes to really understand the effects of double shifts, short-staffing, mandatory overtime, and patched-together medical teams with more and more responsibility for sicker and sicker patients. To understand the fatal effects. I squeezed my eyes shut. *Like lying awake at night, knowing I'm responsible for an old woman dying alone on a hallway gurney.* I exhaled slowly and pushed the image from my mind.

And then there was Sam—though I'd never admit it and let Edie Greenbaum win a bet—to clear from of my mind. Firefighter Sam.

There was only a smidgen of ache when I thought of him now, and much less than the three-alarm burst of anger. But still there was a lingering stir of my senses, the image of enormous shoulders, curly hair, dimpled grin, and the God-knows-why enticing memory of musky cologne and smoke. Damn. Sam and that X-rated sandwich, two perfect reasons to cruise.

Edie crammed the hearing aid back into her ear and tugged at my waistband once more. "My Lord, dear, did you say something about genitals? Sandwiches? You were assaulted by a chef?"

"No, *no*." I flashed her an innocent smile and said a silent apology to my grandmother. "I said that I'd had a . . . food reaction. Yes. To, uh, peanut butter. Common allergy. And actually, I'm here to keep my best friend company. We usually work together back in California, but she spends her vacation time aboard cruise ships as a sickbay nurse. Her name is—"

"Marie Whitley." A husky voice announced behind us. "And, sure, Edie's my buddy."

We turned to see Marie salute us and grin, an unlit cheroot waggling between her teeth. Her gray eyes glittered from beneath a fringe of dark bangs and a nicotine patch clung like a barnacle to the side of her neck.

A snort escaped through my nose as the full effect of her uniform hit me once again. In the seven years of our friendship, it was the closest thing to a dress I'd ever seen Marie wear, such as it was—the cruise line's prim middy, navy culottes, and knee socks. A slightly chunky, almost-forty woman in a uniform fit for parochial school; I guess it proved how badly she wanted to sail. But, of course, she'd added a touch of her own. A sailor hat, complete with silver embroidered anchor, was secured over her short curls and tipped rakishly over the lushly lashed eye winking at Edie Greenbaum.

Edie giggled and then hugged Marie before sauntering away to join the assembled yoga group. I heaved a sigh of relief, then pulled the terry band off my ponytail and patted it against my forehead. I was clammy with sweat all of a sudden.

"You know Edie the Snoop?" I asked, lifting my fingertips once again to my neck. It still felt like my heart was pounding. Marie nodded her head, dark brows rising.

"Insulin dependent diabetic, but not nearly as interesting as being sexually assaulted by a chef. Pastry, I hope." Marie pulled off her sailor hat and smacked it against my shoulder. "What the hell was that about, Cavanaugh? Can't I take you anywhere?"

"Nothing, I . . . no, *look*." I nodded my head toward the yoga group who had begun to twitter and gather around the man sitting on a weight bench. "Can you believe that? It's The Gigolo."

"Dance host."

"Whatever."

I watched as Luke Skyler slid out of his white karate robe, which was immediately and lovingly folded by one of the Yoga Ladies. My face grew warm and I told myself that it was anger and nothing more. Unbelievable, the man had no body hair. Okay, a few tufts, kind of golden and downy . . . I bit my lip and glared as he beamed at the gathered group, his teeth flashing white against his tan. I ran my tongue across my lips. "It's revolting how those old women behave around him."

"You're drooling."

"No, I'm . . ." Luke lifted the barbell, biceps bulging, and my voice dropped an octave, "*not*. And the guy's pathetic—maybe actually dangerous."

"Oh, for crissake. You're not still obsessed with the idea that he's trying to fleece those women, are you?"

"Has he asked *you* to dance?"

Marie wrinkled her brows and shot me a look.

"Okay," I conceded, "but I'm willing to bet that if you wore a drop-dead stunning emerald necklace, he wouldn't care that you're gay."

I felt the ship drop from beneath me again and my head floated, fluffy and weightless. Man, that was a bad one. Why wasn't Marie feeling it? How did she stand so still?

I grabbed onto the treadmill's handrails and my heart pounded in my throat like a jackhammer as my legs went watery-weak. The room turned hazy, dark. What happened to the lights? *I can't see.*

"Hey, Darcy . . . what's wrong?"

Marie's voice floated through fathoms of water and I waved my arms, paddling through the dark liquid to hear, but it was no use. I was sinking. The matting of the treadmill, dark and rubbery as the broad side of a whale, rose toward me and slammed into my cheekbone as everything went black.

TWO

"I was carried in here by The Gigolo? Please tell me you're joking." I raised my head from the sickbay stretcher and touched my fingertips gingerly to the throbbing spot on my left cheekbone. "Marie?"

"Swooned right into his arms, so to speak." She pulled one stethoscope earpiece aside. "Hey, hold still. The doc said one more normal blood pressure reading and I can cut you loose. You'll just have to drink a bunch of fluids. We could still get a quick dinner and make the eight o'clock show."

"What happened, anyway?"

"Rapid heart rate—really racing, kid. Maybe up to one-eighty beats. Dropped your blood pressure like an anchor."

I grimaced.

"Sorry, sailor talk. Comes with the uniform."

I looked over at the cardiac monitor and watched my heartbeat, displayed in neon green, blipping across the dark screen.

Weird to be on this end. It was supposed to be someone else's heart up there.

"It's fine now," Marie confirmed, "Ever since we got you lying down. Didn't even have to give you any drugs to slow it. Isn't this the same thing that happened a couple of years ago? That time in the city?"

I nodded and then clucked my tongue, remembering. Our run in the infamous Bay to Breakers race in San Francisco. Seventy thousand runners, mostly costumed; 12K from sea level at Embarcadero, up Heartbreak Hill, and then on to Golden Gate Park. Not a distance I hadn't done before, but—I shot Marie a look. "Yeah, probably wouldn't have gotten dehydrated if I weren't dressed up like . . . a frigging *taco*. All that sweaty plastic lettuce. Whose great idea was that?"

Marie raised her palms. "Hey, you had a choice, remember— the Chihuahua mask was too itchy for Your Highness. So I got to have hat hair from hell."

I sighed and glanced back at the monitor. "Anyway, it's because of that heart murmur, mitral valve. Pretty mild, but gets it cranking along once in a while. No big deal. I'm fine."

"Agreed." Marie fiddled with her stethoscope, a slow smile spreading across her face. "Hot topic of gossip, of course, but fine."

I slid my legs over the edge of the stretcher. "Gossip?" I groaned. "Oh, you mean because of that gigolo?"

"Luke Skywalker. That's what the Yoga Ladies are calling him now." Marie shook her head. "Can't believe it. This one woman, who had to be pushin' eighty, said, 'Oh, honey, he could sure make me feel "The Force."'"

"Ee-ew. So he picked me up and carried me right in here?" I tried not to imagine it and then tried even harder to ignore a ridiculous prickle of heat.

"No, actually I think he bench-pressed you a couple of times for the fan club first."

I took a swing at her and missed just as a curtain slid open between the stretchers to reveal the wide-eyed smile and cheery "Yoo hoo" of Edie Greenbaum. She was sitting, with the sleeve of her glittering pantsuit rolled up, next to a balding man bent over what looked like a lapful of sequined fabric. He glanced up and smiled and I could see that he was holding a needle and thread. Sewing? He winked as he caught my surprised look and then grinned to reveal a gold-capped front tooth.

"Can we go now, Marie sweetie?" Edie asked. "Has it been long enough after my little shot?" She fluttered her hand toward her husband. "Bernie's got to get this costume back and he still needs to set the props for the show." She peered down over her glasses and giggled. "Besides, I think I hear those silver-dollar slots calling my name."

"Oh, sorry. Of course you can go. I was just getting Darcy squared away here." Marie peeled the Velcro cuff away from my arm.

"Well you go ahead with that, dear." Edie stepped down from the stretcher and moved forward to place her hand over mine. "And we're so sorry to hear about your heart condition, aren't we Bernie?"

Her husband looked up from his sewing and smiled at me again. His dark eyes were warm as just-poured chocolate pudding and made me think about my grandpa, gone long ago. "Absolutely. And we're sure glad that Luke was there, although—" Bernie

Greenbaum straightened in his chair, his chest swelling like a banty rooster, "I would have been very happy to have rescued you myself, young lady. I was a scout leader in my day."

Jeez. I bit my lip and avoided Marie's eyes, then slid my fingers out from under Edie's. "Thank you, but really it's not a 'heart condition' at all. I'm fine."

"But such excitement." Edie purred. "Well, we'll be going now." She paused at the door and looked back over her shoulder. "I'd use a touch of cream makeup over that bruise on your face, dear. No one will know."

"Edie, darling, don't embarrass the girl," Bernie clucked, taking his wife's arm. "She doesn't need you to mother her." He winked and then waved at me and I noticed that he still had a thimble on his finger. "Darcy's lovely the way she is."

I shook my head and groaned after the couple left, then peeled the monitor pads from my chest. "So why can't Edie give herself her own insulin shots or have Grandpa do it?" I rolled my eyes. "He *was* a scout leader after all."

"Squeamish. Both of them. Bernie is pretty helpful though. Makes her watch her diet—not easy on a cruise ship—and monitors her sugar tests." Marie sighed. "But a sewing needle is the only kind he's comfortable with." She shrugged. "You're not going to believe this, but they actually live on this ship. Or are considering it anyway. Quite the trend with retirees now."

"You're serious?" I asked, amazed.

"Yeah. Think about it: retire at, say, fifty-five, give up your mortgage, and use retirement money to lease a cabin. Sort of high-rent homeless. Where else can you get a room, utilities, entertainment, and God knows a shit-load of food for maybe a hundred bucks a day? The Greenbaums have been cruisin' for quite a while now, looking for the right 'home ship.'"

I chuckled. "Hey, maybe you and Carol should consider that. Matching sailor suits?"

Marie smiled and for an instant I saw it—that undeniably tender look that appeared in her gray eyes whenever she thought about her longtime partner. It never failed to amaze me and maybe even bugged me a little, since I was pretty sure that I was never going get lucky like they were. Marie would wear a taco suit for Carol a hundred times over. And a nicotine patch, too.

"Nah," Marie said, folding the BP cuff. "She's still not sure about this whole cruise ship thing or whether I should even do it again. It's a pain when her schedule keeps her from coming along with me." She smiled. "Two more weeks and I'm back in California." She picked at the edge of her patch and sighed. "As a non-smoker."

"Well then maybe I'll consider this myself when I retire from the orthotics business. Think of all the arch supports and bunion plasters I could hawk on a cruise ship."

Marie growled, "I am *not* going to discuss that stupid scheme of yours again. Or that obnoxious podiatrist who's trying to talk you into it. Dr. Foote, who the hell is he kidding?" She folded the aftercare instruction sheet into an airplane and sailed it toward me. "Hey, you want a quick tour of this place before you go?"

"Sure." I smiled, remembering that it had been Marie who'd shown me around our own ER seven long years ago. Veteran nurse and scared-spitless new graduate in pink scrubs.

Marie led the way. "Not exactly our Morgan Valley Hospital, but kind of nicely organized."

"If you say 'ship-shape,' I'm going leave right now."

We ended the tour in front of the "crash cart" and I shook my head, amazed. "You weren't kidding. Very compact, but you seem to have everything you'd need. Really, more than I'd imagine you'd need: defibrillator, temporary pacemaker . . ." I ran my fingertips along the contents of a drawer and whistled. "You've got a whole airway setup here; endotracheal tubes, Ambu bag, and suction." I scanned the labels on a row of vials. "And all the drugs."

I lifted a vial tucked next to the selection of insulin so that I could read the label. The glass was still refrigerator-cold. "Succinylcholine?" I raised my brows at Marie. "You'd really give a paralytic out in the middle of the ocean?"

"Hey, you've seen the Yoga Club—exclusively senior membership. And hell, that midnight buffet is cholesterol surrounded by a pineapple peacock and an ice sculpture. These people have heart attacks, Darcy. If they go down, we've got to control the airway, right? Keep 'em stable until the helicopter comes."

I grimaced. I hated giving paralyzing drugs. Something so claustrophobic and creepy about it, even when we give a sedative first. I often wondered what our patients would think if they knew that it's basically curare, the same stuff that Pygmies dip their arrows in. And I didn't want to even imagine what it must feel like to—

Marie tugged at the hem of my tank top. "Hey, let's get you out of here. I don't wanna miss the Elvis impersonators."

* * *

I rushed around the tiny cabin, blowing on my nail polish, then paused to watch Marie slowly lace her patent leather shoes. "You're wearing glitter socks?"

"It's formal night. Besides, the socks match my bow tie." Marie turned and grinned, fluffing the ruffles on the front of her tuxedo. "Why? Do you think it's too much?"

I shook my head. The woman had the biggest sock collection I'd ever seen. "They were talking about me in the hallway," I mumbled, holding one of my earrings between my teeth and trying to fasten the other with the pads of my fingertips. I should have done my nails earlier in the day; they weren't going to ever dry at this rate. And my hair—I'd had to do it so fast. Just kind of threw it up there. I hoped the pins held.

"Who was talking about you?" Marie clicked the buttons on the TV remote and groaned as another security message began warning passengers to protect their valuables.

"Some of the passengers. I heard them when I was walking back to the cabin. Looks like our homeless little diabetic wasted no time."

"What were they saying—hey, did you see this Elizabeth Taylor infomercial? Sounds just like her, doesn't it?" Marie had started stuffing things into her fanny pack.

"They were talking about my 'heart condition.' No such thing as patient confidentiality apparently." I gave up blowing on my nails. They'd have to dry on the way to the showroom. No more time.

"That's all?" Marie asked.

"What?"

"That's all they were talking about?" Marie's voice sounded suspiciously casual.

"That's enough isn't it—why?"

Marie took a sudden interest in the lapel of her tuxedo.

"Why?" I repeated, smoothing the waistline of my strapless emerald Carolina Herrera—death on a nurse's paycheck but, again, I was feeling reckless lately. I checked my nails: no gouges so far. "What else would they be saying?" I stepped toward her.

"Oh, something I heard outside the casino." Marie puffed out her cheeks and went back to studying her lapel. "Only a couple of people talking, no big deal."

"Tell me!" I grabbed her chin, risking my nails. Dammit, I knew her too well.

"Okay, okay." Marie smiled. "Just that you were assaulted by a chef, and now . . ."

"Now, *what?*"

"Now it's pretty obvious that because of the trauma, you've become a lesbian."

* * *

For once there wasn't a line for the elevator, and I managed to avoid the eyes of the few people we met in the corridors who were undoubtedly eager to confirm my sexual preference. Could this get any worse? Not that I wasn't familiar with humiliation. It had been pretty humbling to show up unannounced at my out-of-town lover's house, wearing just a raincoat and a smile, to find that his mysterious "roommates" were a Labrador retriever and a wife. *Thank you, Sam.* But this cruise was about new beginnings. Being made a fool of was not part of the deal.

We stepped inside the elevator and I double-checked the ship's schematic posted on the wall. It was so confusing sometimes; what was on each deck, which way was fore and aft. Yes, our cabin was on D-Deck and we were headed four decks up to the dining rooms. My stomach was rumbling and tonight was the Pasta Parade. Ooh. A trendy slant on good ol' macaroni and cheese.

"Can't believe we're alone in this elevator and not squashed in like usual," I said. "Everyone must still be at the early show."

I glanced at my glittery Fossil watch and then back at Marie. Cute tuxedo and only Marie had the panache to carry it off, but we probably did look like a gay couple. Well, who cared what people wanted to gossip about? Even if I didn't exactly know what I wanted to do with my career or the rest of my life, I did know who I was. Right? You betcha.

"*I know who I am*, Marie." I nodded my head sharply.

Marie looked at me like I was crazy. "That's . . . good? Hey, look out, your earring—"

I felt the pearl slip from my ear and slide down the front of my dress. Oh shit. "My nails. They're still too wet. You'll have to get it." I held my breath.

"What the hell?" Marie's brows rose. "And why are your cheeks puffing out like that?"

"Please . . . shut up . . . and . . . get it." I exhaled quickly and inhaled again. "I'm holding my breath to wedge it there, keep it from slipping down . . . further. Hurry."

"No thanks."

"Oh for godsake, Marie. It'll slip down through my dress and I'll lose it. It was Grandma's. Just reach in and grab it."

The elevator door re-opened just as Marie, her arm wrist-deep in my cleavage, shouted "Gotcha," and her fingers closed over the earring. Edie Greenbaum and her yoga group stood staring. Directly behind them was Luke Skywalker

It took forever for the elevator to climb the floors to the Whaler's Deck and I had never heard it so quiet. Damn that Marie. She kept making little snorting and snuffling noises, biting her lip to keep from laughing. Worse, I could feel the gigolo dance host staring at my back.

One of the Yoga Ladies finally cleared her throat and turned to me as the elevator glided mercifully to a stop.

"I love what you've done with your hair, dear. A very different kind of upsweep. Sort of looped to frame your face. Lovely. What does it remind me of?"

There was another painful silence. Marie's bow tie quivered as she tried desperately not to laugh.

"Princess Leia," the dance host said.

THREE

DINNER WAS A DISASTER. I swore I could hear everyone whispering, but at least the showroom had been blessedly dark. And now I'd finally gotten away. I stared into the mirror of the ladies' room and scowled. Great. I looked like an Irish banshee. I grabbed my hair by the ends and shook it. The remaining hairpins plinked onto the surface of the cherry wood vanity letting my hair tumble over my shoulders, full and wildly curly from the ocean humidity. I moaned and opened my compact. The bruise on my cheekbone was as purple as Aunt Maureen's plum jam. Princess Leia? Arrogant jerk. How dare he say that?

I could still hear the tittering of the old ladies as they swept from the elevator, elbowing each other and scrambling like they were fifty years late for the prom. One woman, tanned and elegant, even had a simple tiara tucked into her silvery blonde hairdo. Prom Princess? It was formal night, "Meet the Captain Night," and they rustled down the floral Aubusson carpets in gowns of lace, silk, and taffeta, carrying furs that left a scent trail of cedar and mothballs. And the jewels: diamonds, emeralds, and sapphires in rings, bracelets, and pendants; pearl chokers twining around a dozen crepe-y necks. No wonder the ship kept running that infomercial. These guests could be real prey for a smooth operator, like . . .

"Marie?" I snapped my compact shut and stepped toward the toilet stalls. "You aren't smoking in there, are you?"

"Moi?" The marine toilet whooshed like a jet engine and Marie emerged and headed for the sink, holding her tuxedo jacket at the hem and fanning the air with it as she walked.

"I swear I smelled cherry. You know, like your little cigars? Oh, never mind. Hurry up, I've decided that we need to do a little detective work."

"Detective . . . ?"

I jammed my compact and comb into my knockoff Kate Spade and waited as Marie dried her hands. "I, for one, think it's more than a little suspicious that a man as young as Luke Skyler would take a position as a dance host. They don't even get paid, right?"

Marie shrugged. "Inside cabin. All the pâté you can wolf down."

"And the opportunity to get cozy with a bunch of rich widows?" I clenched my jaw. Dammit, now I was reckless and on a mission. "C'mon, I have this sudden urge to tango."

* * *

The Electric Lobster Disco was on the Lido Deck above and we took the mid-ship glass elevator that offered a breathtaking view of the ship's amenities. Unbelievable. It carried us up alongside a marble spiral staircase that surrounded an atrium with red cyclamen, speckled yellow orchids, ferns, and full-size potted palms. A string quartet was tuning up as we exited next to a bevy of portrait photographers, eager as paparazzi for the guests to line up for photos with the white-uniformed ship's captain. And . . . he wasn't half-bad looking either.

"It's amazing, isn't it," I said, peering out into the crowd, "how they can get all this stuff onto a ship, break a bottle of champagne over the bow, then pack on a couple thousand passengers and still manage to make it float?" I glanced overhead warily, wondering how much a swimming pool weighed. I hoped our cabin wasn't underneath one. The elevator doors closed behind us and we walked on past the gilded and jeweled doors of the Mermaid Spa and into a corridor lined with glass and sparkling with tiny white lights. My mind was boggling.

"Shopper's Row," Marie said as we walked past clothing boutiques, duty-free liquor and perfume shops, and jewelry stores with cases displaying Rolex watches, Swarovski crystal, Lladro porcelain, and "Today's Special," loose South African diamonds.

"Would you look at all those ladies lined up in there—hey, it's the Prom Princess, that woman with the tiara, see?" I pointed. "She's already got her shipboard charge card out."

Marie nodded. "And you can bet some of those women will walk out with a couple thousand dollars worth of 'trinkets' dropped in the bottom of their purses. Maybe you're right; they're pretty ripe for the picking."

Cigarette smoke billowed from the neon-lighted entryway as we approached the Treasure Island Casino and we could hear laughter, the cogwheel whir of tumblers, and the chink-chink of tokens.

"They don't make their money on the midnight buffet," Marie explained wryly and then took a half step backward, nodding. "Look, it's Edie Greenbaum."

Sure enough, pink-haired Edie was perched on a stool wearing her glittery pantsuit, little legs dangling like a marionette. She fed a handful of tokens into a slot machine shaped like a huge clam and jabbed at the buttons.

"I didn't see Bernie," I said, walking on. I could hear the music from the disco just ahead.

"Naw, he's probably still down in the theater, taking down the props." Marie chuckled. "Or shimmying out of his blue suede shoes."

"Huh?"

"Didn't you see him in the show? Last impersonator on the right."

My jaw dropped. "You're kidding. The one with the short legs who couldn't keep time to the music?" I grimaced. "Poor old guy. He didn't even *look* like Elvis—painful to watch. Why would he want to do something he's so lousy at?"

Marie reached for the door to the disco and shrugged. "Whatever floats your boat, I guess. Oops, sorry. Sailor lingo. Slips right out." She grinned and held the door, waving me ahead. "Let's go watch your con man at work."

An Asian waitress in a shiny yellow fisherman's slicker seated us at a table near the ocean-view window. Marie grabbed a handful of cocktail peanuts and goldfish crackers, then snagged a lobster canapé as a waiter passed within reach.

"Got to pack on a few more poundsth . . ." she lisped through a mouthful, and then swallowed. "If I don't come back like a little pork-chop, Carol won't believe I've quit smoking."

"Hey, I don't believe it either. But I'll keep quiet if you help me find The Gigolo, okay?"

A three-man combo played a forgettable seventies hit and couples crowded the small dance floor beneath a ceiling strung with crab pots, trawling nets, and glow-in-the-dark lobsters. A huge lighted aquarium in the wall crawled with the real things.

"Do you see him?" I asked after ordering our drinks.

"Not yet, but the other two dance hosts are over there. Herb and Dan, I think."

I spotted them. One was paunchy and wispy bald and the other olive skinned, gray at the temples, and wearing a turquoise and silver bolo tie with his tux.

"Now that's exactly what I mean," I said, pulling the peanut dish out of Marie's reach. "It makes sense for guys like that to be out there trotting the single ladies across the dance floor. They're retired and probably widowers themselves. Free cruise, free eats, and they get to travel without taking a chunk out of their Social Security. But," I narrowed my eyes as a man in a well-cut tuxedo passed by our table, "as for *him* . . ."

Luke Skyler swaggered slowly toward the dance floor balancing two glasses of champagne. He knelt on one knee beside a table and presented one of the fluted glasses ceremoniously to a woman with a shawl and a fuzzy gray perm. He lifted his own glass like he was making a toast, then threw his head back and laughed.

I didn't need to see it to know that the old woman was blushing furiously; I could tell by the way she fluttered her hands and covered her mouth. And was that the woman's charge card that Luke set down on the table beside her purse? "The pig," I seethed, and then turned to see if Marie was watching, too.

Marie was staring at me. "Why does this guy get you so pissed, Darc'? Is this a Sam thing again? All good-looking guys are dishonest?" She rolled her eyes. "That's the sort of thinking that eventually evolves into, 'I'll never fall for that again. I'd rather run away to be a sales rep for an obsessive podiatrist.'"

"Phillip is not obsessed."

"Phillip Foote," Marie said, rolling her eyes, "has an eighty-pound arch support mounted to the top of his Range Rover."

I cleared my throat and smirked. "Know anyone who has a hundred pairs of socks?"

I returned Marie's sheepish smile and sighed. "This is not about Dr. Foote and it isn't about Sam, either." I stirred my Long Island iced tea. "Have you forgotten the mess my family went through with Grandma Rosaleen a few years ago? I thought I told you about that. Back when she was still living in LA?"

Marie's brows scrunched. "Before the Alzheimer's?"

"Back when it was mild, when it was just losing her glasses on top of her head and forgetting to pay the gardener." I took a sip of my drink and shook my head. "Way before she painted her eyebrows with lipstick."

Marie nodded. "Yeah, and put the kitten in her refrigerator. God, I remember that one. Man, I hope it wasn't caused by being a nurse for like—"

"Forty years. She hung in there for forty damned years." I groaned and took a much longer swig of my drink.

It was strange about Alzheimer's, how randomly memories are lost. Basic functions like how to knot a shoelace are suddenly gone and yet other memories are intensely magnified. Each time I visited Grandma I could count on two things: lemon-glazed ginger cookies and nurse stories. Her eyes would light up as memories tumbled out. The baby boy she delivered in the back seat of an Edsel (*Named him Eddie, of course*), the exact style number of J.C. Penney's sturdiest white support hosiery, and every single word to an Irish lullaby she'd sung to Kathleen Murphy, the cancer patient who'd died in her arms. *Toora-loora-looral . . .*

Face it, some days Grandma Rosaleen couldn't remember how to put toothpaste on a toothbrush but she always remembered how it felt to be a nurse, and how "being there" had made a difference in so many people's lives. My chest squeezed. How could I tell her that I have to quit?

"But what's all that got to do with the dance host?" Marie asked, reaching for the peanuts again.

I glanced at Luke Skyler on the dance floor and frowned. "Grandma met this guy, after being widowed forever. Good looking and a lot younger, a semi-retired plumber. Union big shot, supposedly. She was thrilled; we were thrilled. He carved their names on her elm tree, brought her jelly donuts at the crack of dawn, and took her to Paris." My lips tightened with anger as the memories blossomed. "Of course, then he took her for every damned cent she had."

"Ouch."

"We found out later that he'd done it before." I shook my head, "And kicked ourselves for being too stupid to see it coming." I glared toward the dance host. "But I see it now and I'm not going to let it happen again."

Marie jumped as her pager beeped under her jacket. "Oops, keep forgetting about that thing. Be right back."

She returned to the table a few minutes later and picked up her fanny pack. "Got to get down to the sickbay. Sounds like another lady's had a mini-stroke." She shook her head. "That's like the fourth one in the last three weeks." She glanced at the dance floor. "Don't know how long I'll be, but promise not to handcuff anyone without me, okay?"

I maneuvered my chair so that I could get a view of the dancers without looking too obvious. The lounge was crowded, but maybe only a half dozen couples were out on the floor. It was pretty obvious that the large majority of patrons were single women.

I flicked a fingernail against my glass and smiled. Single women? Hell, I was one of them myself. The big difference, however, was that I was immune to the fatal attraction of romance. Inoculated, vaccinated, and no longer subject to the fever, weak knees, fuzzy brain, and ultimate heartache of that disease. I lifted my glass in a toast. *Thanks, Sam.*

I looked back toward the dance floor and smiled as a figure caught my eye—the lady I called the Phantom Dancer. Now there was a woman after my own heart. No doubt she'd been inoculated, too. Decades ago.

At first I'd wondered if the woman was drunk, or maybe crazy. Or both. A few times now, the Phantom Dancer had shown up like this and made her way to the dance floor unaccompanied. Dressed in a drop-waist beaded dress with heavy shoulder pads, patent pumps, and opera-length pearls, she looked like a dowdy time-capsule debutante. Her hair brushed her shoulders, ashy blonde and sort of swept back like bird wings; Marie had called it Farrah Fawcett Retro. Tucked behind her ear, like every night, was a trademark red carnation.

I smiled as I watched her now dancing alone to a Bee Gees tune, tight little calves treading in place, arms extended above her head and rhythmically snapping her fingers. You had to get really close to see the lines beneath her heavy makeup, the vertical creases above penciled lips, the age spots on her forearms, and the ill-fitting dentures that shifted precariously when she gave a shy smile. Probably a retired nurse. Lousy pension, no dental plan.

"Somebody's old-maid aunt," Marie had guessed, and we'd chuckled when the dutiful dance hosts tapped her on the shoulder for a dance. She always refused. That was the really cool part. The Phantom Dancer was totally comfortable alone. Okay, she probably *was* demented and someone should check her refrigerator regularly for kittens, but the point was that she was having a good time.

And so was the Prom Princess, dammit. I watched as Luke Skyler guided the woman with the tiara across the dance floor in a smooth fox trot. He had a way of making any woman look graceful, but I guessed that this particular lady was no stranger to handsome men and glamorous settings. She reminded me of some aging actress, Candice Bergen maybe, silvery blonde with fine-boned, almost regal features. Sophisticated, with that undeniable self-confidence that comes from a rich weave of life experience. And flawless heritage, probably.

I groaned. My own fabric was more of a crazy quilt and you could bet your ass that as the daughter of Bill the Bug Man Cavanaugh and a novice-nun-turned-Vegas-blackjack-dealer, I was never going to have that kind of class. But at least I'd finally learned—the hard way—not to gamble on the honesty of cockroaches. I squinted at the dance floor.

The couple moved with an agility that made the other dance hosts, and their Yoga Lady partners, look like so many cattle on the hoof. Luke's hand held one of hers formally midair and the other was pressed low against the waistline of her bronze silk gown. De la Renta, I'd bet, and from nowhere in the galaxy near eBay.

The music ended and I watched as the Prom Princess raised her arm to look at her watch. Her beaded handbag swayed on its cord with the movement. She spoke a few words and then laughed, raising her arm once more to straighten Luke Skyler's bow tie.

I groaned aloud and my fingers tightened on my drink glass. *Con man, gigolo . . . foxtrotting phony.* How long until he had this woman's shipboard charge card? I glanced around for the security team. Weren't they watching for something like this? Were they blinded because this guy was an insider?

Wait. What the hell? I half-rose from my chair to get a better view. Yes. Luke was opening the door to the darkened deck for the Prom Princess, who had slipped into a fur jacket. And then he followed her outside.

It took me a few minutes to navigate the barroom floor, stopping twice to say "No, thank you" to circulating waiters with trays of crab puffs and mini-wedges of Brie. But I finally made it to the brass-handled deck door and stepped outside. The air was icy-cold and thick with fog, and I shivered with the shock of it against my bare shoulders. I felt myself shrink half a cup size and wondered if my Carolina Herrera could hang on. Marie couldn't bid for a tropical cruise? I scanned the darkened deck. Where could those two have gone? If I could find out what was going on and report it to security, then maybe . . .

I shivered again, and then reached for the teak deck rail as the ship rolled under my feet. A fine spray of salt water stung my face and lips. I knew I was at the bow of the ship and that we were almost a day's sail from Nova Scotia, but I couldn't see a blessed thing except fog and darkness. I glanced up toward the navigational bridge and prayed that the crew's vantage point was way better. And that they were more observant than the security team.

Marie had scheduled a land tour in Halifax, the Titanic victims' cemetery. She'd been almost psychotic with anticipation as she read the brochure. *"Man, look at this: sank three-hundred miles off the coast from there. Ooh, look Darc', we get to see the grave of that musician. You know the one who played on the deck till the ship went down?"* I glanced back out at the dark sea. Whales and now icebergs?

A foghorn blast made me jump and my eBay Jimmy Choos slid on the wet deck. *Oh, no.* My legs splayed and I heard a tiny rip in the back of my gown as I struggled to right myself.

I felt the man's hand on my elbow before I heard his voice. It was deep and full of amusement.

"So, the ladies tell me that your heart tried to run away with you."

Luke Skyler paused and I could feel his lips against my ear. "They're saying that it was because I took my shirt off."

FOUR

I JERKED MY ELBOW out of Luke's grasp and the force sent me sliding across the teak deck like Bambi on a frozen pond. I heard the rip lengthen at the back of my dress, and felt an immediate and undeniable gust of frigid air between my thighs. *Damn.* I grabbed the deck rail tightly and whirled to face him.

"How dare . . ." My words were swallowed by a shiver, and I watched Luke step closer into the pool of deck lights. His hands were raised in mock surrender and he was smiling. He stopped in front of me and removed his jacket.

"I'm sorry if I scared you, Miss Cavanaugh. But here, slip this on; you're freezing." He extended the tuxedo jacket and nodded.

"No, I'm f-f-fine."

"Right, and you're wearing blue lipstick." His chuckle was soft, deep, and his voice had a very slight accent. Southern?

I raised my fingers to my lips and then quickly reached for the offered jacket. Hell, I really wasn't losing anything by taking it; this was a matter of survival. It was true, my lips were numb, and if I were going to get any information from this guy it would have to be quick. Right here and right now. And I couldn't exactly go waltzing back into the disco with my naked backside flapping in the breeze.

"Thank you, I . . ."

"Here, let me." Luke stepped toward me and opened the jacket so I could slip my arms inside.

I stifled a moan just in time, tucking my chin down into the tuxedo collar and hugging my arms around myself. *Mmm*, it was still warm from his body and smelled of . . . what was that, pipe tobacco and *Obsession?* I looked back up at him and tried to think of what I'd wanted to ask. What was it? Luke's face was lit by the railing lights and my brain was turning to day-old macaroni and cheese.

Damn, he was even better looking up close. He stood gazing down at me in a formal shirt and suspenders with his hands on his hips and his bow tie rakishly askew. His short hair was well-cut and sandy blonde, tousled a bit and shot with sun streaks. Eyes were blue, and crinkled at the corners like he was barely suppressing laughter.

I'd guess that he was maybe thirty-five. And the rangy-handsome features were familiar somehow—a strong jaw, smirky mouth, and that sort of Roman-statue nose. Who did he look like? Marie was forever teasing me about my passion for movie trivia and celebrity look-alikes. *"Not everyone looks like a friggin' film star, Darc."* But still, who?

"Better?" Luke asked. He smiled again—white teeth against tanned skin—accentuating the deep dimples, and the chill breeze lifted an unruly whorl of blonde hair over his forehead.

Dammit. Matthew McConaughey. How distracting was that? I clenched my hands inside the jacket's miles-too-long sleeves. *Okay, on with it.*

"Didn't I see you come out here with an—um—elderly woman?" I glanced past him down the deck both ways. Could the Prom Princess have gotten away so fast on this slippery deck? Where was security?

Luke laughed. "I don't think Loretta would appreciate being called elderly."

"Where is she?" I leaned toward him and jutted out my chin.

Luke leaned forward, too. "Excuse me? Maybe I should be asking a question. Like why you were following us?" He had stopped smiling. And the look in his eyes had changed. Kind of cold. And what, defensive, or worse . . . *threatening?* He looked over the rail, a seven story drop, and then back at me. I stammered.

"Um. I wasn't following. I, uh, thought maybe there was a short-cut this way. You know, back to the casino?" Blast it. What was I doing out here anyway? A lot of good it would do to avenge my sweetly demented grandma if I got pitched overboard by a real lunatic. I took a step backward. And Luke stepped forward again, his voice a gruff whisper.

"She's *gone.*"

The ship lurched and Luke slid toward me, grabbing my shoulders. We slid on until the railing smacked into my ribs and stopped our momentum. I could see whitecaps on the sea even through the fog. His voice was very close, the words nearly drowned by a sudden foghorn.

"Loretta's gone to be a mermaid."

Oh my God! I tore my gaze away from the ocean and tried to free my arms from his grasp as the ship rocked once more. "No!" I yelled and struggled again. It didn't matter about my torn dress; I needed to get back through that door and into the safety of a crowd. No one was going to find me out here. Time for action. I gritted my teeth and brought my heel down as hard as I could on his instep.

Luke cried out and released me. "What the hell?"

The door opened behind us and Marie stepped onto the deck. Relief flooded through me like a tourniquet released. The anger returned.

"Mermaid?" I said, hating it that my voice quavered. I cleared my throat and took a step backward, away from him and safely toward the door. "*Mermaid* for godsake? You think that's clever?"

Luke Skyler looked as bewildered as Marie did. He rubbed the injured foot against the back of his other pant leg and grimaced. "Mermaid Spa? The women's spa? You've got a problem with that place?"

He shook his head. "I don't know why you needed to know, but I was trying to explain—before you stomped on my foot—that Loretta went to the spa. I walked her down there. You're right; the deck is a short cut. She was in a hurry to get to their last appointment; won it in one of the promos or something." He tested his foot on the deck and grimaced. "Damn. You're dangerous."

I looked at Marie, then back at Luke and swallowed hard. Oh shit. "I'm sorry, I . . ."

"Hey, let's forget it." Luke strode past me and took the door handle from Marie.

"Wait, take this." I slipped out of the tuxedo jacket and held it up, my mind cartwheeling. Did I have this all wrong?

He took it from me silently, stepped through the door, and then stopped and turned toward us again. "Oh, and if all that was because you thought I was trying to hit on you?" He smiled, and the mocking laughter crinkled his eyes. "I'm afraid you have that wrong, too."

Ooh! I didn't know whether to curse or cry. I watched the door close behind him, then balled my hands into fists and stomped my Jimmy Choos on the deck. Damn that man!

"Hey," Marie grinned, pointing at my shoe, "careful, isn't that registered as a lethal weapon? You gonna tell me what happened out here?"

"Maybe in a little while." I hesitated, watching the doorway, still shaking my head. I sighed and my breath hung in the air in a frozen puff.

"Okay, then at least tell me why your ass is nearly hanging out the back of your dress."

"Oh shit, I almost forgot." I groaned and tried to twist around to see the tear. "What am I going to do?"

Marie grinned and unzipped her fanny pack. "You are so privileged to know me."

"Adhesive tape? You carry adhesive tape with you?"

"Ship's nurse—I've got everything in here but a spare anchor." She pulled the roll free from her pack, knocking half a dozen cherry cheroots to the deck.

"Marie?" I pointed at the cigars.

"Hey, you want the Electric Lobster Disco to see your fantail?"

Minutes, and maybe two feet of tape later, I wiggled a little to test the repair.

"I think it'll work so that you can get back to the cabin without being arrested," Marie said.

"Yes, it's great, thanks. But there's something else we need to do first. Right now." I pointed down the deck.

"I think it's too foggy for shuffleboard."

"No. The Mermaid Spa. We need to find out if there's really an outside entrance." I glanced over the ship's rail and suppressed a shudder, wondering if I'd really been dangerously close to an Atlantic swim. "And we need to see if the Prom Princess is there."

The deck was lighted enough to walk but was growing more slippery each minute as we headed aft. I kept one hand on the ship-side rail and called back to Marie. "I swear it's starting to ice up."

"Code Alpha."

"What?"

"Code Alpha; that's what we call ice on the decks. Hey, hold it, there's the door to the spa right ahead of you. See the handle shaped like a fish tail? I remember now, it's sort of private but definitely an entrance."

"One point for The Gigolo, but we need to see the Prom Princess before I'll really believe she's not whale bait." I pulled at the door handle. "Damn, it's locked."

Marie glanced at her watch. "Pretty near to closing time."

I pointed upward. "Then let's peek through that porthole there."

I held onto the handrail as Marie attempted to stand with one foot on the rail and one on my shoulder. My collarbone creaked and I made a mental note to smack Marie's hand next time she reached for the peanuts.

"Why am I the one up here?" Marie groaned. "It's you that knows what the Prom Princess looks like."

"Because you're a ship official. Less conspicuous."

"Right, to be looking into a massage room? Wait, wait, I see someone."

"Hey, stop wiggling. You're making me slide." I tightened my grip around her glitter sock. "Why are you laughing like that?"

"The Phantom Dancer." Marie's legs wobbled again and she snorted through her nose. "You know how she always wears that red carnation?"

"Yeah, why?"

"She has a little flower-print satin robe and slippers to match. Eew, freckles and wrinkles; there should be a law."

"Who else do you see?"

"Nobody, only the manicurist closing up. No, wait. Is the Prom Princess sort of tall and slender, and . . ."

"Looks like Candice Bergen?"

Marie groaned again. "Okay, she's there. Fiddling with the cucumber slices on her eyes. Can we go now?"

* * *

Edie Greenbaum was waiting for the elevator as we headed toward the stairs down to our own deck. She balanced a tray stacked high with appetizers: chilled jumbo shrimp, mini quiches, South American tapas, and calamari rings. A steward followed her, carrying a coffee pot and table settings. Something about him looked familiar.

"Bernie's back is bothering him. I keep telling him that he should let some of the younger fellas move all that heavy stuff," Edie explained, licking cocktail sauce from her fingers. "Doubt we'll make it to the midnight buffet, but don't want to starve." She thanked Marie for holding the elevator doors and then stepped inside.

I poked Marie's arm. "Wait. Wasn't that our cabin steward? Virgilio?"

"You mean the guy who's been making those animal sculptures out of your lingerie? Definitely him."

I rolled my eyes. "Don't remind me. But aren't they just assigned to one deck? Edie's on G-Deck. Shouldn't she have her own cabin steward?"

"Me-ow," Marie narrowed her eyes, "aren't we getting prissy and territorial now?"

"Oh, you know what I mean. He's usually too darned busy to go anywhere else."

"I told you before. The Greenbaums are like family here. And you can bet your ass they're good tippers. All the staff pretty much caters to them." Marie stopped and pulled out her cabin keycard. "I'm beat—no way I'm hiking those stairs next time."

Minutes later I crawled into my twin bed and switched off the light. Marie's lava lamp cast oily shadows on the cabin walls. I glanced over at her. She was rubbing at her nicotine patch. "Hey, you never said how that lady did earlier. You know, the mini-stroke."

Marie yawned aloud. "Fine. Just like the others—symptoms were pretty much gone by the time we examined her. Almost can't diagnose it as a mini-stroke, Doc says." She yawned again. "We send them out with enough aspirin for the rest of the cruise and have them come in daily for pressure checks."

"Too much rich food, probably." I was yawning, too.

"Or the Luke Skywalker effect."

"Shut up."

The phone woke us an hour later.

Marie grumbled as she pulled on her rumpled culottes and middy blouse. "They don't get no friggin' sailor hat at midnight."

"What is it?"

"Another damned mini-stroke. What else? You know, sometimes this is not worth the free eats." She fastened on her fanny pack and closed the door behind her.

I watched the molten orange globs of the lava lamp stretch, separate, then drift upward and remembered when the doctors had diagnosed Grandma Rosaleen with mini-strokes. There had been brief memory lapses, sudden weaknesses, and then eventually they'd realized that it was so much more than that. This past year was the worst. A familiar ache crowded my chest. It was so hard to accept the changes in my bright, feisty grandmother. It was like losing her.

So much was gone. Physically she was still there, of course. In Dad's guestroom, only blocks from Mom's condo. My divorced parents live far enough apart that they can't easily scream at each other but still close enough that they can get soused on major holidays, sneak into each other's bedrooms, and then tiptoe home without threat of a DUI. No one has to tell me that I inherited relationship failure from my family. Anyway, the new medication helps Grandma quite a bit, and on a good day she'll say, "Yes, of course. You're my little Darcy. You're a nurse. Like me." But even then, her eyes swim with tears like she knows she's lost something. Damn, it kills me.

I reached out and touched the warm glass of the lava lamp and remembered the feel of the black velvet stripe on my grandmother's nursing cap. *Blue stripe when you're a student nurse, Darcy, then black after you raise your hand and take the Florence Nightingale Pledge.* Wait. Had I raised my hand? I tried to remember. It could be the perfect loophole. If I didn't raise my hand for the pledge then maybe it could be annulled.

The little stripe. It had been a black ribbon stuck tight to the stiff edge of the tri-fold nurse's cap, just the width of my fingernail at age four. Kitten soft. Grandma would come over to baby-sit after a night shift, white stockings swish-swishing as she came through the door, and she'd hoist me onto her lap in the rocker, hugging me against the starched and pleated bib of her uniform. She'd smile, showing the same tiny space between her front teeth that I had. *We Cavanaugh women can spit like the devil when we need to, honey. Don't you forget it.* And nod patiently as I counted for the umpteenth time the little row of gold pins: a school pin from Emmanuel Hospital, pins for years of service, special appreciation, and advanced training. She'd sighed as I tried on the nurse's cap, pigtails sticking out below, saying that almost no one wore caps anymore. She'd said that a lot of other things were changing, too—*Oh, Grandma if you only knew*—but that change could be good and that nursing would always be a "noble calling." Or maybe just endangered, like that little velvet stripe.

It was after 2:00 AM when I was awakened by the sound of Marie's return. I switched on the bedside lamp and squinted.

"Sorry, I was trying to be quiet." Marie sighed. She reeked of cherry tobacco.

"That's okay. Hey, you sound funny, what's wrong?" I watched as she sank down onto her bed. It looked like she was going to cry. Cry? That wasn't like her. Marie threw things; she didn't cry.

"It was the Prom Princess."

My hand flew to my mouth. "She died?"

"No, much worse than that."

Marie hurled her fanny pack across the room and it knocked over the lava lamp. I squelched a smile. That was more like it. "What happened?"

"She woke up from her little mini-stroke and accused me of stealing her jewelry."

41

FIVE

"So it looks like I'll be turning in my sailor hat." Marie shouted back over her shoulder to be heard above the din.

I shook my head as I balanced my tray and followed her across the Lido Deck's Coney Island Café. The clatter-chatter of the breakfast crowd was louder than foghorns. Steam from a silver mile of chafing dishes condensed on the windows. It was going to be tough to find a table this morning since there was no eating outside. The captain had called the Code Alpha at 6:00 AM, after one of the Yoga Ladies slid on her fanny alongside the entire length of the deck's swimming pool and broke her glasses.

"Prunes," Marie muttered, grabbing a table beside a full-size rearing carousel horse.

"What?"

"You can always tell the fifth day at sea." She nodded toward the ladies at an adjacent table with a half-dozen crystal compote dishes. "Stewed prunes. We run out of them."

"Don't change the subject." I spread orange marmalade on my croissant and glanced across the table. Marie looked awful after almost no sleep. They'd called her in for the Code Alpha briefing and then asked her to stay afterward to talk with the security staff. "What did they say?"

"Asked me a bunch of questions, then casually suggested that for my own 'protection' I start my days off a little early." Marie shrugged her shoulders and blew on her coffee. "I only had one more day to work until then anyway; you know I planned the next several days so we can do the land tours."

"So what did the Prom Witch have to say anyhow?" I asked, picking a crumb from my pink tie-front cardigan.

Marie squeezed her eyes shut for a second like her head hurt. "Loretta Carruth, 'of the Newport Carruths,'" Marie frowned, "basically said that she was missing an heirloom topaz necklace and a matching bracelet. And, of course, her Judith Leiber handbag." She lifted her hand to her brow and moaned. "Oh shit. With the loose two-carat South African diamond in the bottom of it."

"Oh my God. What about her tiara?"

"Cubic zirconia and still on her lyin' head."

"But—"

"Wait, there's more." Marie tapped her coffee cup and looked around. "If you see a bar steward, I really need a shot of Bailey's in this. It seems like the Prom Princess isn't the only one whose been reporting stolen items."

"What do you mean?"

"You know those stupid Elizabeth Taylor infomercials promoting the cabin safes? Well, apparently there's been a real rash of stolen valuables in the past few weeks. Fraudulent charges on guests' cards, too."

"Where ... who ... how?"

Marie smiled. "Easy, Nancy Drew. You think they'd tell me? Hell, I'm like a *suspect*."

"Damn, I don't believe this." I rolled my head back and forth. My neck was still sore from my belly flop onto the treadmill. A person waving from a table nearby caught my eye and I groaned. "Oh, jeez, it's the Greenbaums." Bernie was wearing one of those elastic back braces over his sweat suit. It made him look more pathetic than ever.

Marie waved back and I followed suit, trying to think of something polite to say. "We caught your Elvis act last night, Bernie," I said. "It was, um, really unique."

Bernie smiled and then hiked up one side of his lip, exposing his gold tooth. "Uh, thank yuh, thank yuh very much," he drawled, shimmying in his chair.

I forced another smile and whispered out the corner of my mouth. "What the hell was that—an encore or a mini stroke?"

Marie laughed for the first time in twelve hours.

I said a silent thank-you when the Greenbaums went back for more prunes and an old couple, in matching Bar Harbor sweat suits, snagged their table.

* * *

"Flying monkey," Marie said after opening our cabin door. She pointed to a satin sculpture draped over a coat hanger and suspended from the ceiling.

I groaned. "It's my half-slip. Unbelievable. Virgilio. Why in the world does he do that?" I looked sideways at Marie. "And if you say 'whatever floats your boat,' I'll adhesive tape your lips together. Don't tempt me."

"I was going to say, 'artistic expression' but now I realize that it's probably the inevitable mental illness that comes from living below decks like a friggin' mole. A lot of the stewards do it, I hear." She groaned and sank down on her bed, closing her eyes. "God, I'm exhausted."

"Oh no you don't. No dozing off until you tell me the rest of the Prom Princess story. Did you actually see her jewelry and purse in the sickbay?"

"Everybody keeps asking me that." Marie opened her eyes. "The truth is, I don't know. You know I don't give a rat's ass about jewelry; never really notice. She was still wearing her spa robe when I got there. I remember the stupid tiara, but 'heirloom jewelry'? Couldn't say."

"Wait," I sat down on my own bed and leaned forward. "You mean she had her mini-stroke at the spa?"

"That's what the doc said. Some of the crew put her in a wheelchair and brought her down in the elevator. Still had a cucumber slice stuck to the side of her snooty face. I remember that."

"So does anybody remember if she had her valuables with her?"

"None of the crew. But the problem is that she, Mrs. Carruth of *the* Carruths—whoever the hell they are—claims that she very clearly remembers having them with her."

"Could she remember?"

"When I got there she was awake. Kind of groggy and still complaining of feeling weak and achy, but she was moving all her parts and was lucid enough to know the date and the President's name. You know the drill."

"Groggy?"

Marie smiled. "Okay, that was shipmate-polite for sloshed. Soused, three sheets to the wind." She shook her head. "The spa package includes all-you-can-slurp champagne mimosas. Plus, someone remembered seeing her drinking even before that; in the disco."

"With Luke Skyler," I hissed through my fingers.

"What?"

"That's why I was out there on the deck looking for the Prom Princess, remember? Because she went out there with him. Dammit, I knew it."

"Hold on, Darc." Marie shook her head, watching as I tucked my rosy tee into the top of my jeans and checked my face in the mirror.

"I knew he was up to no good," I mumbled around my lip-gloss wand. Why on earth was I primping?

Marie sighed and flopped back on the bed. "You can't prove that he had anything to do with it any more than I can prove that I didn't."

"Well, I sure as hell am going to try." I grabbed my purse and my jean vest and reached for the door.

"Where are you going?"

I curtsied and flashed a syrupy smile. "Well my goodness, it seems that I owe a certain dance host an apology. Now, don't I? For that awful accident when I stepped on his foot."

Marie yawned. "Oh shit. Why do I have a bad feeling about this?"

"Go to sleep."

"Darcy?"

"M-hmmm?"

"Take the flying monkey down, will you? It's gonna give me nightmares; you know, like in Oz. When the little buggers carried Dorothy off?"

*   *   *

I studied the shipboard newsletter in the elevator on my way to the lower decks. "At Sea Day." What was on the schedule today and what does a sleazy dance host do in the daylight? Or should I be wondering where a jewel thief hides?

The first thing I needed to do was take a few slow breaths and calm down, not go off half-cocked as my pest-killer Dad likes to say. But dammit, it made me furious to see Marie put in this bad light. If there was anyone I trusted with anything, it was Marie Whitley.

Sure, people got annoyed at her wisecracks and her crazy irreverence. And, face it, there were still the small-brained people who couldn't look past her partner preference—her parents included—and I ached for the brave front that she showed in the face of that monumental hurdle. Part of me—the pathetic, macaroni and cheese-bingeing part—was probably more than a little jealous of what she and Carol had together. Ironically, they were probably the most conventional couple I knew. Ten years together. I couldn't manage more than ten months. Yep, Marie had the real deal—white-picket-fence permanence. I smiled, remembering. She'd done that, spent weeks building a picket fence and not that prefab plastic stuff, either, but the kind that had me picking splinters out of her fingers for an hour. She'd done that for

Carol, that spring after her breast cancer scare. It was the only time I'd seen Marie frightened. That's love in my book. And if there were a way to help my good friend out of this mess, I'd find it. Even if it meant schmoozing that jerk Luke Skyler.

The lower decks, A through C, were pretty spartan, mostly crew quarters, sickbay, ship's laundry, and so forth. Kind of conspicuous to go nosing around there, especially since I swore I could suddenly see a lot more of the security folks walking the corridors. Marie mentioned this morning that the ship had hired a whole new security team. Nepalese, is that what she'd said? Yipes. I watched as a pair of them rounded the corner, walking toward me. Short, really sturdy military types, dressed in black and carrying radios. And guns. I stepped back into the elevator and pushed the Up button.

There was a sushi-making demonstration on the Whaler's Deck, bingo in the main-floor theater, and Big Band era name-that-tune game in the Lobster Disco. Not likely. I needed to think like an inscrutable Nepalese. Out of thirteen decks, A through Sun Deck, what would draw a gigolo? Rich women. And where would they be?

All right. The elevator door opened onto the Promenade Deck and I saw the gilded sign, "Art Auction This Way." I grinned. I could see it now, hot McConaughey look-alike watching women in Chanel suits and heirloom jewelry waving white-gloved hands to bid on Monets, Renoirs, and Van Gogh's Starry Night. He'd be there.

Ninety minutes, later my stomach growled as I made one last round of the bars and headed back to the auction. Where was that guy? He couldn't exactly get off the ship. I'd been to all of the obvious places. I scanned the stupid auction crowd until my eyes burned; I still couldn't believe that sweat-suited yoga grandma had outbid everyone. An art-deco-framed canvas of a rabbi poised to circumcise the statue of David? Enough was enough. I'd walk down to the Java Café and get Marie a couple of those chocolate-dipped macaroons that she liked, kind of make up for the morning's dismal failure. I was no Nepalese.

I wove my way through the crowd in front of the photo gallery. Every blessed passenger must have posed with the captain. I was passing the entryway to the library when Luke's voice startled me.

"Buy anything?"

I hated it that I jumped. "What?" I asked, turning to where he stood in the library doorway.

Luke grinned. "At the auction. You stood there so long in front of that one painting." He was wearing wire-rimmed reading glasses, and through them I could see his eyes crinkle at the corners with amusement. "Michelangelo would have sued, don't you think?"

My faced burned. He'd been watching me? All these hours he'd been watching me watch for him?

"No." I smiled and brushed a strand of hair away from my face, stalling for a moment to catch my breath. "I didn't buy anything. But I'm glad I ran into you. I owe you an apology."

He removed his glasses and smiled down at me again. He was wearing a pale-flecked fishermen's knit sweater over a teal turtleneck that made his eyes appear an even deeper blue. Tropical water on a white sand beach sort of blue, warm, and fluid. *Easy girl, this is the enemy. How do you think he suckers all those women?*

"You're not trying catch me off balance so you can stomp me again, are you?"

"Swear." I smiled and crossed my heart.

My stomach growled like a wild thing and Luke chuckled, reaching for my arm. "Lunch?"

*　*　*

The ice had disappeared from the aft Lido Deck and sunshine slanted through the clouds. We carried our trays to a table near a freestanding stove an arm's reach from the railing. In the distance, the northern New England coast was visible through coast-hugging fog in burnished autumn colors of copper, saffron, and pomegranate red as if some careless woodsman had set it afire. I wasn't willing to admit it was romantic. I wasn't *that* reckless.

I crumbled a corn muffin between my fingertips and let it drop onto the surface of the thick crab bisque, watching the steam rise.

"My grandmama liked hers that way, too," Luke told me with a soft sigh. The collar was turned up on his dark wool pea coat and the chill breeze sifted his hair, leaving his tan cheeks ruddy. He'd missed a little patch below his jaw line when shaving, and the growth there was golden in the sunlight.

I felt my breathing soften, picturing Luke as a towheaded youngster tugging at the hem of his grandmother's apron. I watched his face, feeling the heat rise again in my own. Wait, what was I doing?

I looked back down at my soup bowl and pressed my lips together in a tight line. Blast it! This guy would not sucker me. I was immune to these charmers. Childhood memories? Sure. What was he going to parade out next, puppy stories and a recital of the Boy Scout motto? I would not be stupid again. The grandma vignette could be thrown onto the scrap pile along with Firefighter Sam's woolly tales of his "roommates." What I needed was information to help Marie. Starting right now.

I cleared my throat to speak but saw that Luke had turned his head to watch as a woman stepped out onto the deck. She was maybe seventy, with lacquered henna hair and a fur coat draped across her shoulders. A steward put a hand under her elbow to assist her and two waiters moved forward like drones to a queen bee. VIP? This lady looked familiar. From where?

The deck steward offered a chair and she sat down, waving the swarm of buzzing waiters away. She fumbled to produce a pair of yellow sunglasses from her handbag and used her left hand to adjust them over her eyes. Diamonds the size of clover blossoms flashed in the sunlight. I was riveted to the look on Luke's face. Spotting his quarry? He turned back toward me.

"I'm sorry, you were saying?"

"I was going to ask you a question," I said slowly. I'd be subtle, with no accusations. Simple shipboard curiosity. His eyes were making my brain fuzzy again.

"Yes?"

"So what's the deal with you and all these rich old ladies?"

Oh my God. I wanted to suck the words back as soon as they rolled from my tongue. Did I say that? I squeezed my eyes shut and felt my face catch fire. What was wrong with me? If I'd been standing in a London alley with Jack the Ripper, would I ask, "What's the deal with all that slashing?"

Luke Skyler chuckled deep in his throat and stirred his soup. "Delicately put." He looked up at me and smiled. "I'm a dance host. Cha-cha, merengue, rumba, and 'Waltz Across Texas'? The way you've been watching me, I'd imagine that you'd figured that out by now." He glanced down as he stirred his soup. "And now I get to ask what you do."

I hesitated. Sorry, Grandma. "I'm an orthotic sales rep."

Luke's smile faltered and his head snapped upward, brows scrunched, like I'd said something totally unexpected.

"Orthotics," I explained, "the kinds of things that a podiatrist prescribes? For foot problems, fallen arches, and plantar fasciitis." I fought the demon urge to glance over my shoulder at the Queen Bee. "Foot fixes for the elderly?"

Luke had composed his expression and smiled at me, letting out a soft breath. "Good. Want to keep them dancing. And your roommate, Miss Whitley, how long is she going to stay onboard? She's not a full-time employee, correct?"

I swallowed and stared. Damn him. What was going on here? I was supposed to be asking the questions. What did they do on those TV lawyer shows? Redirect.

"But that's not nearly as interesting as what you do, Mr. Skyler."

"Luke." He was staring into my eyes.

"Luke." I felt my face warm up again and hoped he thought it was from the sunlight. "Isn't it sort of a gypsy life to just sail the ocean catering to passengers? You're so much younger than the other dance hosts, and I understand that the cruise line doesn't even pay you." Blunt, but I was back on target. His move now.

The Queen Bee was laughing behind us and Luke turned briefly to observe before answering my question. "Wages? No. But it's a great way to meet people. See places. I've come into some money, so wages are really not an issue."

I bit my lip to keep from groaning aloud. *I'll just bet you've come into some money, mister.* I'd started to ask another question when there was a loud crash and the unmistakable sound of breaking glass behind us. Luke rose spring-loaded from his chair and knelt beside the Queen Bee.

The woman apologized for the commotion, her voice oozing like honey, and explained how she'd accidentally tipped the tray over due to clumsiness caused by a fiberglass cast on her right arm. Cast?

I watched as the woman turned to expose her injured forearm in its fur sling. Now I remembered her. At the auction, dammit. She made one of the highest bids of the day. I clenched my teeth as I watched Luke grin up at the woman. He'd been scouting the auction after all, from an inconspicuous seat in the library. Smart, slippery snake.

Luke returned to the table a few minutes later and looked down at his watch. He started to speak, but I cut him off. *Oh no you don't.* No mercy now. I had a few more questions. "So, I wondered if . . ." The Queen Bee rose from her table and took a step toward the ship's door and Luke stood up. He glanced down at me and smiled. "No, I'm the one who's wondering now." His smile faded. "I'm wondering if you found out all you needed to know."

My mouth went dry. *Act casual.* "What do you mean?"

"Last night," he said, his voice without expression, "when you and your friend were out there in the dark peeking through the spa window."

SIX

"YOU TOLD HIM WE were cleaning the port holes?" Marie lowered the huge binoculars and stared at me. *"Cleaning the port holes?"* Her round face reddened and her knuckles blanched white.

"Hey, you're not going to throw those things at me are you?" I shook my head and groaned. "I knew you'd react like this; see why I didn't tell you until this morning?"

"Couldn't you have come up with something a tad more believable? Shit, he saw us outside the spa? I'm gonna get arrested for sure." Marie pulled the hood of her madras windbreaker up and watched over the Whaler's Deck rail as the ship docked in Halifax.

"No, wait. I thought about this all night. I admit the porthole thing was stupid. I couldn't think that fast. But I've been analyzing this. Why would Luke Skyler tell anyone we were out there? Men aren't allowed in the spa; why would he risk having anyone know that he was hanging around there, too?"

"Because you've read him all wrong and he's just a Good Samaritan?" She pointed to the dock below. "Look, bagpipers."

"Good Samaritan? Like hell. You saw him last night at the show, sucking up to the Queen Bee."

Marie grimaced and hissed through clenched teeth. "Can you *stop* it with those stupid nicknames? You sound like . . ." Her face slowly softened and she reached out to squeeze my shoulder. "Sorry, I really need to get on dry land. Hey, you've got our tickets for the Titanic Cemetery, right? I see the buses down there."

I managed a cough and a mumble.

"What? You've got them, don't you?" Marie narrowed her eyes.

Oh hell, I'd have to spill it sometime. About the whole plan. It was for Marie's benefit after all. I beamed and tried to look enthusiastic. "I traded them in for something better."

"You what?"

"It's not healthy to be focusing on disasters, so I traded them in for the tour of Peggy's Cove, instead." I feigned interest in the cropped hem of my suede jacket.

"Peggy's Cove?"

I pulled the brochure from my pocket. "Quaint fishing village on the scenic Nova Scotia coast. Most photographed—"

"Most photographed lighthouse in Canada," Marie mocked, interrupting. "I've been there twice."

"But not with me."

Marie sighed and picked up her backpack. "You're right. C'mon. Maybe we could wash the lighthouse windows while we're there."

We joined the crowd filing down the gangway and heading toward the buses in the distance. Clutches of bagpipers whined and droned, beckoning the passengers to linger in the Port's gift shops. I spotted the tour guides' signs just beyond the exit, past counters laden with a dizzying array of clan tartans, hockey logo sweatshirts, and miniature jugs of maple syrup.

"Do you think my face is too round for one of these Mountie hats?" Marie stopped and grabbed for my sleeve. "Hey, hold on. What's the rush? You're like a bloodhound on a scent. *Uh oh.*" She set the stiff-brimmed hat down and stared.

I smiled and raised my brows.

"Now I get it." Marie narrowed her eyes. "Do you wanna tell me the truth about this sudden change of tours?"

"So I'm still trying to save your ass. Is that all right?" I sighed. "Last night at the show I heard the Queen Bee and Luke talking about going to Peggy's Cove."

"And?"

"Oh for godsake, Marie. She's his next target. Don't you see that? I'll bet you anything they're already on that bus together. I want to get a seat close enough to hear his spiel."

The Peggy's Cove bus was the last one along the curb and Marie snorted as we passed the group boarding for the Titanic Cemetery Tour. We followed two of the Yoga Ladies up the steps and slowly made our way to the few remaining seats near the back of the bus.

The Queen Bee, in a lamb's fleece jacket with matching arm sling, was seated halfway down the row on the driver's side, in the aisle seat beside Edie and Bernie Greenbaum. Luke Skyler was not aboard.

"Great," Marie said as we squeezed past shopping bags and found our seats. "Guess that sort of blows your theory. I could have been at the Titanic Cemetery wearing a very cool Mountie hat."

I was silent as the bus doors closed and the driver pulled away from the curb. "Sorry," I mumbled at last.

The tour guide keyed the mike, cleared her throat, and then suddenly pitched backward as the driver stepped hard on the brake. The passengers tipped forward and let out a collective groan as the driver apologized.

"Sorry, folks."

The doors hissed as they opened to let Luke Skyler step aboard.

"Just because he's on the bus, doesn't mean he's stalking her," Marie whispered as we watched Luke amble down the aisle. "So wipe the feathers off your chin, kitty cat."

"Why else would he be here?" I asked, smirking.

"Lobster and blueberry cobbler. Same as me."

"Right." I elbowed Marie and barely contained a squeal as Luke paused beside the Queen Bee and rested his hand on her shoulder. He smiled, spoke a few words, and we could hear her gush and titter as the bus started back up. Luke took the last empty seat directly behind her.

"And Marie?"

"Yeah?"

"I just thought of another reason he wouldn't want to tell anyone we were outside the spa."

Marie rubbed her hand across her eyes. "Okay, why?"

"Because maybe he needs to find something out first." I lowered my voice and felt goose bumps rise on my arms. "Maybe someone *told* him we were out there and now Luke needs to know if we were watching him steal from the Prom Princess."

Luke turned around and looked directly at me, then pulled a skiing magazine from his knapsack and never raised his head the rest of the way to Peggy's Cove.

"Hey, wake up, we're here." I nudged Marie who was softly snoring on my shoulder. And tried not to notice the amused clucks and knowing smiles of passengers filing by us. I shoved

Marie again. "Get off of me. You're ruining my chance of dating any man south of Newfoundland."

Luke fastened his down parka, hefted his knapsack, and followed the Queen Bee off the bus while we trotted close behind.

"He's never gonna get a chance at her while she's with the Greenbaums." Marie paused to adjust her binocular strap. "I mean look, Edie's got a death grip on her only free arm."

"You're right," I agreed, folding my arms over my breasts and remembering that day in the gym; for a pink-haired Munchkin, Edie Greenbaum had quite a grip. "What's Bernie doing, waving his arms like that?"

"Looks like a little re-enactment from last night's *Annie Get Your Gun*. The guy never quits, does he?"

Luke walked past us and nodded to me, wayward spikes of golden hair bobbing with the movement. I felt my throat constrict. He wore an ice-blue quilted parka over a navy striped rugby shirt, and paused for a moment to remove a pair of aviator sunglasses. The scent of his cologne lingered, mingling with the salty air, and I breathed in softly realizing that my hands were trembling.

Damn him. I pulled my gloves from my pocket and slipped into them like armor, reminding myself again that Luke Skyler was dangerous. I watched as he walked away toward the lighthouse and then clenched my teeth and tugged at Marie's sleeve. He was following the Greenbaum threesome.

We headed up a road hemmed by rusty red sea grass, past the chiseled angel's wings of a maritime monument, and on toward the lighthouse rocks. I raised the zipper on my jacket and felt the damp wind whip my hair across my lips as I scanned the little fishing village tucked into Margaret's Bay.

No wonder it was the subject of countless calendar photos. Wonderful. It practically sang of oilskin slickers, sea salt, and brandy-laced coffee in ancient mugs. Even below the day's gray sky, Peggy's Cove was as awash with color as an artist's palette. My eyes took in the ramshackle boats and bait stands that seemed to be held together by a magic mucilage of heavy paint: primary reds, blues like summer-faded denims, and mustard yellows. Lobster traps were stacked high on the docks, their braided ropes coiled neatly by fishermen's fists. I imagined watermelon in the hands of children with paint-freckled faces, and I could almost hear their bare feet slapping the surface of the sun-warmed pier. Marie shouldn't complain that I'd chosen—

"This is as far as I go," she told me, stopping.

The path had begun to climb in earnest and had changed from sandy earth to solid rock. Huge boulders like sunning sea turtles overlapped each other and led upward toward the lighthouse.

"See?" Marie pointed toward a well-worn plaque at our feet.

WARNING

Injury and death have rewarded careless sightseers here.
The ocean and rocks are treacherous.
Savor the sea from a distance.

"But," I glanced ahead up the trail and could see several passengers continuing on. "The others . . ."

Marie shook her head and pointed down at her shoes. "Not in the shoes I'm wearing. We can see fine from here."

The lighthouse was a white, octagonal concrete tower rising maybe fifty feet, with a vertical trio of windows and topped with a red cupola. From behind the windows, its beacon flashed electric green across the foggy sky.

I leaned past Marie and scanned the path and the boulders beyond. Where were the Greenbaums and the Queen Bee? I'd lost sight of them somehow. And Luke?

I tested the traction of my Doc Marten boot against the first boulder. "They're exaggerating with that plaque. Do you see the Greenbaums?" I stretched the strap taut against Marie's neck and lifted the binoculars to my eyes to scan the area around the lighthouse again.

"Hey, you're choking me. And no, I don't think they would be stupid enough to go any further." Marie pulled the binoculars from me and began to walk away.

"Wait, where are you going?" I shouted against the wind.

"To 'savor the sea from a distance.' In the café. Over Irish coffee."

"Well, I'm going on up there," I told her, nodding toward the lighthouse.

Marie turned and frowned, her brows scrunched together. "Oh, come on. I've heard it's not even that great a view."

"You've been here twice and never gone up?"

Marie kicked the toe of her shoe against a rock, then looked back up and shrugged. "Okay, I hate heights."

I shook my head and laughed. "Well hell, I'm scared spitless of whales. Do you think I'd get very close to the edge? I'll be careful, I swear. And I won't be long."

"You'll listen for the bus horns, okay? We've only got, like, twenty minutes more. And you won't want to miss the lunch stop, trust me."

I tested the sole of my boots on every rock and watched for clumps of algae and wet spots as I climbed upward. There was a handrail for the first hundred yards and then it was more like being a mountain goat. The ocean roared in the distance and the wind whipped my hair against my face until I stopped and pulled it into a ponytail using my fleece ear warmer as a band. I could hear the drone of a bagpiper entertaining the passengers outside the café below. I shivered. Maybe Marie had the right idea. A hot cup of coffee with a splash of Bailey's Irish Cream sounded pretty good right now. My foot slipped slightly and I spread my hands like a tightrope walker, regaining my balance easily. See? No big deal.

There were only a few other tourists visible now and most of them were on the way down. I stopped and looked back at the café and moaned. The Greenbaums. And the Queen Bee. Standing next to the bagpiper. Where was Luke Skyler?

No one had moved toward the buses, so I decided to continue on even if I wasn't tailing the Queen Bee after all. I was a sightseer, right? And though I wouldn't admit it to Marie, there was a little closing ritual I had planned. A "Sam thing," Marie would call it. It needed to be done.

I reached the base of the lighthouse and looked out across the bay. Marie was wrong—it was way worth the climb. Amazing.

I let my gaze drift out to the silver-gray horizon and then back to the tidy cove with Lilliputian buildings and toy boats. Even our cruise ship would look doll-size from up here. I put my palm on the white concrete of the locked lighthouse, cold and damp from the sea air, and tilted my head backward to blink up at the green beacon. I walked around the building's base to be certain I was alone and then sat down on a rock outcropping a safe distance from the edge. A snowy white gull hung in the air just beyond me. I pushed up the sleeve of my jacket and sweater to reveal the silver Italian charm bracelet. *Okay, now.*

"Don't ever take it off," Sam had told me as we lay together one afternoon after lovemaking, "and don't ever stop thinking of me." I shook my head and the ocean wind roared in my ears like it would whisk away the memory of his words. He was married. All those months we were together.

I'd asked myself the questions a thousand times. Why had I blindly accepted the conditions of that relationship without question: calling him just on a cell phone, meeting him only at my apartment or the little inn miles from his home? Had it made that much sense, his stories of slobby roommates and erratic call schedules? Had I needed to believe him so much? Was a half-hearted commitment all I was really ready for? *Or was I just plain stupid?*

I shook my head and the wind whipped a loose strand of hair across my lips in a sharp sting. Bagpipe music droned in the distance like a dirge. Was I stupid? I'd asked Sam exactly that six months ago, the day after knocking on that door and looking into his wife's eyes. I'd screamed and beat my fists against his chest and asked, *"Was I stupid—did you count on that?"*

"No," he'd said, trying to hold me as I struggled. "Not stupid, Darcy, just trusting." Like that made it okay somehow, erased the hurt. Like it wasn't a totally fatal flaw. Trust. A lot of things boiled down to that, probably—trusting Sam to be honest, even trusting that the problems in our healthcare system could be fixed before I was forced to bail out.

I touched the charms one at a time. The diamond chip, my birthstone—April. A stylized blue running shoe I'd bought after my last half-marathon. The gold caduceus, for my nursing career. What would the symbol be for an orthotic rep? And the red charm—raised enamel and rimmed in gold. A firefighter's hat. For Sam. Don't Ever Stop Thinking About Me Sam.

I stood and stretched the links apart using my fingernail to pry the charm out. I held it for a moment between my fingertips and took a slow breath, a test breath. Nope, no more pain. I smiled and tossed the charm toward the edge of the cliff. *Good bye, Sam.*

It bounced on the rock and stuck tight. Shit.

I tested the rocks ahead of me with the toe of my boot. Reasonably dry, even though the air felt more like drizzle than fog now. I crept forward a few feet more, squatted down, and reached for the charm. It slid away from my fingertips into a shallow, moss-filled crevice. The wind picked up and obliterated the bagpipe music below. I hadn't heard a bus horn, had I?

I duck-walked another step toward the edge and stretched my fingers out again. I could see over the edge now, and onto the slope of jagged boulders that swept down to the whitecaps beyond. My fingers pried the charm from the crevice and I felt my breath escape. I pinched it tightly. *All right.*

I'd raised my hand to make the toss when a horn honk made me turn. The sole of my boot twisted on the mossy surface and slid out from under me. *Oh my God!*

My belly slammed hard onto the rock's surface and my body slid backward until my legs dangled over the ledge. I struggled for a breath and dug my fingernails into the rocky surface. There was nothing to grab onto. My scream was smothered by a painful cough. *Please, God.*

Legs appeared in front of me, but I was afraid to lift my head and risk another backward slide. I blinked and focused on all that I could. Blue jeans, high-top hiking boots. Deep voice. Familiar? Oh God. Luke. He was going to shove me over the edge.

SEVEN

"Don't fight me," he growled.

My fingertips dug at a crevice in the rock and I raised a painful palm to slap at Luke's arms. He was going to have one hell of a fight if he tried to push me over. "No!" I yelled and then tried to hike my knee up to wedge the toe of my boot against something solid. Just get a toehold and give myself some sort of chance.

The bus honked again in the distance, and . . . *what was that*? Footsteps, coming closer? Luke turned his head, but kept a fierce grip on my upper arms, his parka sleeve brushing against my lips. If I was going to do something, it had to be now.

"It's okay, I've got her," he shouted out against the wind.

Got me?

Luke pulled hard on my arms, yanking me forward. "If she'd stop fighting me." He glanced down, did a double take, and frowned. "You were going to *bite* me?"

Hard to deny with my mouth full of his sleeve.

Within seconds I was standing upright, weak in the knees and shivering uncontrollably. My hands stung like fire and my teeth chattered so badly that I bit my tongue when I tried to speak. "I . . ." My body was wracked by another chill as the wind whipped my words away. I looked up at a small group of men, maybe fisherman and a uniformed park ranger, and tried to smile. Tears filled my eyes instead. *Oh my God.* What had just happened here?

"Let's get you back down there," Luke said, his voice suddenly gentle. He slid his parka over my coat and fastened the snaps all the way to my chin while I stood shivering and mute. Then he brushed my hair free of the collar and laughed softly. His face was inches from mine, his breath warm against my skin. "This is getting to be a real sick pattern, you know. Attacking your rescuer?"

Marie had climbed as far as the end of the handrail and I saw her wave furiously as we approached. She lowered her hand and stared, eyes wide, at Luke's arm wrapped around my shoulders. I was going to have some explaining to do.

"Don't ask me anything yet," I muttered as Marie and I moved along the bus aisle past the Greenbaums to our seats. Her elbow nudged my ribs as we watched Luke assist the Queen Bee.

I squeezed my eyes shut and rubbed my scraped palms together gingerly. I didn't know what to think. Had Luke really come to the lighthouse to rescue me or had the fishermen and ranger simply interrupted a . . . murder attempt? Was he the jewel thief or did I have it all wrong? My head throbbed like a cheap tequila hangover.

I peered down the aisle as the bus started up. Luke had taken a seat beside the Queen Bee. I didn't want to think about that anymore. I just wanted to close my eyes. There was a heater vent right under my seat and it felt so good to be warm again. I smiled; bless her, Marie was already jabbering away about lunch.

* * *

The entrance to the Sou'Wester Sea Shack was shaped like the mouth of a whale and I got nicked by a splintery tooth as I ducked through its jaws. The salt-on-hot-grease aroma of crispy French fries and the twang of a steel guitar wooed us as the doors swung open.

Marie clasped her hands together like a believer kneeling at an altar. "I'm *saved*. Country music, and . . ." she pointed to a chalkboard menu and moaned, "lobster seven frigging ways. Thank you, Lord."

I excused myself to wash my battered hands and resurrect my lipstick, and then returned to find that Marie was already seated at a table topped with a red-and-white check tablecloth, with the Greenbaums, the Queen Bee, and Luke Skyler. They were all wearing plastic bibs.

"I ordered for you," Marie grinned. "Classic whole lobster, since you've never tackled it that way."

"To lobster." Luke grinned, hoisting a glass of beer, "One of the few meal choices that invites you to choose your own victim."

The Greenbaums raised their glasses and murmured in agreement, and the Queen Bee watched Luke's face, giggling like a starstruck groupie. *Like Grandma Rosaleen and her con man.* Why were these women so foolish, and why wasn't anyone doing anything about it?

I thanked Marie for ordering my chardonnay and took a very unladylike swig, glaring at Luke over the brim of my glass. Victim? He obviously planned on toying with us all. Like hell. We'd see who had the last laugh.

I turned my attention to the little band assembled near the expansive ocean-view windows. Touring celebrities, according to a posted flyer. "Top Country Band in Newfoundland," it read.

Newfoundland? It was a province whose time zone changed in a half-hour increment. How many country bands could it possibly have? But, hey, they *were* good. Really good. I smiled at the lead singer, a forty-ish man in a striped western shirt, and shook my head as one of his cohorts—a man in his seventies I'd bet—played a washboard adorned with a yellow happy-face while sucking on a shoulder-mounted harmonica. My grandma would love this.

The meals arrived and I found myself face to face with my lobster—neon red, claws like a prizefighter, squatting above a bed of French fries, coleslaw, and a half-stump of steaming corn. Its twin antennae saluted me above beady little eyes and I grimaced. The Cavanaughs were the kind of people very used to our fish arriving safely behind plastic wrap and a bar code. No outdoorsy hunting and fishing genes in the pool. Dad's idea of a "great catch" involved a nest of termites and a spray nozzle, and I'm pretty sure that my mother's favorite sunset was painted on the ceiling of Caesar's Palace. Whole lobster was definitely a New England deal.

"I have to break its legs off?" I asked warily. "I'm sort of used to them coming only as a tail. No shells, no face, just a lemon wedge and a little saucer of butter."

Edie clucked her tongue. "You've got to *name* him first, sweetie. Little tradition for the newbies. Then don't worry, we'll show you how to eat it."

Luke presented his metal nutcracker with what I'm sure was unnecessary theatrics and then crushed his lobster's claw with a resounding crack. "Don't baby that woman, Edie. I've seen Miss Cavanaugh in action. Stomping and biting. A little dismemberment should be a real yawn for someone like her." He raised his glass and smirked at me. "To your newest victim then, Darcy. What's his name going to be?"

I sneered and squeezed the handles of my own nutcracker, then smiled when the loud crack made Luke's eyes widen. "Cassanova," I said, meeting his gaze.

"Ooh," the Queen Bee winced, "That was his head, dear."

Despite the carnage, the lobster was the sweetest I'd ever tasted, each mouthful succulent and dripping with butter. And after my third chardonnay, I was sucking on the little soda-straw legs like a pro. Even Bernie Greenbaum's incessant puns seemed hilarious. I glanced over at Luke and watched his face morph from fuzzy twins into focus again. One of him was more than anyone should trust.

He'd led the conversation during the meal, telling stories of his travels, then drawing out the others and listening with interest. Even Marie, the twit, was baring her soul, talking about her New York relatives, her stint aboard the ships. The man was good.

Well, drunk or not, I wasn't going to be played for a fool. No sir.

"What?" I set my nearly drained glass down. Why was everyone staring at me all of a sudden?

"Luke's asked you to dance, dear." The Queen Bee raised her penciled brows. "It's too awkward for me with this darned cast. But you go ahead and dance with him especially since . . ." she paused and fluttered her fingers like she'd witnessed a cloud in the shape of the Virgin Mary, "he just *saved your life.*" There was a murmur and then a burst of applause, and then someone waved a hollowed-out lobster carcass and whistled.

The Newfoundland band waved us forward and the room began to thrum with stomping feet and the deafening chant of "He-ro, he-ro, he-ro!" *Oh for godsake.* What else could I do, but dance with the jerk?

My face flamed. I stood as the crowd cheered, and then paused for a moment until my head stopped swimming and the stripes on Luke's rugby shirt were no longer revolving like a slot machine. I smoothed my snug black cardigan to make sure it covered the top of my jeans and, warily, let him take my hand to lead me toward the tiny dance floor.

They lowered the overhead lights until the fading coastal sunlight was all that lit the room, casting rusty shadows over the weathered wood walls and across the washboard player's craggy face. The music started, the Queen Bee's request: "Wind Beneath My Wings." Great. "Did you ever know that you're my hero?" the lead singer began, and the room breathed a collective *awww* as Luke's arms closed around me.

He held me like . . . like a gigolo I guess. Like a man used to holding women. And having those women really like it. Not that *I* liked it. Or cared that he held my hand so gently and that he was close enough that I could feel the warmth of his skin, and smell the scent of his hair. He smelled like fresh rain, warm musk, and maybe blueberry cobbler. Boyish, clean, and honest. *Honest?* Oh jeez. Where in the world was I going with this?

Luke's palm was warm where it rested below the belt loops on the back of my jeans, and his hands really were gentle now, so unlike that painful grip at the lighthouse. Warm, yes. There, along the small of my back. And lower, to where my short sweater ended and . . . was he moving his fingers a little, to the rhythm of the music? For that matter, dammit, was the *floor* moving, too? I groaned. I should never drink three glasses of wine. Why hadn't Marie stopped me?

"Did you say something?" Luke asked, tilting me slightly away so he could look into my face. He had dark blonde lashes and there were little matching flecks, like California gold dust, in the blue of his eyes. Deep blue; deep like a plunge from a sea cliff.

"No. But I guess I should say thank you," I whispered. "You know, for what happened at the lighthouse."

It seemed like Luke held his breath for a moment. "What *did* happen up there, Darcy?" His brows furrowed and I could feel his hand tighten against the curve of my back.

"I don't know what you mean."

"What were you doing up there all alone? So close to the edge?"

"Nothing really, I . . ." I felt his arm move to bring me closer against him. Until his cheek was warm against mine and his lips brushed against my ear when he whispered.

"You weren't throwing something away?"

I stopped mid-step and my legs turned rubbery-weak. I tried to move away and stumbled over his foot. He caught me and gripped my arms hard for the second time that day. He'd been watching me? How long . . . and *why*?

I didn't realize that the music had ended until I heard the crowd applaud. And then they cheered as Luke lifted my hand and pressed it to his lips.

* * *

I was glad to get back on the bus and head back to the ship. Funny how it seemed almost like going home, after the day's turmoil. This time it was I who fell asleep leaning against Marie, in the seat behind Luke and the Queen Bee and listening to Bernie Greenbaum leading lively a rendition of "A Hundred Bottles of Beer."

I wasn't sure if it was the tour bus's jolting stop that woke me or the sirens and flashing lights. What was going on down there? I joined the others staring through the bus windows at the dock. We'd pulled up alongside the cruise ship and the driver's radio was squawking with static and a chorus of authoritative voices.

"Got to stay on the bus until the ambulance pulls away," the driver growled over his shoulder. "So sit back down, folks. But no more singing, for cripes sake."

"It's not just an ambulance," Marie whispered. "Look. Cops."

A trio of patrol cars was parked near the gangway, and my eyes moved across the logo on one of the dark blue doors—a lighthouse, maple leaf, Nova Scotia's coat of arms, and the wording below: *Halifax Regional Police.* A large German shepherd pressed his nose against the glass from inside.

The passengers murmured and rose from their seats again and I craned my neck to see. Paramedics were guiding a stretcher down the gangway, balancing a portable oxygen tank and securing a mask against their patient's face. An elderly man tried to keep pace beside them, his bespectacled face pale with obvious worry.

One of the Yoga Ladies toward the front of the bus squealed. "Oh my ga-awd, it's Helen. Helen Kravitz! That's her husband, Karl, there with her." The passengers moved like a tidal wave toward the windows again.

"Hey," Marie touched my shoulder. "Kravitz? Aren't they the old couple two cabins down from us? The ones that had the banner on the door for their fiftieth anniversary?"

"Mm-hmm, yes, I think that's right." I was scanning the passengers. Where was Luke?

"Okay." The bus driver pushed a button on his radio. "They're going to let you get off the bus here in a few minutes. So get your belongings together." He turned back to the group and lowered his voice, "And since we're talking about belongings . . . I

71

shouldn't really be telling you this, but be very careful, folks. See those police cars there? Well, it seems like while that poor lady was in the infirmary with a heart attack, some rotten bastard went through her cabin and stole everything she had."

The tour guide lined us up and let us pass in an orderly fashion one by one from the bus. It was easy to see that, somehow, Luke Skyler had exited before us.

EIGHT

"Gee, I wonder who would send flowers to Princess Leia?" Marie asked.

"What?" I stepped out of the steamy bathroom wearing my old chenille robe and rubbing at my hair with a towel. My mouth fell open.

Marie nudged the door shut with her foot and balanced a huge vase of flowers, an autumn mix of bronze mums, bittersweet, and multicolored snapdragons, framed by gold-dipped cattails and slender branches of fiery maple leaves. It looked like some wood sprite had snatched a fistful of Nova Scotia and presented it on a whim. A tiny metallic lobster sticker glimmered on an envelope affixed to a cattail stem.

"Shall we guess?" Marie set the vase down and pressed the envelope to her forehead, swami-like. "Let's see, I'm getting a vision. Ee-ew, Dr. Foote?" She grinned at the look on my face. "No? Then maybe our lazy little Virgilio? To apologize for creating absolutely nothing with your lingerie today?" She nodded toward my satin nightgown, draped strangely untouched across a chair.

I snatched the card, feeling my face grow warm, then sat down on my bed and lifted the edge of the envelope. It couldn't be. Could it?

"Well?" Marie prodded.

The handwriting was small and unfamiliar. It read, "*Have dinner with me in a galaxy far, far away. Starlight Bistro. Eight p.m. Please? Luke.*"

I handed it to Marie and buried my face in my hands. The scrapes on my palms still stung, a reminder of the morning's episode with Luke and the confusion that still remained.

"Well, well. So are you going to go?"

I threw my towel at Marie. "You're awfully eager to foist me off on some shady character, aren't you?"

"Hey, I never bought into that theory in the first place, Darc'. And besides," she grinned, "the dance host was cracking lobster with about fifty witnesses today when that burglary went down." She waved her arms in the air and did a little touchdown dance. "And I was too, don't ya love it? Yes! Thanks to Mrs. Kravitz, maybe I'll get my sailor hat back."

I flicked a fingernail against the edge of the card. Marie had a point about Luke, and the burglary. Did it really take him off the hook? "And what would you be doing if I decided to join him for dinner?"

"Doing?" Marie's gaze darted to her watch.

"I mean we usually have dinner together. I wouldn't feel right leaving you."

Marie shrugged. "To tell you the truth, kid, I was gonna leave you anyway. See, there's this little poker game. Howie, the night nurse, begged me to come." She shook her head. "The guy's trying to recoup some losses—I swear, he'd take bets on thermometer readings if he could get anyone to ante up. But the point is that I'd planned to skip dinner tonight because they're going to have all this great stuff like barbecued chicken wings, fried cheese, and jalapeno poppers." She grinned. "You know, real food."

I raised my brows. "Wait. That game's in the Havana Club, right? The cigar lounge?"

Marie tapped her watch. "You'd better get cracking, Princess. We don't want to go looking like something the dolphins dragged in, do we?"

* * *

The Starlight Bistro was on the Promenade Deck and was one of three specialty restaurants that had limited seating and required reservations. It was aft, and boasted a huge dome-shaped ceiling of glass like an astronomer's observatory, with the ability to open when the ship cruised warm waters. The tables there, unlike in the formal dining rooms, were intimate and screened by arrangements of fragile white willow branches strung with seashells and tiny star-shaped lights. The moon shone through the panes overhead and the room was bathed in candlelight. Strains of Vivaldi's *The Four Seasons* floated overhead. Yes, it screamed "Gigolo."

I glanced at my watch—*too early*—and ducked into the ladies room near the bistro's entrance. What was I doing anyway? I looked at my reflection in the huge mirror framed with glittering starfish. Was I about to make a fool of myself again?

I swept powder lightly over the fading bruise on my cheekbone and applied some gloss to my lips. The top of the hankie hem dress hugged my breasts and its turquoise color made my eyes look more teal than green in this light. I blinked my lashes; the trace of shimmery shadow was just enough. Sam would have said, "*Per-r-fect.*" But then Sam was a liar. Ask his wife.

I raised my hand and let my fingertips trace across the side of my jaw before tossing a wavy tendril of hair over my shoulder. How had Luke's face felt against mine when we danced? How about his fingers, there at the back of my jeans . . . Damn, what was I doing? I jutted my chin and pressed my lips together. I was immune to the effects of a smooth operator like Luke Skyler. A near-death experience on a sea cliff couldn't change all that. And there were still so many questions to answer about his involvement with the old women. I was ready.

The ladies room door opened behind me and two elderly women entered and then paused to stare at me.

"Oh look, Gracie, she's primping for that dance host. Isn't that sweet?" One of them stepped closer, her birdlike fingers tugging at my bodice to get my attention. What was this? Were seniors given some special license to handle people at will, for godsake?

"Skitter along now, dear," the woman cooed. "He's waiting in there for you. At the table."

I barely stopped myself from groaning aloud, tossed my compact into my purse and reached for the door. No such thing as privacy, that's for sure.

"Did you see that, Gracie?" the woman was asking as she opened the toilet stall door. "*Mine* used to stand up like that, too, real perky, I swear. Flat as flapjacks now, dammit."

* * *

Luke stood as the headwaiter ushered me to the table. I felt my pulse quicken and resisted the urge to sprint away. Did he have to look like that?

He stood there like some sappy romantic hero, broad shoulders and a tan houndstooth jacket, candlelight on his face, and his expression openly admiring. The whole effect made him look like Prince Charming in the bedtime story my grandmother read to me a thousand times.

Great. I was pre-programmed for relationship suicide.

"You look beautiful, Darcy." Luke said after I was seated. "And I'm very glad that you came." He smiled and shook his head. "I wasn't sure you would."

I took a deep breath and smiled. No sense in being nervous. It's not like I could avoid men altogether. Throwing an Italian charm into the ocean—okay, trying to—wasn't some magic spell that would suck them all from the face of the earth. I was healed; I was wiser. And so what if I was just plain curious about this guy? I could do this.

"Of course I would come," I told him. "And I want to thank you for the flowers; they're gorgeous."

"Little gesture of apology," he said, the hint of a drawl presenting itself again. "I think we've gotten off on a bad foot."

I laughed. "Well, that's certainly diplomatic. I think you mean that I stomped that foot and then fought like a wildcat any time you've gotten within arm's reach since."

He clucked his tongue, nodding. "And I'll bet you beat your brothers at arm wrestling."

I laughed again thinking of them, Will and Chance Cavanaugh. "Every time." Wait. *How* . . . "How'd you know that I have brothers?"

"Lucky guess. But a woman needs to be a little . . ." Luke smiled, "kick-ass nowadays, doesn't she?" The sommelier arrived and presented a pinot noir for approval. Luke sipped, nodded, and waited while the wine was poured. "She's got to be careful she isn't taken advantage of. Not only by men. By anyone." He shook his head. "My father would say, 'These are not gentle times.'"

I took a sip of my wine, quiet for moment. *A woman's got to be careful?* Where was he going with that? Toying with me again? I watched him as he lifted his own glass. The candlelight flickered across his face. Unreadable.

"You mean like that woman today. Mrs. Kravitz, the one who was burglarized?" I raised my brows. "By the way, how'd you manage to get that driver to let you off the bus ahead of everyone else?" I watched Luke's Adam's apple move up and down before he smiled.

"So you missed me? I'm flattered."

"No, really. How'd you do it?"

"Would you believe I had a dance lesson to teach? A cha-cha emergency?"

"No."

He smiled and held his glass by the stem, swirling the dark liquid. "Oh, but you have to. Like I'm supposed to believe that what you do is sell bunion plasters." He looked away as the waiter arrived to take our dinner orders.

By the time dessert arrived, we'd found common ground on a surprising number of things including an appreciation of music from classical to bluegrass, a secret weakness for sloppy joe sandwiches, and the fact that both of our grandmothers had spanked us with wooden spoons.

"Swear to God," I giggled over the brim of my glass as I watched Luke press a fork against the last bits of toasted pecan. He had great hands. "Grandma Rosaleen had to be the fastest swat on the West Coast. Did you ever get whacked while the spoon was still . . ." I grimaced, remembering, "actually wet with something?"

"Hush-puppy batter," Luke said without missing a beat. He grinned and his eyes crinkled. "Gritty damned stuff stings like a sonofabitch."

I watched his eyes as the waiter poured more coffee and re-arranged the little silver containers of sugar and cream. A warm sensation crept into my chest and I took a breath to diffuse it. *Be careful, Darcy.* What was it about this guy? How could he seem so . . . what? Genuine? Yes, all right, genuine and *warm,* really. Approachable. And then all at once, he'd kind of close down. No, it was more than that. It was like he would slam into reverse and invade. Circle and sniff. Like a predator. What was he up to?

He exhaled softly and leaned toward me, making my confusion tumble headlong toward distraction. "I'd love to dance with you again, Darcy."

The adjacent piano bar had a small wooden dance-floor, potted palms, and soft-lit Moroccan décor below slow-swirling ceiling fans. A tuxedoed pianist smiled and nodded as we entered, his fingers moving over the keys to release vintage Sinatra. Fewer than a dozen people were scattered across the room and only a single couple was dancing.

"Slim pickings for a dance host," I teased and felt instantly sorry when Luke's smile faded at the remark. No, not a remark—it was a jab. *Stop arm-wrestling, Darcy.* "I'm sorry, I was joking."

He waited while I set my wrap and evening bag down and then took my hand and led me to the dance floor. He was just the right height to dance with comfortably, my chin a little below his shoulder so that he didn't have to stoop and I didn't have to rise on tiptoe. If I weren't just-burnt cynical, I'd have to say that we were the perfect fit.

I felt his hand move low at the waist of my dress as he brought me closer and we moved into the rhythm of the music. The wool jacket was soft under my fingertips, and I was near enough to feel his thigh brush between mine as we pivoted together in a turn. His cheek rested against mine and I breathed in the starchy scent of his shirt and a trace of cologne.

"I'm *not*." He said, his lips brushing against my ear.

"Not what?" I opened my eyes, unaware until that second that I'd closed them.

"I'm not a dance host."

I leaned away from him. What was he telling me? Good God, was he confessing something? I knew it.

"Not tonight." He grinned down at me and his incredible eyes crinkled at the edges. "Tonight I'm a fellow wooden spoon survivor." He moved me back against him, his fingers warm along my back, and whispered in my ear. "And the man who is very privileged to have the beautiful Darcy Cavanaugh in his arms."

The pianist was expert at judging his audience and let one song blend fluidly into another in a romantic medley, until I was unsure of how long I'd been in Luke's arms. I only knew that my head was too heavy to leave the soft berth of his shoulder and that somehow my arms had twined around his neck until I could feel the soft tickle of his hair against my hands. The ship's movement rocked the dance floor gently and I could feel the thrum of the piano strings as we passed near. Somehow my pulse was keeping pace with it all, one rhythm indistinguishable from another. Luke's lips moved against my neck.

"We should be far enough from shore now to see a great view of Halifax," he whispered. "Want to go outside and look?"

The aft deck beyond the piano bar was dark and nearly deserted, although we could hear voices from the Sports Deck above and the Lido below. There were vacant deck chairs and some ember-red space heaters near the railing. The piano music continued, drifting from overhead speakers. From the rail, the city of Halifax glittered with lights, like—*thanks, Grandma*—like Cinderella's kingdom. I sighed.

Luke helped me into my beaded shawl and his hands lingered across my shoulders. The heater next to us glowed.

"So," he said, his voice soft. "Next port is Quebec City. Have you been there?"

"Never," I said, surprised that my voice sounded husky.

"It's great," he said, smiling down at me. "Very quaint, very French. Old streetlights, bakeries, horse-drawn carriages, and ice-skating in the square." He reached down and tucked my shawl around my shoulders tenderly. "I'd like to show it to you."

I listened to the music drift overhead, the hum of the ship's engines and soft laughter from the decks above. Romantic ambiance. They could bottle this stuff. I remembered the feel of Luke's arms on the dance floor and reminded myself that, after all, I'd come on the ship to relax, to forget, and to get a new start. Who was to say that a pleasant diversion like Luke Skyler wasn't exactly what I needed? If I was careful, of course. I looked up and saw amusement on his face.

"Why," I asked, smiling, "are you looking at me like that?"

Luke reached for my hand, held it gently, and traced his thumb over my palm. His face was lit by moonlight and he chuckled softly. "I was thinking how amazing it is to be standing this close to you and not have to dodge your feet, or your teeth or . . ."

I started to speak but stopped as Luke's finger touched my lips, quieting me.

"Shh . . . wait. I was going to say that it gives me hope." He smiled again and brushed a strand of hair away from my face, letting his fingertips trace along my jaw.

"Hope?" My skin prickled and I could feel my pulse in my throat. I knew these signs too well. I was doomed.

"For this." Luke leaned toward me and pressed his lips lightly against the corner of my mouth. Then he moved back a little to look down into my eyes, brows raised.

Before I could react, a chorus of shrieks split the air overhead and the side of the ship was suddenly daylight-bright with the white glare of sweeping searchlights. The ship's public address system began a staccato series of bursts, short, then long.

What was happening?

Luke thrust his arms out and stepped in front of me, his eyes on the side of ship where the lights had focused. "Go back inside, Darcy. *Now.*" His voice was brusque, authoritative.

"But . . ." My heart hammered in my chest. The decks above thundered with footsteps, and the door behind us opened, spewing dozens of boisterous passengers nearly trampling each other to get to the rail and stare upward. I saw Luke's head turn side to side as the passengers pressed forward, his eyes squinting in the searchlight's glare, jaw clenched, expression agitated. Desperate?

I lost sight of him as the crowd elbowed me forward, and I fought to maintain balance until at last my body was pressed against the outside rail. I squinted and craned my head upward until I could finally see where they were all pointing.

A man's body was hanging from the deck railing above, suspended alongside a row of portholes; rope around his neck and face blue-gray in the light's glare, eyes rolled back, lifeless. His arms and legs dangled, sliding across the side of the ship with its movement, like an abandoned puppet.

"It's that little cabin steward," a woman breathed beside me, her fingers pressed to her lips. "You know, from D-Deck. Virgilio."

The ship moved under our feet and my stomach lurched. My head was fuzzy. Could this be happening? Oh my God, Virgilio! I reached for the ship's rail and frantically scanned the passengers around me. Where . . . ? Luke was gone.

NINE

"Well, nothing like a helicopter landing on the roof at midnight to kind of perk your appetite." Marie sat down and handed me a breakfast sausage.

"No thanks," I grimaced. "I'm still kind of queasy about the whole thing. You didn't see him *hanging* there. His face . . ."

"No, but I've sure seen a lot of faces just like it, back in the ER. You, too. Part of our job."

I jabbed my straw at my grapefruit juice and stared at my friend. "And does that prove my point? Why I'm sick of that kind of work; why selling orthotics, hell *anything,* would be better than being an ER nurse?"

Marie frowned for a moment and then sighed. "They don't all die, Darc." She tilted her head and peered up through her fringe of dark bangs, her voice lowering to a thick whisper. "That old woman dying was not your fault. There's no way anyone could have known that would happen. We've been over and over this."

I swallowed hard. "I was in charge of the place and I couldn't find her a bed. That patient—she has a name, *Anna Lozano*—

'crashed' out there in the hallway because no one noticed until it was too late." I whispered through clenched teeth, "*Don't* try to make it okay."

"Hey, listen." Marie shook her head. "She looked stable when she came in, right? And God knows you had no extra nurses to stay out there with her. Who were you gonna kick out to make room, the two-year-old with the seizures? The man on a ventilator? What if you hadn't been there for them?" She sighed and reached for my hand. "Quit beating yourself up about this, Darc'. Everyone knows you're the first one to jump in on a bad case and the last one to leave. You're the best Charge Nurse we've ever had. I'm serious. Besides, she was a 'No Code,' never wanted to be resuscitated anyway. You would have been going against her wishes."

I chewed my lower lip and took a deep breath, flinching against the logic. I'd re-lived it a thousand times. Wanting to "die with dignity," didn't mean dying alone. And I couldn't get past that.

The sight of the obituary in the morning newspaper had hit me like a fist in the stomach. I'd wadded it up and thrown it away without reading it afraid, irrationally, that it might somehow list my own name as Cause of Death. By evening I'd pulled it from the trash can, wiped away the coffee grounds, and traced a shaky finger down the columns. I held my breath and read about Anna Marie Lozano, retired schoolteacher, pianist, and avid gardener. *Over three hundred tulips in her garden. Beloved grandmother.* And then on Tuesday, I put on my black dress and sunglasses and drove twenty-five miles to a small church in San Jose; the first time I'd ever gone to a patient's funeral. I stood in the back, behind a wicker basket of silk tulips, holding my rosary and hearing nothing. Because I was whispering, over and over, every single word of the Irish lullaby that my grandma had sung to her dying cancer patient.

I slid my hand away from Marie and shook my head. "She died alone and that wasn't right. This is not what I signed on for. I can't be part of that."

Marie was silent for a moment and nodded, giving my forearm a squeeze. She shook her head slowly then grabbed the sausage and waggled it like a little cigar, a wicked grin spreading across her face. "Hey, I told you how I did at the poker game, but you didn't say how you scored at dinner last night."

I felt the heat creep into my face. Only part of the reason I couldn't sleep had to do with poor Virgilio. Most of it was because of Luke. Sure, I was remembering how we'd laughed together at dinner, the feeling of being in his arms on the dance floor, and that surprisingly tentative kiss. Was he waiting for permission? But what really kept me sleepless was second-guessing my own reaction. If that grisly incident with the hanging hadn't happened, what would I have done?

I felt my pulse quicken and glanced away from Marie's inquisitive eyes. Where had Luke gone last night? For that matter, where was he this morning? He'd seemed so sincere, and so kind of Southern-gentlemanly last night—attentive, protective almost. And then poof, he disappears? Did I read him all wrong?

"Well?"

"Jury's still out," I said, ready to change the subject. "But hey, I keep thinking about Virgilio. Suicide? Did he seem depressed to you?"

"Naw, I wouldn't say that unless underwear origami is some sort of symptom. But I did hear some stuff about him just now, while I was in the breakfast line."

"What do you mean?" I glanced around the room quickly. No Luke.

"I overheard Edie Greenbaum and some of the Yoga Ladies. They were saying that Virgilio had marriage problems. That he'd found out his wife was cheating on him while he's been at sea."

"Ouch. Did he leave a note or anything?"

"Don't know." Marie shrugged. "Maybe he just left a sad little panty sculpture."

I stared at her. "Dammit, girl. You want me to ask Dr. Foote about a job for you, too? That was pretty harsh."

Marie shook her head. "Okay, but I got an earful from the ladies all right; even heard the Prom Princess comparing mini-stroke symptoms with two other former patients. Kind of interesting."

"How so?"

"They were talking about winning free coupons for the Mermaid Spa." Marie pursed her lips and whined through her nose in imitation, "'How perfectly *lux-uu-rious* the herbal wraps are dahling, the cucumber masks and all those yummy champagne mimosas.'"

"And?" I tapped my fingernail against my juice glass and scanned the dining room once more. Where was he?

"And," Marie continued, "they said they were sort of squeamish about the 'vitamin shot,' but decided to have it and wondered now if it made them too relaxed, what with the champagne and the steam and everything. And maybe all of it together had caused them to have a mini-stroke."

"Vitamin shots?"

"That's what they said."

"The spa staff is allowed to give injections?"

"Not that I know of. Acupuncture, yes. I know they have some-one who does that. Maybe that's what they meant." Marie turned her head. "Hey, isn't that your dinner date?"

I raised my head, hoping that Marie hadn't noticed the way my breath caught. It was Luke, but why did he look like that?

He set his tray in front of the coffee machine and filled the second of two large mugs with steaming brew. He was wearing the same blue dress shirt and slacks as last night, without the tie and jacket, and his hair was as rumpled as his clothes. His face was somber, unshaven. He rubbed his hand across his eyes and yawned.

"Looks like he slept in a life raft," Marie whispered. "Or maybe the damned helicopter kept him up, too. Did you hear it land again around four AM? Like *RiverDance* on the roof." She shook her head. "Took old Virgilio away, but did it have to come back?"

"Hmm? Oh, yeah, don't know why, either." I lowered my eyes before Luke could see me watching him. He was heading our way. What should I say?

I didn't have to worry. Luke nodded almost absent-mindedly in our direction and then carried his tray out of the room without looking back. I felt my face flame.

"Your mouth is hanging open." Marie shook her head. "This guy's some great conversationalist. The Clint Eastwood of dance hosts."

I crumpled my napkin and jammed it into the empty juice glass. What was that about? He couldn't even say hello, good morning, thanks for the cheap thrill? I felt like an ass. No, I was an ass. Continuing a long history of asshood. I growled through clenched teeth.

"I totally agree," Marie said. "So what's going on with that guy?"

I buried my face in my hands briefly and then tried to smile. "Hey, same old, same old." I narrowed my eyes. "Probably has a wife and four kids stashed somewhere below deck." I stood up and tugged at Marie's sleeve. "I need to go work out. Want to come?"

We passed the Greenbaums in the hallway. Edie was wearing her animal-print leotard and sneakers, and Bernie bowed at the waist and then tossed me a flirty smile, his gold tooth flashing.

Marie nudged me after they passed. "Chin up, Cavanaugh. Who needs Eastwood when you've got Elvis?"

The gym was crowded enough that I had to wait for a treadmill while Marie ambled on toward the stair-step machines. I rolled my eyes. One of the old women was eating a Danish as she paced the treadmill. She turned and I saw that it was the Queen Bee, complete with a polka-dotted arm sling to match her gym shorts. The woman looked up and smiled warmly, removing her headphones.

"Here, sweetie, you can take over on this. Edie insisted I try it, but this is just not my idea of fun."

"No, I can wait, really," I answered, realizing for the first time that this woman's smile was very much like my grandmother's. "I can see that you've barely started."

"I know, and it was nice of Edie to show me how, fix all the settings and everything. But actually, I'd rather go shopping. Here, I'm pushing the Stop button right now."

I thanked the Queen Bee and plugged my headset into the radio jack on the treadmill. I'd finally remembered to bring it, although it looked like this machine had only one station available. Forties band music, sounded like. Not my choice, but better than having to talk with anyone. What I needed now was to shut everything out and run. Sweat, get my heart pumping. *Without* the aid of Luke Skyler. I'd be damned if I'd waste any more time thinking about his kind of schizo behavior.

I'd run about two miles in about sixteen minutes—good pace—and noted that my heart rate was holding steady at one-thirty. Exactly right. The music really wasn't too bad either; the old tunes, with lots of brass, were just the right tempo. Wait—what was happening?

My earphones screeched with static and the music broke. Ouch, it was loud. I lifted the earpiece away and peered around to see if anyone else was having the same trouble. No one had looked up. The screeching stopped and instead a woman's voice came through the earpiece.

"*Darling,*" it said in a syrupy, somehow familiar voice. "*You're very lucky today. You are about to be pampered like a movie star.*" The voice gave a throaty giggle and I recognized it. That Elizabeth Taylor impersonator. Like on the infomercial. What was this?

"*You've won a Mermaid Spa experience. Massage, herbal wrap, and all the champagne you can drink, sweetheart. A coupon will be delivered to your cabin today with the details. Congratulations, Mrs. Thurston.*"

The music started again and I shook my head. Mrs. Thurston? What the heck was that about? I glanced around the gym. Nothing looked out of the ordinary. People walking on the treadmills, Marie on the stair-stepper. The ship TV channel was playing a spa advertisement; maybe it had cross-connected into my music station. Had to be that.

I ran a few more minutes, closing my eyes and listening to the music, then blinked them open to see Luke appear in front of my treadmill. He smiled and pointed at my headphones and I slid them down around my neck, reaching for the handgrips. The sensors read my heart rate, a humiliating betrayal in digital red. One hundred and fifty. I slowed the machine to a walk.

"Sorry," he said, "I didn't mean to make you stop." He'd changed into his workout clothes, low-slung drawstring pants and karate robe, and he'd shaved. His voice sounded sleepy and made the soft drawl more apparent. He ran his fingers through his shower-damp hair and smiled again.

I tried to ignore his soapy clean scent, and the fact that—*oh jeez*—the robe was partially open across his chest. Crap. I did not want him, I did not want . . . I snatched my palms from the sensors before it could alarm and alert the whole stupid gym.

"No. No problem," I said, trying to keep my voice casual, aloof. "I was . . . finished . . . anyway." *Breathe, Darcy.*

"It's just that I . . ." he paused and stared as I patted my face with a towel. "You look so pretty like that. Anyway, I wanted to apologize for running off last night."

I stepped off the treadmill. I wasn't going to listen to his explanation or apology or whatever it was he was trying to do. I didn't like the effect he had on me. It couldn't be good. No, blast it. It was more like the kind of thing that could lead you to throw things from the top of a lighthouse cliff.

"No problem." I started to walk away and he caught my arm.

I looked down at his hand and back at his face.

Luke let his hand drop. "Sorry. I didn't want you to think I'd abandoned you out there last night."

I looked him square in the eye and jutted my chin. I'd set him straight and get out of here. "I don't know what you mean," I said, narrowing my eyes. "I'm a careful woman, remember? Kind of 'kick-ass.'?" I shook my head and smirked. "Hardly even noticed you'd gone."

I slung my towel over my shoulder, turned, and walked away. I knew he was watching me. Damn, the entire gym was watching us both. I could feel his eyes, but I didn't care. I'd had this sort of epiphany while running on the treadmill. The truth, to the tempo of Grandma's favorite music. I was not responsible for any of these people. Not for the old widow ladies and their jewelry, poor dead Virgilio, Bernie Greenbaum's continuing humiliation on stage, and *especially* not responsible for interpreting Luke Skyler's erratic behavior. Hot-cold, menacing, charming, whatever. I wasn't responsible. And wasn't this what I'd been trying to convince myself of anyhow—in my career, too—that one person can't expect to make a big difference? If I'd ever thought so before, I was fooling myself. I walked on toward the punching bag and reached for a pair of gloves.

"That's why nurses eventually burn out, don't you see?" I asked thirty minutes later, salty with sweat and taking one last jab at the bag. Marie caught my gloved fist and held it captive.

"What are you talking about?" She asked, holding out a towel. "Here, dry off. Your ponytail's dripping."

"We're overly responsible, trusting, compulsive . . . fixers," I puffed, taking the towel, "which leaves us vulnerable to . . ." I glanced quickly in the direction of the weight benches. *Gone, finally.*

"Dance hosts?" Marie raised her brows.

"What?"

"You said that as nurses we are vulnerable to . . . ?"

I flung the towel back at Marie and scowled. "Oh for godsake, where do you come up with these crazy ideas?" I held my glove to her nose. "Does this look vulnerable to you? And watch out, I can spit through my teeth, too." I grinned. "We are invincible." I yanked off my boxing gloves and nodded. "Let's go back to the cabin and stuff some snapdragons into the trash can. I think I'm allergic."

We arrived at our cabin just as the black-suited Nepalese security team stepped out of the door.

TEN

"So you sell shoes to the elderly? Is that correct, Miss Cavanaugh?"

I glanced in total disbelief across the small cabin to where Marie was being questioned. We were being interrogated, for godsake. *Just a random security check*, my ass. These guys were carrying mace and guns. What was going on here?

"Miss Cavanaugh?" The security officer—*Gombu,* his badge read—tapped a pencil against his notebook and cleared his throat.

"Shoes?" I squinted at him. "No, I don't sell shoes. I'm a registered nurse."

Gombu pressed the eraser end of his pencil to his notebook and nubbed through the pages, frowning. "You are not an orthotic sales representative?"

"I told you . . ." I shook my head. This was bordering on ridiculous. Where the hell did he get . . . ? My stomach dropped like an elevator and goose bumps rose.

I crossed my arms over my chest and narrowed my eyes. "I don't believe I should say anything more without my lawyer present."

Even if I didn't have one. *Shit.* My throat began to constrict and my mouth went sticky dry.

Gombu's face tightened in what he probably thought would pass for a smile. "That will not be necessary, of course. As we said, this is simply a random—"

"Marie!" I whirled around and my voice strained like I was starving for oxygen in Katmandu. "We won't be answering any more questions without benefit of counsel, will we?"

The last pair of combat boots marched out of the cabin and Marie closed the door behind them, watching as I sank down onto my bed with a groan.

"What the hell is happening, Marie?"

"Wait, I'm thinking."

"I can't think; my brain is melting. This 'random check,' wasn't random, was it?"

"I don't think so, kid." Marie ran her fingers through her hair and sighed. "At least I've never seen it before."

I got up and walked over to the vase of flowers. I touched a fingertip to a bittersweet leaf and saw that my hands were shaking. I turned back to Marie. "What sort of questions were they asking you?"

"Routine stuff at first; you know, confirming where I live, etcetera. But then some kind of odd things. Like do I like baseball and do I ever use the batting cages up on the Sports Deck?"

I pinched a snapdragon blossom and watched it open its throat in a silent scream. "They asked me if I was an orthotic sales rep."

Marie scrunched her brows. "You've been *telling* people that?"

"No." I plucked the flower and dropped it to the floor. "I only told one person that. Luke Skyler."

"But . . ." Marie pushed a pile of socks aside and sat down on her bed, "why would he tell that to the Men In Black?"

"Not sure. Maybe because he was questioned and we were seen together last night? I don't know." I pulled the band off of my ponytail. "I think what we need to figure out first is exactly what they're investigating."

"I'm assuming it's the thefts," Marie said. "You know, the Prom Princess and the others?"

"Not the heart attack victim's burglary?"

"Why? We weren't even on board." Marie shook her head.

"But her cabin was only a few doors down."

The knock on the door made us both jump. Marie opened it to reveal the new cabin steward, Virgilio's replacement, balancing two huge cardboard boxes.

"Your costumes, misses. For the party tonight."

I groaned as Marie closed the door and set the boxes on the table. "Oh Lord, the Halloween party. I forgot all about it." I reached for the lid of the topmost box. "What costume did you finally get me, Xena or Cat Woman?"

Marie squeezed her eyes shut.

"Well, okay, I'll take a peek then," I said as Marie grabbed my arm.

"Wait, Darc'. I sort of . . . uh, forgot. Until the last minute."

"What do you mean?"

"I mean we didn't get our first choices."

*　*　*

96

I stood in front of the full-length bathroom mirror yanking at my costume. Sequins, flouncey netting, and fish scales. A mermaid?

I draped the huge satin tail across my arm and took a halting step toward the door. The glittery fabric tugged across my hips and four guilty pounds of macaroni and cheese. My cleavage, encrusted with tiny seashells, rose like high tide every time I breathed. I yanked the fabric up to cover the small shamrock tattoo on my left breast. Mardi Gras, sweet sixteen—big mistake. Damn, could it get any worse? I squeezed my eyes shut against a wave of déjà vu. Yes. It could.

Halloween 1980, first grade. Holy Spirit School. Holy Spit. I'd almost forgotten. Six years old, I'd kept my costume a secret—had godawful diarrhea from the sheer anticipation of showing it off. Grandma's handcrafted nurse's costume. Wonderfully complete down to white stockings, black ribbon cap, and the satin lined winter cloak that all the nurses had worn at Emmanuel Hospital. And then I'd stood there on the playground surrounded by a clutch of howling grade-school cartoon heroes: Batman, three Supermen, Spiderman, and smug little Missy Foster as Wonder Woman. Missy had magic bracelets and a golden lasso and I had a plastic thermometer.

I'd pressed my hands over my ears, enduring the laughter and the taunts. *"Is that a cape? A cape! Hey, everybody, Darcy Cavanaugh thinks nurses are superheroes!"* And I kept my temper and my eyes dry as they followed me chanting, *"Nurse, nurse, Darcy Cava-Nurse!"* But when that horrible, squinty-eyed third grader, Rusty Daniels, dressed as Darth Vader, grabbed the cap from my head and mooned me from under his black cape—*"Hey, Cavanurse, take my temperature?"*—I finally lost it. Big time. Howling like a banshee, I planted my little white lace-up nurse's shoe square in the crack of Vader's dark side and shoved for all I was worth. *Bless me Father, for I have sinned . . .* It took eleven stitches to close the wound after Rusty's chin hit the playground asphalt, and I was the only six-year-old ever to be suspended from Holy Spit. I would go to hell for sure and I didn't care, because Rusty Daniels would be there, too. And I'd kick him in the butt again.

I tugged at the scanty green bodice and rolled my eyes. A mermaid. I was going to kill Marie. If I could manage to flop out of the bathroom.

"At least you're not a Holstein." Marie sighed as I appeared.

I clamped my hand over my mouth and laughed until I dropped my tail and stumbled over it.

"This'll teach me not to procrastinate, I guess." Marie turned slowly around for inspection, a dizzying blur of black and white spots. "So, be honest. Do I make you crave a cheese plate?"

"Oh, man," I said with my voice curdling into laughter again, "what's that on your feet?"

"These? Not part of the costume. I'm proud to say these babies were mine. Convenient, huh?"

"You already *owned* cow socks?" I stared at the black and white anklets.

"Gift from a friend with impeccable taste." Marie wiggled her toes. "You like?"

"But why are there ten little individual toes—all pink? Kind of like . . . Oh, Lord." I shuddered.

"Udder-ly cool, right?"

I punched the button to the elevator and hugged the fishnet shawl around my bare shoulders. I felt naked.

Marie twirled her bristle-tipped tail. "At least the Ninja Squad will have second thoughts about our being suspects. Nobody dressed like this would be smart enough to be jewel thieves."

"Stop it, okay? I'm only going to this party because I'm starving and I think it would look suspicious if we stayed in and ordered room service. I'll be damned if I let those security people intimidate me."

Marie ducked out of the elevator, beyond my reach, and grinned back over her spotted shoulder. "Ooh, you look just like a little puffer fish when you're angry, babe."

*   *   *

Dry ice clouds billowed from the entrance to the Lobster Disco and the din of funereal organ music made it necessary for us to yell to each other to be heard.

"So, do you think the dance hosts will be doing the Monster Mash?" Marie shouted, nodding toward the dance floor.

"I don't want to see any dance hosts. I just want to eat something." I rearranged a tiny starfish that was poking my left boob and smiled at Marie. "Okay, and maybe do enough snooping to find out who else was questioned and why."

"But no peeking through port holes. Deal?"

"Deal." I snagged a table as a pair of witches vacated the chairs. "Here, sit. Let's see what they've got in that big cauldron on the bar."

It was something with rum, and it smoked when I stirred it with a little eyeball swizzle stick. And man, it was powerful. I was feeling a serious buzz by the time we were halfway through the buffet line.

I caught a glimpse of the food ahead; what had the menu said? Lobster crepes, poached salmon, prime rib, and a scarecrow made entirely of fresh fruit. Heaven. If I could stay upright long enough to get there. I balanced my plate and my huge satin tail and turned sideways to let witches and Draculas and Cat Woman—*hey, that was my costume*—squeeze by.

"Looks good." A deep voice spoke over my shoulder and I half turned. Velvet frock coat, ruffled shirt, broad hat, and long dark curls. Small hoop earring. Captain Hook?

"Yes," I agreed, my eyes on the buffet. "It's supposed to be great food."

"No," the man chuckled. "I meant the *costume*. Your costume. Looks good on you."

I turned around to face him and felt my head spin to catch up. The man's eyes were blue, the crinkles at their corners unmistakable.

"You," I said, feeling my fingers tighten on my tail.

"Guilty as charged." Luke removed his hat and swept it across him as he bowed. "Captain Hook at your service."

"Well," I inhaled to make my slutty bodice feel more secure, "it so happens that I have absolutely no need of service. Of any kind. Thank you."

I stepped ahead to find that I'd reached the buffet table and that Marie was no longer in front of me. I scanned the crowd as I began to fill my plate. The Cat in The Hat, Alice in Wonderland, Big Bird, Tweedle Dee and Tweedle Dum—*jeez, that's the Greenbaums*—but no Holstein cow. Great. The room was crowded shoulder to shoulder. I'd never find Marie. And where could I sit? If I didn't start eating soon, the cauldron rum would be the end of me.

"Hey, I found a table. Just to eat?" Luke pointed to a table next to the lobster tank. "Please?"

I looped my tail over my arm and followed him, telling myself that it was a medical necessity; too much exercise and not enough food. My needs were primal, not social. This was not capitulation.

Half an hour later, Luke pretended to spear a marinated prawn with his hook and I couldn't stop myself from laughing. The rum had softened my resolve and the feeling of food in my stomach made me want to forget everything. I savored the last morsel of crepe, sweet lobster bathed in sherry sauce, and smiled at Captain Hook.

"Mmmm, I've gone to Heaven," I pronounced, taking another sip of the rum. I should stop drinking it. It was making me giggle and my tingly lips said words before my brain could edit them. I was headed for asshood again. "And by the way, where *did* you go last night?"

Luke watched my face and waited a moment before he spoke. "I wanted to explain that," he said. "I tried to, this morning, in the gym." He smiled and shook his head. "But my grandmama, the one with the hush puppy spoon, said it's never wise to try to explain bad behavior to a lady wearing boxing gloves." The drawl emerged again, sweet as the crepe.

His eyes twinkled and I hated him for it. What was it about this guy? Sincere or slick? And why was it that I needed to know, when my common sense told me that the best thing was to turn tail—pardon the pun—and run?

"So?" I asked.

"You mean, where was I last night?"

"Mm-hmm." I could see two of him now. He'd pulled off the hat and wig, and the rum had given me kaleidoscope vision creating two tousled blonde heads, four blue eyes, and two mouths . . . a thousand sexy lips. *Oh God.*

"It's a funny story, really," Luke laughed, leaning toward me. "The truth is that—"

"That you are a naughty boy!" Miss Piggy, with blue eye shadow, long lashes, pink snout, and fur stole, hooked an arm around Luke's neck and nuzzled his ear. "You promised me a dance, and they're going to play 'The Monster Mash.'"

I watched as Luke tried to extricate himself from the pig's grip. Then the woman turned and I caught a glimpse of her other arm. In a jack o'lantern print sling. The Queen Bee.

Luke looked over at me helplessly. "I did promise. Will you wait here for me?" He dodged the woman's grasp. "I really want to talk with you, Darcy."

Before I could answer, the Queen Bee tugged Luke from his chair and propelled him toward the dance floor. I realized I was clenching my hands. I was jealous of a senior citizen? Asshood supreme.

"I found you." Marie pulled out the empty chair and sat down, biting into a jumbo shrimp. She crossed her legs and bounced her foot up and down in time with the music.

I looked down at her sandals. "What happened to your cow socks?"

"Oh, in my fanny pack. Toes were sweatin' like a bitch. So, have you found out anything?"

"Hmm?" My head was beginning to pound in rhythm with the ship's movements. Up, down, back and forth. *Ugh.*

"About the interrogations?" Marie prodded.

"No." I glanced over at the dance floor long enough to see that Luke was watching me over Miss Piggy's pink shoulder.

"Me neither. Only some gossip about Edie Greenbaum's shipboard charge card being rejected earlier in the casino." She grinned and fiddled with her cow horns. "A couple of stewards dressed like Jawas—you know, those great little burlap bag guys in *Star Wars* with eyes like flashlights? Anyway, they said there she was, dressed like Tweedle-Dee and sputtering with indignity and complaining to the manager about the mistake. She finally opened up her purse and pulled out a wad of cash instead. Tried to double her bet out of spite." Marie shook her head. "Retirement must be nice."

I'd opened my mouth to make a snarky crack about nurses' pensions, when the ship moved again and my stomach followed like a limbo to the drumbeat in my head. Sweat beaded on my forehead. *Oh no.* "I think I need to . . ." I closed my eyes.

"Whoa, are you going to puke?" Marie scooped the ice out of the drink and wrapped it in a napkin. "Here put this against your face. Take some deep breaths. Maybe it will pass."

"No," I took a halting breath, "let's go now. I can make it." I stood slowly and glanced toward the dance floor. Luke was nowhere to be seen.

We threaded our way through the crowded room and out into the corridor toward the glass elevator. More room, more air. *Ahh, way better.*

"Want me to carry your tail?"

I smiled and ran my hand across my face. No more sweating. "No thanks, I'm doing better now."

Marie stopped abruptly and fumbled with her fanny pack. "Wait. Stop right there. This is so great. I want to take a picture of you in front of the spa. The *Mermaid* Spa."

I turned to look. We were standing right in front of the gilded and jeweled door to the spa. I rolled my eyes as Marie produced the yellow cardboard camera.

"I love it," Marie laughed. "You should do an ad for them, Darc'. Hell, at least you should get a free coupon."

I laughed, mostly because I was glad the seasick feeling had passed. "I almost did."

"Hold still. You almost did what?"

"I thought I'd won a free coupon to the Mermaid Spa today. In the gym." I struck a sultry fish pose as Marie raised the camera. "I heard it over my earphones after the Queen Bee let me have her treadmill. Only they said some other woman's name—" I clamped my hand over my mouth and stared at Marie.

"What? Are you getting sick again?" Marie lowered the camera.

"No. But the Queen Bee . . . what's her *real* name?"

Marie smirked. "Ah, so now you finally admit that all those nicknames are stupid, huh?"

"Dammit, Marie. What is it? What's her last name?"

"Thurston. Why?"

I grabbed my tail and Marie's arm. "We've got to get to the sickbay. Hurry. We need some information."

ELEVEN

"Ouch." I stumbled in the dark and my knee smacked against a metal mop bucket with a loud clang. "So basically, anyone could break into the sickbay?"

"Hey, quiet." Marie's penlight focused on a recessed inner door handle and she glanced over her shoulder at me, whispering. "And yes, I suppose anyone could if they knew this utility room connects to the nurse's quarters." She smiled as the door opened, "And if they knew Howie never bothers to keep it locked on his shift."

I stepped through the doorway and glanced quickly around. "You're sure he's not in there?" I whispered, nodding toward the exam room beyond.

"Naw, he's playing poker with the Jawas. He's got his pager and the number's posted right outside in the corridor. All a passenger or crewmember has to do is dial the number. Pretty cushy job on the night shift; you can sleep through most of it." Marie put her hands on her hips. "Okay, we're here, and against my better judgment I might add. So what are you looking for?"

"File cabinets?" I stepped into the ward area and looked around. Six empty stretchers, blankets folded neatly. Door to the corridor closed. Good. "Treatment information." I nodded. "We're going to do a little research on the mini-stroke victims."

"Wait . . . medical records?" Marie's brows scrunched. "No way, Darc'. We shouldn't be—"

"No," I said quickly. "We aren't looking for names. Just an idea of how many victims there are, what they were doing when the symptoms began, and, more importantly, *where* they were." I raised my brows. "I'm trying to help you here, Marie. We can't have you being suspected of jewel theft, for godsake."

"There's a log sheet," Marie said, eyes still a little wary. "But we're *not* opening files. Don't let me hear you saying any last names, okay?"

"No problem."

The computer and rack of color-coded manila folders were on a desk next to the medication cupboards and the crash cart. Marie shook her head at an opened drawer on the red metal cart. "Howie's a hell of a poker player, but a total slob. Look, I'll bet those are Edie's insulin syringes on top of there."

"Why would he have the crash cart open?" I asked.

"Restocking probably, checking for drug outdates. That's his assignment." She reached for a couple of clipboards. "These are the logs of the last few months' treatments."

I scanned down the list: dozens of motion sickness patches applied, moleskin for blisters, soap suds enemas, and toothache treatments. Nothing too exciting.

"Hey, here's a certain Princess," Marie said, running her finger down a sheet of paper. "She was in the spa all right. 'Patient states she had finished a steam bath and was relaxing in an herbal wrap when she suddenly felt very weak.'"

I looked up from the clipboard I was holding and smiled. "And here's two more. Three weeks ago, a Mrs. S. who—let's see—yes, began to feel like her arms and legs were heavy and couldn't move after a massage in the Mermaid Spa."

"Eleanor F.," Marie said, tapping her finger against a paper, "came in for a blood pressure check because she was worried after experiencing a brief episode of 'extreme weakness,' in the spa the evening before." She looked up. "That one wasn't even reported as a mini-stroke, Darc'. Makes you wonder how many more episodes there were like that?"

"That's right." Goosebumps rose on my arms. "And I don't think this is a coincidence either." I grabbed a pen and made some notes.

Marie scrunched her brows. "You think the spa staff's being negligent in some way, like serving too much alcohol to these women?"

"More than that." My heart beat faster. "I think that these so-called mini-strokes and the thefts are somehow related."

"What? . . . How?"

My mind raced. "I told you that I was offered a free spa coupon. Well, it wasn't meant for me. It was meant for Mrs. Thurston, the Queen Bee. And when you were accused of stealing jewelry, it was by the Prom Princess, who won a free spa experience, too. Remember Luke telling us that?"

"Damn," Marie eyes widened. "So you're saying that all the mini-stroke patients might have been robbery victims, too? But how do—"

"How do we prove it?" I smiled, folded my sheet of notes and tucked it into the bodice of my costume. "We simply take our list of information and—"

Marie clamped her hand over my mouth and pointed to the outside door, whispering, "Oh shit."

I froze as the sound of footsteps halted outside the door and the handle moved up down and then stopped. There was a mumbled voice and a click-whir as a keycard was inserted into the sickbay door. Marie reached into her fanny pack, found the penlight, and gave me a shove, snapping the light switch off as we headed back toward the utility closet.

Seconds later, I peered over Marie's shoulder through the crack of the closet door and into the sickbay beyond. My mouth went dry and my pulse pounded.

What the hell had I been thinking? Snooping at records was against the law. Didn't they tell you that in nursing school even before they taught you how to do a bed bath? And lately there were very scary federal penalties.

Marie jabbed me with an elbow. The door to the sickbay opened and the light switched on. Three Nepalese security officers stepped into the room, their boots thumping against the polished floor. Two of them moved immediately to the desktop and the treatment logs, and the other surveyed the crash cart then reached for his radio. He turned toward the desk before he spoke. It was Gombu.

"Okay, bring him in here," he said, and the radio dissolved into static.

There was the sound of footsteps again, and a tall man dressed in a ruffled shirt, brocade vest, duster coat and cowboy hat entered the room. Riverboat gambler. Howie. I could hear Marie's breathing quicken.

"So, Mr. Carson, you say that you haven't been in this room for several hours?" The black-suited man rested one gloved hand on the butt of his gun and used the other to gesture around the sickbay. "This room was locked and is exactly as you left it, before you went to the party?"

Howie patted his pager, his voice defensive. "I'm still on call. But yes, I haven't been here since maybe eight o'clock and I locked it before I left. I told you that already."

The two other men stepped aside to allow a full view of the desk. Howie's eyes widened.

"You left those records out?" Gombu pointed to the crash cart. "And those drawers open?"

Howie stepped forward and waved his hands. "No way." He shook his head. "I swear I don't know how that happened. Did you check with the doctor?"

Gombu said nothing, his face unreadable. He turned away from Howie and watched as one of the other men stooped to pick something off the floor.

I heard Marie swear softly. *Oh God.* A cow sock? She'd dropped one?

Gombu frowned at the teat toes and then held the sock out to Howie. His tone was a barely concealed sneer. "And was *this* here when you so carefully locked up?" Gombu nodded toward the other officers. "Perhaps we'll ask Mr. Carson to accompany us around the corner to our office."

Marie waited for several minutes after the footsteps receded before she opened the door to the corridor, and then spoke in a whisper. "It's clear out there. We need to get the hell out before they come back. Separately. You go first. Take the elevator. I'll take the stairway. Go."

"Marie, I'm sorry."

"Go." Marie shook her head. "Look, I want to get out of this cow suit and call Carol. And then sulk with a shitload of beer. *Alone.* No offense, okay?"

The elevator doors closed and my stomach dropped below sea level. I held my mermaid tail and my breath and broke out in a cold sweat when a passenger at the next floor stepped aboard dressed in black from head to toe. Wait—not Nepalese. Flora Perkins as a black panther. I needed to get a grip, fast.

I was such an idiot for starting this spying escapade in the first place. And now Marie was going to be under far more suspicion. Because of that cow sock. No, dammit, because of me. How could I fix this?

"Ooh, shiver me timbers," Flora giggled as the elevator crowd moved back for yet another passenger to board. "If it isn't that darling Captain Hook."

I quit studying a line of green sequins on my tail and looked up. Luke.

"So who abandoned whom, now?" He whispered, stepping to the rear to stand beside me. "I thought you were going to wait for me until I ditched Miss Piggy."

"I . . ." I swallowed hard and blinked furiously, astounded at the tears that filled my eyes. Oh no, this was all I needed. I had to get off this elevator.

"Hey," Luke ducked down and looked into my face. "I was just kidding."

"No," I rubbed the edge of my tail across my eyes, "it's nothing, really." Only that I was about to become Public Enemy Number Two.

The door opened and Luke took my hand and moved ahead through the passengers. "Excuse us, please. This is our stop."

I leaned backward and tried to pull my fingers away, but the Yoga Panther gave me a little shove forward. "Isn't that the cutest thing? Captain Hook and a Mermaid." The answering titters and awwws completely drowned my protest as I stepped from the elevator and someone tossed my tail unceremoniously out onto the carpet.

"I feel like an idiot." I glanced down at my seashell encrusted bodice and tears threatened again. "And I look like . . ." I picked at a trio of scallop shells, "like something out of *Finding Nemo*." I sighed and looked up at him. "But thank you. I really did need to get off that elevator. Where are we?"

Luke hadn't let go of my other hand, and he squeezed my fingers gently. "First of all, you look beautiful, kind of like . . . some mythical . . . sailor's dream." He smiled and then his face reddened with obvious embarrassment and he glanced away, letting go of my hand. He cleared his throat and his voice was suddenly deeper. "Secondly, we're on the Sports Deck. Not too many people playing basketball I'd suspect, so no crowds. And," he added, pointing, "there's a bar down there. Buy you a glass of wine?"

He was right. There was almost no one in the corridors as we made our way aft; the gym doors were closed and the small video arcade soundless except for a few isolated hums and beeps emitted by waiting machines. We reached the bamboo-framed entrance to a little Polynesian bar and Luke opened the door so that I could step inside.

We sat in bent willow chairs at a table next to an aquarium of swirling fan-tailed goldfish. Music, maybe mandolins, floated overhead mingling with air that smelled of ginger and coconut. I sank back into the flowered cushion and sighed. I glanced over at Luke and watched the light from a floating candle play across his profile as he ordered our wine.

"Better now?" He asked, turning back toward me. He'd taken off his frock coat and rolled up the shirt's billowy sleeves; all that remained of his costume was the small hoop earring. It looked natural on him somehow. Like a Pirate King.

"Much better." I smiled. What was it about this man that made me feel sort of—what was it, *cared for?* It was a new feeling, and I was certain I shouldn't trust it. But Sam had been so different, all shoulders and swagger and swat-you-on-the-butt kind of playful. A definite fistful of daisies, grocery-store-greeting-card kind of man.

I watched Luke lift his glass toward me. Sam would never have called me "beautiful like a mythical . . ." *anything.* The only myth Sam Jamieson ever knew was that one about marital fidelity.

"To wooden spoon children," Luke said with a smile, "and the few of us who remain intact."

"So where in the South did you grow up, anyway?" I asked after taking a sip of my wine. Coastal chardonnay from California. Home. If I didn't go to prison.

"Virginia," he said, the look in his eyes drifting far away. "Charlottesville—Jefferson's Monticello? Near there, anyway. Out in the country."

"A farm boy?" I teased, not able to picture him like that.

"Gentlemen's farm." He smiled. "Horses. You can't have two sisters and live in Virginia and not be stumbling over saddles and buckets of grain and," he shook his head, "great damned mountains of horse manure. You're looking at a man who can wield a mean shovel."

"Marie's partner has horses," I said, wanting suddenly to see his eyes light up like that again. *Sisters, grandmama . . .* what was it in the way he spoke of these women, almost reverently, that made my heart soften? "She has one horse anyway. And a donkey. Marie took me riding once. Of course I got to ride the donkey. Can't really say it impressed me much."

"A donkey?" Luke laughed and leaned his chair back on two legs. He swirled the pale wine in his glass, his gaze far away again. "You haven't lived until you've galloped a well-bred horse flat out across a grassy meadow, bareback, holding onto a fistful of mane. Feel the wind in your face. And all that power between your legs."

Oh Lord. I choked on a mouthful of wine and felt my face flame.

"Hey, you okay?" Luke tipped forward and offered me a napkin, oblivious, thank God, to where my mind had just drifted. What could you expect from woman in tacky sequins?

He tilted his head. "Hear that?"

"What?" I fanned myself with the napkin and squeezed my knees together.

"Music. From the piano bar on the deck below us." He raised his brows. "Where we . . . danced the other night?"

I fanned faster. Yeah, and where we also . . . wait a minute. I glanced toward the window. "We're on the Sports Deck? Isn't that where—"

Luke finished my sentence. "Where the cabin steward hanged himself."

I leaned across the table toward him as it all came rushing back. Virgilio's dead body, Luke disappearing, the Nepalese searching our cabin and questioning me.

"Yes," I said slowly, "and never mind about telling me where you disappeared to that night, Luke, no matter how 'funny' the story is." I narrowed my eyes and set my wine glass down. "Just tell me this: what did you say to the ship's security officers about me?"

TWELVE

"You're saying that you have something to hide?" Luke rubbed his fingertip along the rim of his wineglass and watched my face.

"No, I . . ." My hand curled into a fist in my lap. Damn him, he was questioning me again. How did he do that? Sincere and boyishly warm one minute, then turning to go right for the throat. Who was this guy?

I exhaled slowly and forced a smile. I would not be baited this time. And he would not deter me; Marie was in trouble. "Of course I don't have anything to hide. It's just that it was unnerving to find those men in our cabin and to be interrogated like that."

"And you think that I had something to do with it?"

"One of them, a Mr. Gombu, asked me if I sold shoes."

"Shoes?" Luke's face was expressionless.

"He was flipping through a little notebook and asked me if I was an orthotic sales rep. I didn't tell that to anyone but you." I watched Luke's face for a reaction. Nothing.

"It's a top secret occupation then? Like the CIA?" Luke smiled.

"Dammit." I flattened my palms on the tablecloth and arched my back, rising taller in my chair. A tiny starfish popped loose from my bodice and cartwheeled onto the table. "What I'm saying is . . ."

My words were drowned by boisterous laughter as a group of Disney characters balancing cocktail glasses staggered toward the next table. A flop-eared Goofy pointed at my cleavage and poked Minnie Mouse in the ribs.

"Now that-ths," he slurred through a toothy mask, "what I call a cost-thume. Hoo-whee." Three of the Seven Dwarves clapped their hands and hooted, one losing his beard in the effort.

Luke stood and pulled out my chair. "I need some air. How about you?" He helped me with the fishnet shawl and then aimed a sharp look directly at the Disney group. The table was instantly quiet.

Outside, the night sky was clear and strewn with stars, and potted palms—strung with twinkle lights—continued the Polynesian theme. A trio of freestanding space heaters made it surprisingly warm under the teak overhang.

"I'm sorry, Darcy." Luke said softly from behind me as I spread my hands toward the heater's orange glow. "I shouldn't tease like that. Comes from living with sisters, I suppose, but that's no excuse. You were serious."

I turned, not realizing he was standing so close. I pulled the iridescent shawl tighter like it would protect me. "Why would you tell Gombu *anything* about me?" I asked.

Luke shrugged. "They're questioning a lot of people, not just you and your roommate. And I have to assume that we were seen dancing together the night before? Gombu understood that you were also a nurse. Like Marie. I corrected him, that's all." Luke rested his hand on my shoulder gently. "And I'm really very sorry if it upset you."

"I am a nurse." My mind raced. Why did the Nepalese want to know that?

Luke raised his brows. "I'm confused. Didn't you tell me . . ." He sighed and a brief smile flickered across his face.

"I lied," I said with a shrug. "Well, maybe it wasn't a lie. More like jumping the gun, I guess." I watched Luke's brows furrow. "I'm thinking of making a career change. This trip is kind of a hiatus. Maybe like it is for you?"

Luke chuckled and shook his head. "It irks the *hell* out of you, doesn't it?"

"What?"

"To think of an able-bodied man wasting his time as a dance host."

"Well, you . . ."

"Might as well be carrying a cardboard sign: '*Will dance for food?*'"

"I didn't say—" My lips stopped moving as Luke pressed his finger against them.

"You didn't have to. It shows. Because you're a hard-working, independent young woman. With a lot of integrity and a strong sense of right and wrong." Luke nodded. "Absolutely nothing the matter with that. Almost Southern, really."

He lifted his fingertip from my lips and let it linger on a tendril of hair alongside my face. "And, yes, I am on a sort of hiatus. From very respectable employment." His thumb traced my jaw line. "Does that make it okay?" He was whispering suddenly.

My skin warmed under his touch. "Okay?"

"To kiss you?"

My breath caught as he cupped my face in his hands, raising it so that he could look into my eyes. My pulse quickened. I nodded very slightly and closed my eyes. The deck swayed under my feet and I wasn't at all sure that it was the movement of the sea.

Luke's fingers slid to the nape of my neck, twining into my hair as he brought my face to his. His cheek was a little rough with beard growth but his lips were soft and warm as they pressed first against my brow, then to the tip of my nose. I heard him chuckle softly after kissing the corner of my mouth.

"I've never kissed a mermaid before," he whispered, his lips moving beside mine.

I smiled and then his mouth covered mine, lips far from tentative now. I parted my mine and returned his deepening kiss, feeling his tongue find mine. He pulled me closer against his body and I reeled with an incredible rush of textures, sensations—beard, lips, tongue, velvet against sequins . . . warm skin, cold salty air, the rocking of the sea and. . . was I breathing? Who cared?

"Your tail . . ." he whispered, finally, sounding breathless, too.

"Wha-at?" My voice wouldn't work and my eyes refused to open. I couldn't even think. I didn't want to.

"Be careful," Luke said, his breath returning to form a laugh. "I think I'm standing on—"

I took a step backward and my tail stuck tight under his shoe, yanking the top of my dress downward. "God!" I squealed, trying not to topple over and attempting to cover my half-exposed breasts.

"Here, sorry." Luke reached out to steady me then stopped and stared. "What's *that*?"

My hands flew to my chest. What did he mean? The stupid shamrock tattoo?

A slip of paper fluttered to the deck and Luke grabbed it before I could. *Paper?*

"So where else would a Mermaid keep her grocery list? Makes perfect sense." He laughed, holding the paper to the light. "Let's see . . ."

I swallowed hard and squeezed my eyes shut. *Oh shit.* The victim information list. From the sickbay. How could I explain?

I saw Luke frown before handing it back to me with an exaggerated shrug. "Looks like you're going to starve." He turned toward the bar's door, his voice suddenly different. Analytical, businesslike? *Changing again.* "Speaking of that, I'm sort of hungry. Want to see what's left at the buffet?"

I shoved the paper back into my bodice and nodded, my face flushing. Damn. I had an amazing fake Kate Spade bag, and I couldn't carry it tonight?

* * *

The silence between us felt awkward as we rode the elevator down to the Lido Deck. Was I imagining it? It would have been hard to talk with all the costumed passengers packed in next to us; the squealing as a vampire squirted fake blood and a roar of laughter as someone dropped an entire sack of candy corn underfoot. I glanced over at Luke. Maybe I was imagining it. He wouldn't know the significance of those names anyway. No need to worry.

We exited the elevator and I excused myself to use the ladies' room but took the opportunity to call Marie instead. I let the cabin phone ring a dozen times and hung up. Maybe she was still having that beer. Worrying about being arrested. I frowned. Even if I wanted to tell Luke the truth, how could I? If anyone knew that we'd been in the sickbay and it somehow got back to the security . . . No, I couldn't tell anyone. Not yet.

The party crowd had diminished but the buffet had been replenished, dessert now the focus. Luke threw me a boyish smile and filled his plate with a mound of goodies: pecan tartlet, apple crepe, brandied chocolate cherries, and cream-cheese-stuffed apricots.

The steward poured steaming coffee as we took a seat. I closed my fingers around my cup and looked at Luke out of the corner of my eye. "You never did say what 'respectable' career you're taking a hiatus from."

Luke licked a speck of chocolate from his lower lip and grinned, narrowing his blue eyes. "That thing about curiosity and cats?" He touched a fingertip gingerly to a seashell over my breasts and sighed. "Does that apply to mermaids, too?"

"You're not going to tell me?"

"No." He turned his head toward the dance floor and laughed. "Hey look, it's that woman who keeps rejecting me."

The Phantom Dancer, adding only a black satin eye mask in deference to the holiday, twirled alone on the dance floor, red carnation firmly in place behind her ear. She snapped her fingers rhythmically almost like she held Spanish castanets as the beaded fringe hem of her dress licked at her calves.

"Turns me down every time I ask," Luke said, shaking his head.

"She's old enough to be your grandmother."

"Not the point. It's a matter of pride." Luke smiled sheepishly. "For Herb and Dan, the other dance hosts. Not for me, of course."

"She's got Edie Greenbaum going for it, too." I laughed, pointing to the opposite side of the dance floor. Tweedle Dee, padded body, big collar, bow-tie, and beanie hat, was doing her own version of a solo dance act.

Luke turned his head to glance around the room.

"Who're you looking for?" I asked.

"Bernie. Isn't he Tweedle Dum?"

"Was. But he's at that haunted house on Whaler's Deck now, the one the show crew puts on. Probably popping up from some coffin as the gold-toothed reincarnation of Elvis." I grimaced. "You can't blame him for needing an outlet, though. I wouldn't want to live with Edie."

Luke led me onto the dance floor as the DJ began to play a slow song. I looked up into his face as he smiled down at me. It already seemed funny to think of him as bigger-than-life handsome and unapproachably arrogant. *And dangerous?* He didn't seem that way now. Handsome, sure. I glanced at the unruly thatch of blonde hair, the small scar on his chin. Not perfect. But trustworthy? I felt the warmth of his face as he stooped slightly to rest his cheek against mine and nuzzled my neck for an instant. A part of me wanted to trust him, but then I'd trusted Sam, too. I closed my eyes. I needed to remember that.

I opened my eyes to see that we were the only couple left on the dance floor. Edie Greenbaum had drifted away to sit with friends and the Phantom Dancer had ambled off. I started to smile as Luke raised my fingers to his lips, but then something caught my eye and I stopped dancing. I barely stifled a gasp.

A group of maybe ten Nepalese officers, boots thumping, were striding across the disco and heading toward the door to the deck. One was talking on his radio and gesturing for the others to follow. It was Gombu, and the black and white cow sock was easy to spot in his dark glove.

"What's wrong?" Luke followed my gaze to the deck doors.

"Nothing, I . . ." My pulse began to thrum in my head. Where were they going?

My hand trembled and I slipped it from Luke's before he could notice. "I just remembered that I have to check on Marie." I swallowed and forced my voice to stay steady. "She wasn't feeling very well, earlier."

I picked up my tail to walk away. Luke caught my arm. His eyes moved quickly to the deck door and back.

"Wait, Darcy. What's going on? Where are you going, *really*?" An anxious look flashed across his face.

I pulled my arm free and jutted my chin, staring up at him. "To the cabin. I told you." I couldn't stop the picture in my head of Marie being threatened by these scary men. What the hell did they do with those things anyhow? "Please. I'm going now."

"Can you wait a minute? I have to check with the DJ about a dance class tomorrow night, then I can walk with you."

"No, stay. I've got to go." I patted his arm quickly and hurried away as fast as my satin tail would allow. Where would Marie be? I needed to get there before the ninja troop did.

The Halloween festivities were winding down and deck stewards dismantled the stacks of cornstalks and rolled pumpkins like wobbly orange bowling balls into waiting laundry bags. A few costumed passengers twirled their masks and sipped out of plastic cocktail glasses outside the Treasure Island Casino.

No light shown behind the etched glass of the Mermaid Spa. I hurried on toward the elevator. I would try the cigar bar and then go back to the cabin.

* * *

I scowled as I remembered I'd forgotten my purse and keycard and started to knock on the cabin door just as the ship's overhead system began an alarming series of blasts. What now? I banged on the door with my palms and prayed frantically that Marie was inside.

"Well, hell, you're subtle," Marie said, after opening the door and catapulting me inside with a single motion. Her breath reeked of beer and she held a half-full stein in a hand covered by the remaining cow sock. She waggled her fingers in the pink teats and burped. "Par-*don*. Where are my manners? Should have said 'Moo.'"

"Oh good God." I whipped my head around to scan the corridor. "What are you thinking? Get rid of that sock!" I yanked it from her hand. Where could I stash it?

I jumped as the PA system blasted overhead again, and then crammed the sock into the top of my dress. The victim information list crumpled and poked my breasts. My boobs were a freaking crime scene.

"I *don't* know you." Marie shook her head and sank down onto her bed.

I squeezed my eyes shut and ran my hand across my forehead. I was sweating. "The Men in Black," I whispered. "They're goosestepping around with your other sock. Talking into radios."

"So what do we do?" Marie leaned back on her elbow and toyed with the zipper of her fanny pack. A VW Bug- shaped cigarette lighter rolled out onto the bedspread and I followed it with my eyes, my mind racing.

"Burn them," I said suddenly, watching the lighter and reaching into my cleavage.

"What?"

"Burn the sock and the information list." I scanned the room quickly and my eyes stopped on the bathroom door. "Yes, in the shower. And then we'll flush the ashes. Hurry."

"Promise me," Marie said slowly, rising from the bed. "That you will never drink rum again."

The paper caught fire quickly but it took several flicks of the Volkswagen wheels before the sock sparked, then frizzled and finally started to glow. The spots melted black onto white and the teats shriveled, raising a surprisingly dense cloud of acrid smoke.

"Man," Marie said, choking. "I feel like Mrs. O'Leary at the Chicago Fire. What's that smell?"

"Acrylic. Don't breathe it. Wait, what's that noise?" I fanned the air and leaned toward the bathroom door. Voices in the hall? *Shit.* "Okay, hurry. Scoop it up and flush it."

"I can't see to . . ." Marie's words were drowned by the shrill overhead scream of the smoke detector. "Good plan," she shouted, dropping to her knees to join me in a scooping frenzy.

It was mere minutes until the knocking began on our cabin door. We left the shower running, and I leaped forward to rub a washcloth against a soot mark on Marie's cheek just as she opened the door. Dozens of passengers filled the corridor and dozens more filed past our cabin talking excitedly. Had they called the crew?

"We're fine," I called out.

"What?" The Yoga Panther, in a chenille robe and still sporting a penciled nose and whiskers, paused and raised her brows.

"I said thank you for your concern, but we're *fine*. The smoke detector? Someone knocked on our door?" I glanced beyond the woman for any sign of the security staff.

"Don't know what you're talking about," the Yoga Panther said. "Someone was probably letting you know about the news. We're going up now to find out more."

"News?" I looked sideways at Marie and my stomach lurched.

"The robbery. Another one." The Yoga Panther wrinkled her little black nose. "There was a gun this time."

THIRTEEN

"A GUN?" I STARED at Marie as she closed the cabin door.

"Hell, at least they didn't say someone choked to death on a mouthful of acrylic cow teats." Marie sat down on the bunk and watched as I rummaged through the small closet. "What are you doing now, Darc'?"

I turned, holding a pair of black-cropped trousers and my lace print cashmere. "I'm going up there of course. We need to be forewarned."

"Okay, I'll come with you." Marie stood and swayed, putting her arms out for balance. "Whoa."

"No way." I shook my head. "You can hardly walk and, frankly, the less anyone sees of you right now the better." I pursed my lips. "Do you know offhand if anyone else had a cow costume?"

Marie shot me a withering look.

"Okay, stupid question." I smiled and tossed the mermaid suit onto my bed. "Anything even close?"

"Couple of Dalmatians?"

"Never mind." I pulled the sweater on over my head and smoothed its off-the-shoulder neckline. "Let's be optimistic here. Anyone could own a cow sock, right? It doesn't necessarily point to you." I glanced over at the dizzying heap of black and white spotted fabric on the floor and grimaced. "But we should have a story ready just in case."

"You mean why I was in the sickbay tonight?" Marie ran a hand through her short hair. "I've been thinking about that."

"And?"

"And maybe I'd forgotten to record some things in a chart, so I went back to do that?"

"Ummm . . ." I stooped in front of the mirror, pulled my hair up high into a stretch band, and checked the fastener on a silver and onyx earring. "Work on that a little more, okay? Meanwhile I'm going up there to find out what happened with that robbery." I turned back to Marie. "And see exactly where those security goons are."

I opted for the stairs because the elevators were crammed with old people in robes, pajamas, and furry slippers. I watched as a pair of women padded by, their hair in sponge rollers and pin curls. It looked like a senior-set pajama party. Mystery party. They were as curious as I was.

I trotted up the carpeted staircase, tapping my fingertips along the brass handrail and grateful for the freedom of moving without a tail. A mermaid and a cow. If Marie had remembered to get decent costumes earlier, would we even be in this mess? No time to think about that now. I glanced at my watch: 11:00 PM. The bars would still be open. I stepped out onto the Lido Deck and into a sea of pajamas.

An enormous woman in a ballerina costume was the center of attention. Mascara streaked her face. I positioned my head between a shiny maroon smoking jacket and a Hawaiian print housecoat for a better view.

"And that gun was pressed into my neck," the woman blubbered, tutu bouncing with each sob. Pale flesh escaped from the holes in her fishnet stockings like an overstuffed sausage casing. "And a deep voice said . . ." she paused to wail and jab the air with a glitter wand, "'Give me your purse, Fatty, or I'll plug ya.' And then I think maybe . . ." she sniffed, "his other hand lingered on my bosom."

The crowd gasped. Cardboard cameras flashed rapid-fire and the victim's face lit up in a dimpled smile.

"But did you see his face?" A man's voice—Bernie Greenbaum—called out in front of me. "Is there any way we can identify this pervert?"

"Well, no I—" The woman turned as a pair of security officers arrived at her side. Gombu whispered in her ear and then waved his arms at the crowd.

"We have things under control, ladies and gentlemen. As you can see, Miss . . ." he frowned and looked down at his notebook.

"Bliss," the ballerina giggled. "Serena Bliss."

"Thank you." Gombu continued. "Miss Bliss," he frowned again, "is shaken but basically unharmed. Again, we have things under control. And are investigating," he tapped his notebook, "a number of possibly related clues to this unfortunate and rare occurrence."

I ducked down a little and felt my stomach quiver. Clues? Like a break-in at the sickbay? Now we were suspects in an armed robbery? I needed to get out of there before Gombu spotted me. I stepped backward and onto someone's foot.

"Ouch, there you go again."

I turned and saw Luke grin. He'd changed from his costume into khakis and a sweater. Black V-neck, no shirt under it, and sleeves pushed up his forearms. Every inch of skin that showed— believe me, I was looking—was sort of golden brown. His hair looked just-washed and I thought I could smell a faint trace of pipe tobacco.

"So how's she feeling?" he asked.

"Who?"

Luke raised his eyebrows. "Your roommate. Marie? Didn't you rush off to check on her?"

"Of course, I . . . she's fine. Touch of the flu." I muttered and then frowned, shaking my head. "Bovine strain probably."

Luke shrugged. "What? Okay, you're the nurse. But it sounds like it's safe to go have some coffee then." He touched a fingertip to my chin and I could feel it clear to my toes. "Listen to some piano music, maybe?"

I hesitated for a nanosecond and then smiled. Coffee wouldn't hurt, right? Give Marie some time to sober up. And maybe I'd hear some more crime details from the late-night passenger crowd. Sure.

"I guess so. But safe?" I grimaced. "While some madman with a gun is lurking around?"

Luke took my hand and laughed. "The only madman you have to worry about is me." He brushed his lips across my fingers. "I was driven completely crazy by a mermaid."

* * *

We went to the little Moroccan piano bar we'd visited that previous night. The night Virgilio hanged himself. I shivered. What kind of vacation memories were these anyway?

Luke seated me at a tiled table next to a collection of painted urns and a large potted palm. Ceiling fans swirled slowly overhead and the dark-skinned pianist was playing "As Time Goes By." I smiled. *Casablanca*, Grandma's favorite film.

Our coffee arrived in a Turkish pot, brass with a long, black handle. The steward poured it into small demitasse cups, steamy, strong, and dark, and laced with raw sugar.

"So *are* you?" I held the warm cup to my lips and peered at Luke over the rim.

"Am I what?"

"A madman. Is that part of your 'respectable employment'?"

He shook his head and glanced away. "Hey, want to dance?"

"Really, what do you do?"

Luke swallowed a sip of coffee and was silent for a moment. "You're not going to let this go, are you?"

I shook my head.

"Okay." He wrinkled his forehead. "I'm on a sort of hiatus. Like I told you." Luke hesitated.

"From?"

He sighed. "Wouldn't really interest you. Boring bureaucratic stuff mostly. Paper clips, paperwork. Legalese."

"You're a lawyer?" I set my cup down and stared, mouth open.

Luke turned his head quickly to scan the room. "Damn, want to spoil my reputation? I didn't say that, okay?" He winked, stood, and reached for my hand. "C'mon, I'm a dance host."

A bass player had joined the tuxedoed pianist, and the music was soft and sensuous, bone-deep with resonance. Warm and sweet as the Turkish coffee.

I shut my eyes as soon as Luke's arms closed around me. I didn't want to think about hangings, robberies, or destroying evidence anymore. I didn't want to think, period. Suddenly all I wanted was to close my eyes and steep in this wonderful music. In these arms.

"Nice?" Luke murmured against my ear.

"Mmm, very," I answered. I stepped closer to his body and his arms slid low, one warm palm at the back of my trousers. His fingers tightened and pressed me even closer until our hips met fully and perfectly. It seemed like we were barely moving across the dance floor and that everything around us was a blur. There was only warmth and connection, the deep thrum of the bass strings and Luke's breathing against my ear.

I leaned away and looked up into his face.

I wasn't even sure what I wanted to say. But then talking wasn't what I wanted at all, was it? What I wanted was Luke. It was true. All my tough talk about being immune and not susceptible was one big bluff. I wanted this man. And suddenly, it made perfect sense. Now what?

Luke bent his head down and kissed me. My head swam as I reached up and buried my fingers in his hair, kissing him back. If he hadn't been holding me so tightly, I would have crumbled. We'd stopped dancing altogether. It felt so wonderful, and . . . Oh God, someone was applauding. No, not someone—*everyone.*

I stepped away from him with my face burning and watched as the pianist and the bass player began applauding, too. Luke chuckled and squeezed my fingers.

The pianist grinned and spoke into the microphone. "We bill our music as 'romantic,' folks, and I think these two have just proved it." He winked. "What do you think, should we send some champagne to their stateroom?"

I pressed my palm to my face and shook my head. Couldn't the floor please swallow me? So much for being inconspicuous.

Luke slipped his arm around my waist and led me from the dance floor as the patrons continued to applaud. I nodded toward the exit and grabbed my purse from the table.

"It's not such a bad idea, really," Luke whispered as he opened the door.

"Leaving there? Absolutely." I could feel his fingers caress the back of my neck.

Luke stepped into a shadow along the corridor wall and pulled me close, tracing a fingertip across the kitten soft neckline of my sweater before nuzzling my neck. "No, I meant the champagne. And the stateroom. Mine?" He leaned away and watched my eyes. "I've got a balcony and we'd get a moonlight preview of the Canada coastline before I show you Quebec City tomorrow. The Saint Lawrence Seaway is incredible at night. Mountains and lights, and . . .?" His parted lips brushed mine, asking for an answer.

My legs were giving out. Dragging a fish tail was nothing compared to how this suddenly felt. I leaned back and looked into his eyes for an instant before eagerly returning his kiss.

"I've always wanted to see the Canadian coastline," I murmured against his mouth. Okay, corny and pathetic. And true to form. I wasn't even fooling myself.

We passed everyone in the corridors, of course. I shooed Luke's hands away a half dozen times and waved chastely at the file of passengers headed for the midnight buffet—the Greenbaums,

Yoga Panther, Queen Bee, and Prom Princess. Miss Serena Bliss, still in her tutu, appeared to have recovered from the earlier trauma and kept pace. An openly admiring old gentleman walked beside her, leaning on a cane and carrying her glitter wand.

Luke's stateroom was on G-Deck aft, and we passed by a door festooned with a rainbow of balloons and streamers.

"Honeymooners," Luke explained, shaking his head. "Third time around. He's eighty-two."

The floral carpeted corridor was empty and Luke stopped in front of his outside stateroom and backed me gently against the closed door, his hips resting against mine. I'm no genius, but I knew that this was definitely not just about champagne and coastal geography. He pressed his lips to the curve of my neck and slid them very slowly upward. My legs barely held me.

"I want to tell you something," he whispered, his warm lips at the corner of my mouth.

"Not that you've got a wife and two kids asleep in that room?" I felt his breath puff against my face in a laugh.

"What I was going to say," he smiled, leaning away a little and looking down into my face. "Is that I've been going crazy, wanting you, since—"

"Since my sexy swan dive on the treadmill?"

Luke traced a fingertip across the swell of cashmere over my breast and my breath caught like a virgin.

"Yes. Well, since I picked you up off the floor that day and realized how good you felt in my arms." He chuckled. "I didn't realize I had this weakness for stomping, biting little spit-fires in boxing gloves."

"Did you notice I'm not fighting anymore?" I whispered. Corny was fast becoming my second language as I leaned forward into his touch.

"I noticed." He covered my mouth with his own for a long moment. Long enough for me to realize that I'd never been kissed this well before and to wonder what other surprises were in store. "And I also noticed," he whispered hoarsely, "that for some damned reason we're still standing out here in the hallway."

Luke pulled the keycard from his pocket and swept me off the carpet and up into his arms like a hero in one of those Lifetime movies. "Let's go drink that champagne."

I rested my cheek against his chest, my legs dangling deliciously. "So . . . no little wife in there, huh?"

Luke turned the handle and pushed the stateroom door open with his foot. "Nobody but us," he said, carrying me over the threshold and into the room.

The six Nepalese security officers turned as we entered and snapped to attention.

FOURTEEN

"ARE YOU SURE? I mean if you're sick, I could come to your cabin. I'm a nurse, remember." I put my hand over the phone receiver, squinted into the morning light and then rolled my eyes. Marie was standing on the dock beyond me, drumming her fingers on her bicycle helmet and looking impatient.

Luke's tone was curt. "No. I'll be fine. Thank you."

"But you're going to miss Quebec City." And we were supposed to see it together like we were supposed to drink champagne on the balcony of his stateroom last night. *What happened?* "Shouldn't I come by and check for—uh—fever?"

I heard him sigh and my heart sank. Not a good sigh. Definitely no fever; not like last night's anyway. This sounded more like a brush off.

"No," he said. "I think maybe it's contagious. A flu."

He paused and I tapped at the receiver of the courtesy phone with my fingernail, wondering if we'd been disconnected. His voice finally returned, cool and sarcastic. Sarcastic? Was it a bad phone connection?

"Bovine flu maybe. Isn't that what you said your roommate had?" Luke paused once more. "By the way, bovine means cow, doesn't it?"

I returned his goodbye and hung up, staring at the receiver. *Cow?* Oh, God, why had I made that stupid remark? But he couldn't know what I'd meant, could he? Impossible but, damn, the whole thing last night was so confusing. Being lifted into Luke's arms and carried over the threshold, all hot and giddy. Then *wham,* right into the penetrating stares of the the Men In Black like an icy-cold hosedown. Luke had asked me to leave immediately and then didn't answer his phone when I tried to call again and again until about two in the morning.

"Hold your horses, Marie, I'm coming." I picked up my helmet and walked down the boardwalk.

"'The European charm of the Old Walled City of Quebec,'" Marie quoted, tucking the brochure back into her fanny pack and pointing upward. She swept her arm wide. "'And the romantic Dufferin Terrace with a spectacular view of the St. Lawrence River.'" She picked at her nicotine patch and peered at me from under her bangs. "Or aren't we feeling romantic this morning?"

A young couple, with faces rosy from the cold, strolled past us whispering softly in French and totally absorbed in each other. The girl laughed suddenly, eyes sparkling, and gave the curly-haired young man a playful punch on the shoulder. He slipped his arm around her hips and nuzzled her neck. Dammit, that could have been Luke and me—I could fake French, no problem. I sighed and opened the buckle on my helmet. "Why does everything sound so revoltingly perfect in French?"

Marie stared at me, waiting.

"He says he's sick," I groaned.

"So maybe he is. I would be after pulling an all-nighter with our friendly Nepalese." Marie lifted her eyebrows. "You know, all those bright lights in his face and bamboo under his fingernails— Man, hope it wasn't his toenails. Couldn't dance."

I glared. "Stop it. You don't think he's really under suspicion, do you?"

"Hell, Darc', what do I know? You're looking at someone who burned a sock in her shower."

"But . . ." My mind was screaming. I couldn't be wrong again. Could I? "He seems okay. All that stuff I thought before, about fleecing the old ladies and setting up the Queen Bee? I don't believe it anymore, because . . ." Because I would never have slept with a crook?

"Hey, I'm not accusing anybody." Marie reached over and squeezed my shoulder gently. "All I'm saying is that someone on that ship has a gun. It's not a simple pickpocket thing anymore; the rules have changed. The crew and the security staff are downplaying it. Have to, to avoid panic. But the point is that we've all got to be careful." Marie picked up her bike, swung her leg over and pointed. "So you think we can get these babies up that hill?"

We reached the top, our breaths making snowy puffs in the morning air, and paused to look out at the sunlit river and its island, Ile d'Orleans, afire with autumn color. The Laurentian Mountain range rose beyond. At our backs was the Chateau Frontenac, with fairy-tale spires and a dramatic green copper roof, rising like a castle from its manicured grounds. I gulped at the frosty air, squeezing my eyes shut for a moment against a rush of dizziness. *Whoa*, we'd climbed it pretty fast.

"Look," Marie said, pointing at her brochure. "The little chateau's only five hundred eighty-five bucks a night, American.

Bet they have great cigars." She looked back at me and her dark brows scrunched with worry. "Hey, what is it? What's wrong?"

I raised my hand to the side of my neck and sucked in another big breath. Damn. My heart was pounding like a jackhammer and a second wave of dizziness made my legs wobble. "My heart, it's—"

Marie dropped her bicycle, grabbed mine, and then helped me sit down on the lawn. "Here, let me count it and then we'll see what we can do to make it slow down." She frowned and her forehead creased like a scolding mother. "Up late drinking coffee, hardly ate a thing at breakfast . . . did you even sleep at all?" She pressed her fingers into my neck then glanced up from her watch. "One-eighty, at least. Here, I'm gonna start massaging."

I tried to keep my breathing steady and my eyes focused while Marie rubbed her fingertips rhythmically against my carotid artery. Carotid massage. I'd seen it work before, lots of times. *Please, God, don't let me pass out.*

"Let's try one more treatment. The Valsalva maneuver. You know how." Marie watched as I held my breath and grunted, bearing down to increase the pressure inside my chest and abdomen and to slow my heartbeat.

I was aware of voices, people standing over me—hazy, couldn't make them out. Was that Edie? The Queen Bee? My heart lugged, fluttered, and skipped a beat, then finally steadied. *Yes.* The blood rushed back into my head like rain after a drought. "I'm fine now."

"Wait, sit up slowly." Marie checked my pulse and nodded. "Back to normal."

"Well, for goodness sake, Darcy, aren't you too young for this kind of thing?" Bernie Greenbaum, wearing a maroon beret, leaned down, his chocolate eyes clouded with concern. He slid his tongue over his gold tooth and tried to smile as he nervously patted my arm.

"Oh, thank God you're okay, Darcy," the Queen Bee murmured. "And what a blessing that Marie was here. Here, honey, you're not dressed near warm enough. Take my fox."

"No really, I'm fine." I smiled and blinked as the mothball-scented fur swung close to my face. How many people were standing there? I felt like a tourist attraction. "I just need some water. No big deal."

"A heart condition," Edie Greenbaum boomed like she was making a public service announcement, "is certainly a *very* big deal. You can never be certain of the outcome, dear. Why, only last year my youngest niece, Rachel—"

"Well," Marie interrupted, pushing the fox coat and Edie Greenbaum aside, "don't worry, I'll take care of Darcy. And you folks should probably get going. Don't want to miss your tours do you?"

After the crowd dispersed, I stood up slowly. No problem. Steady as a rock. I picked up my bike and looked where Marie was pointing.

"There's a coffee-house down there, someone said. Past the ice-skating rink. You really feel okay now?"

We walked our bikes slowly downhill along a narrow cobbled street, admiring little boutiques with doorways festooned in tiny pumpkins, cornstalks, and bittersweet branches. It seemed as if every other storefront boasted an art gallery. Canvases brushed thick with vermilion, ochre, and cerulean blue leaned against bisque-fired pottery and simple jelly jars made glorious by fistfuls of autumn blossoms. Shoppers lingered on corners, laughing and leaning against street lamps, their colloquial language like impromptu poetry. I wanted to pinch myself, soak it all in. Quebec City. Luke was right. Wonderful.

We stopped in front of a small yellow building across from an open-air ice rink, and the door opened releasing the fabulous aroma of fresh roasted coffee and just-baked pastries. We locked our bikes, followed two young women dressed in ski sweaters and stepped inside.

"Look, it's an Internet café," Marie said, raising her voice above the hubbub and pointing toward several rows of computers near the back of the room. She pulled me into the line forming in front of the service counter.

"No arguing, you are having juice, not coffee. Not a drop of caffeine." Marie's eyes widened as we approached the bakery case. "But for sure you need one of those therapeutic cream cheese and fruit thingies." She grinned. "I'll have one too, for moral support."

Marie mimed our order to a young girl dressed in black, with coffee-cup shaped earrings, and pointed to a chalked menu written in French. I surveyed the crowd, taking in the obvious mix of cultures, ages, the youngest loudly enjoying computer games. I scanned the little clutch of side-by-side monitors, wondering how people could stand that, being crowded so close together, knee to shin.

I heard Marie call my name and started to turn back when a man caught my eye. Hunched over the farthest computer, head bent toward the screen. His hand was moving furiously over a notepad. Blonde man with wire-rimmed glasses and . . . Luke. He'd lied to me.

He spoke without looking up when I approached.

"Okay, miss, I'm pretty much finished," he muttered, obviously mistaking me for the waitress.

"Yes, I guess that about sums it up in my eyes, too," I whispered through clenched teeth.

Luke's head snapped upward and his mouth gaped open.

"Darcy, I . . ."

"Don't bother trying to explain," I said, watching his fingers move to quickly close the program screen. "I'm just glad to see that you've obviously recovered from your illness." I turned to leave and he caught my hand.

"Darcy, please. Wait. I can explain this." His voice was soft and conciliatory with no hint of the earlier sarcasm. He was wearing a brown leather aviator's jacket over a loose-knit sweater; the reading glasses made him look boyish, like an Ivy League undergrad. Why was he always like this—so wily and unpredictable? His thumb moved against my palm and I fought a rush of familiar heat.

I opened my mouth to speak and was interrupted as Marie arrived at my side balancing a plate of pastries, coffee, and a bottle of juice.

"Hey, I think we'll have to eat this on the go, Darc', 'cause—" her eyes widened. "Luke?"

I slipped my hand free and turned to Marie. "You're right, we've got that bus to catch for the tour. I almost forgot."

"But . . ." Luke stood.

"You were right about one thing anyway, Luke." I smiled and stepped away. "Quebec City is amazing. Now I'm going to go enjoy it."

*　*　*

The bus wound through the French Canadian countryside and into the foothills of the Laurentian Mountains and toward the Lake Beauport region. Marie sat near the window and snapped photos, droning like a Gregorian monk at the passing scenery.

"Sugar maple—ooh—red one, yellow with black bark—mmm—orange like fire, purple . . . Hey, can a tree be *purple*?"

"Save some film for Montmorency Falls, you twit." I laughed. "They say it's maybe one and a half times as high as Niagara."

Marie turned and shuddered. "Yeah, well you can let me know, okay? I'm gonna save all my energy for the following stop." She grinned and licked her lips. "'Cabane à Sucre.' Sugar Shack. Hot maple syrup poured onto snow. That's instant candy, babe."

I leaned back against the headrest and closed my eyes, forcing thoughts of Luke from my mind. Damn him. No problem, I'd think of something else. Yes, Dr. Foote and his job offer. What were the names of some of that inventory he'd showed me? Heel wedges, spur pads . . . oh yeah, and some custom-made German orthotic. Velveteen arch support? Yes. I could just imagine Marie laughing at me on that one. Not the same as cardiac life support, but people had to have comfortable feet, right? Dr. Foote—*Phillip*—had even offered to show me how the measuring was done for it, the wax casting of a bare foot. He'd had me take my shoes and socks off and—my thoughts were interrupted by a guttural voice directly across the aisle.

"And really, honey, I thought I was a goner," Serena Bliss explained to the man beside her. "You know how they say your life passes before your eyes? It's true. I saw it like a collage: my sixth birthday with the Minnie Mouse cake; my brother's Bar Mitzvah—unbelievable spread—and that romantic summer in Oregon with the Strawberry Fair." She smacked her lips. "'World's Largest Shortcake.'"

"So you were looking right down the gun barrel?" The elderly gentleman asked, eyes milky behind thick lenses.

I leaned out into the aisle slightly, straining to hear.

"Well, I didn't actually see it of course," Serena conceded. "Impossible with the cucumber mask over my eyes."

"Cucumber mask?" The man watched Serena intently, his face flushing pink.

"It's a little sleep mask, sweetie, like the airlines give you? Only this one's filled with chilled water and fits over two thin cucumber slices." She batted her eyelashes. "Gives us that youthful, dewy-eyed look. Here, touch my skin."

I leaned back and nudged Marie. "Last night's robbery with the gun," I whispered, "was in the Mermaid Spa."

* * *

The tour guide hadn't been exaggerating about Montmorency Falls. A breathtaking expanse of snow-white water roared from the cliffs above and cascaded some 270 feet to the St. Lawrence River below. My face tingled with the icy-cold spray as I held onto the waist-high railing and watched the foam dance over the huge boulders below. I smiled. Marie, of course, had chosen to stay behind and sample the selection of teas at Montmorency Manor.

"Hey, I can hold my pinkie out as good as anyone," she'd laughed and then added, "Besides, you couldn't have safer company;

Bernie and Edie have done that climb a dozen times." She'd rolled her eyes. "That little woman is part goat."

I hugged my fur-trimmed parka closer and took one last look out across the falls, the arching steel bridge, and stone towers beyond. I sighed and my breath suspended in a puff. It would have been so perfect to share this with Luke. Why was he so blasted difficult to understand? Only a fool would try.

I followed the trail back toward the Manor, my feet scattering orange-yellow leaves with each stride, and then paused in front of a bed of claret-red chrysanthemums to tie the lace of my boot. The footsteps of the final tour group receded beyond me. Good, some solitude at long last. I stood upright again and bumped smack into Luke. My breath caught.

"Hi. I found you." He smiled tentatively.

"How . . ." I couldn't take my eyes away from his. They were warm, inviting, and so very different from earlier.

"I have some pull with the tour guides," he explained, "and they let me look at the guest itinerary. Hopped the next bus, and here I am." He frowned slightly. "I need to explain . . . no, apologize first. Darcy, I'm sorry."

I crossed my arms and tried to deny what his eyes were making me feel.

"I was worried last night," I said, keeping my voice as matter-of-fact as I could. "I must have called half a dozen times. You didn't answer." I watched his eyes. Could I even recognize the truth anymore?

"I had to go down to the security office. Answer some questions to clear some things up."

"And?"

"And we cleared them up," Luke said softly. He stepped toward me and I moved half a step backward.

"And this morning? Your 'illness'?" I watched a series of expressions flicker across his face. Was he taking too long to answer?

"A lame excuse. I was involved in something, Darcy." He read the look on my face and gave a quick laugh. "Something, not someone." He reached for my hand and I didn't pull away. "Something I'm caught up in and really can't talk about yet. Business."

"That's why you were in the cyber café?"

"Partly. I was coming to find you when I got a call on my cell phone and had to check some things. On the Internet." He stooped down to look into my face fully. "I swear. Believe me, there was nothing I wanted more than to spend today with you." He touched his fingertips gently to the side of my face. "Except maybe to have tasted that champagne."

"You were coming to find me?" I whispered over the catch in my throat. I searched his eyes, surprised at how much I suddenly wanted to believe him.

"Cross my heart," he said, his gaze never wavering. "I care about you, Darcy. I wasn't really prepared for that." He shook his head. "And I wish I could give you a better explanation about all this business, but could you maybe trust me for now?" He tucked a finger under my chin and tipped my face up toward him. "Just consider that?"

I watched his eyes for a few moments longer, then took a deep breath and launched myself into his arms. I grinned and raised my face for his kiss. What can I say? I'm easy.

Luke's mouth covered mine and he kissed me deeply, his arms around my waist and palms warm against the back pockets of my jeans. He stopped and laughed, then picked me up and twirled me around, brushing an aspen bough and sending a shower of yellow leaves fluttering to the ground. He set me down gently and kissed my brow, my nose, my cheek—a flurry of kisses peppered with laughter—and then found my lips again.

My head spun as I returned the kiss, breathing through my nose so it wouldn't have to stop. He smelled of soap and leather and espresso and I slid my arms under his jacket, feeling the hard muscles of his back beneath his sweater.

My palms kneaded his back, creeping higher until my right hand bumped against something and stopped. What was that? Leather and metallic cold. A cell phone? In a . . . holster? Oh God. I shivered and it had nothing to do with the kiss. *A gun.*

FIFTEEN

MARIE WAS TAKEN AWAY as soon as the ship entered international waters.

"It's the Feds," Serena Bliss mumbled, her mouth full. She pointed her donut toward the café ceiling and powdered sugar sifted down her forearm. "They've got a helicopter up there on the Sun Deck."

I glared and jogged to the stairway once more. Damn. The security staff was still blocking it off; their arms folded and radios crackling. There was no way to get to the helipad. Angry tears rose again and I shook my head. Marie, on the other hand, had been maddeningly calm about the whole thing.

"Look, kid," she'd said while packing a small duffel bag, "it's not like I'm under arrest or anything. I'm being asked to 'assist in an investigation.' Kind of cool?" She picked at the edge of her nicotine patch. Her fingers had trembled and she'd quickly dropped her hand to her side and forced a laugh. "Did you see those guys—dark suits and sun glasses? Hell, this is more like a date with the Blues Brothers."

I glanced back toward the elevators; they had a Nepalese officer in there, too, being sure no one pushed the button to the top deck. Maybe making sure I didn't get back up there again. What else could I have done? Okay, so banging on the security door outside the captain's quarters was a little over the top. But they were taking Marie away!

I stepped back toward the dining room and tilted my head. There it was, the unmistakable *thwoop-thwoop*, then *whine-whir* of helicopter blades. Taking off. *Shit.* My stomach sank and tears spilled over. I walked toward the staircase and leaned on the polished rail.

This was all my fault. If I'd been more diligent about finding the real thief maybe I could have turned the suspicion away from Marie. But no, what did I do? Orchestrate that bumbling break-in at the sickbay and then drop the whole thing to get into a kiss-fest with Luke Skyler. Luke. Who had a gun. And what did I do about that?

I looked up and sniffed as a hand tugged on the hem of my sweater.

"Here's a tissue, sweetie," Edie Greenbaum said, and then sighed.

"Thanks." I dabbed my eyes and let her pat my arm.

"We're all upset, dear," she clucked. "Who'd ever have guessed the troubles that people have?" Edie peered up through her bifocals. "That poor Virgilio, hanging himself because his wife cheated on him. And now Marie." She fingered the beaded cord on her glasses like it was a rosary. "I was just telling the ladies that if that sweet girl needed a little money, she could have come to Bernie and me."

My jaw clenched. *What the hell . . .* she was saying that to people? Blood rushed to my head and it took every ounce of strength I had not to shove the nosy little woman down the stairs. Instead, I settled for blowing my nose and handing the soggy tissue back before turning and bounding down the steps.

The Java Café on the Promenade Deck was nearly deserted; most of the passengers probably busy dressing for dinner. I bit into a chocolate-dipped macaroon and sighed. Yep, dinner, and the table talk would be about Marie Whitley, jewel thief. Moderated by Edie Greenbaum—rotten little gossip. It still totally fried me. Especially after Marie had been so good to her.

"There you are." A hand touched my shoulder and I looked up to see Luke. He was dressed in slacks and a sports coat, a checkered linen shirt open at the throat. And gun under his arm?

I flashed the smile I'd practiced on the bus ride back from Montmorency Falls. Sweet, unsuspecting, and just-kissed confused. That last part was pretty easy.

"You didn't answer your phone." His eyes looked concerned. He glanced down at my hooded cotton sweater, chinos, and snakeskin flats. "Not going to the dining room?"

"I . . . oh, hell." I couldn't stop the tears from brimming again. This was such a mess, and how honest could I dare be with Luke now? I pressed the napkin to my eyes and blinked against a speck of coconut.

"I heard about Marie, of course," Luke said softly, pulling up a chair. "And if it helps, I was able to get some information from the security staff." His hand brushed my arm.

"What do you mean?"

"Only that she should be back in twenty-four hours at the latest." He glanced away and paused as if unsure of what he wanted to say. "She's on her way to the FBI Field Office in Boston; they're the headquarters for upper New England."

I wrinkled my brows. "How do you know all of this?"

Luke shrugged. "Hey, I've been on the ship awhile. People talk and I find out things. A dance host is viewed as pretty non-threatening, you know." He smiled. "Anyway, I've been assured that she'll be fine, Darcy." He rubbed the back of his hand gently along my cheek and my heart bounced in my chest. "Now, please, can I convince you to come have dinner with me?"

I squeezed my eyes shut for a moment. It would be so easy to say yes. I wanted that more than I could say. Dinner, lingering over coffee, dancing, and the long-awaited champagne? But the rules had changed now. There had been a helicopter on the deck and a gun under Luke's jacket. What I had to do now was sort it all out. To help Marie.

"I don't think so," I said, and watched disappointment register on his face.

"Later, then?"

"No." I glanced away and swallowed. "Please understand, Luke. I need to be alone for a while."

I watched him walk away and then asked the coffee steward for a pencil. I grabbed a stack of ship logo napkins and made a list. Good way to start. Logical, careful, and calculated. I tapped the end of the pencil against my coffee cup and listened as a string quartet warmed up just yards away. What had happened chronologically?

Prom Princess. The heirloom jewelry and loose diamond. In the spa? No, wait. I crossed out the word "spa" and frowned. Crime scenes should be another column. This first column was for victims.

Mrs. Kravitz, the heart attack victim. I dotted the "i" and chewed on the end of the pencil. And Virgilio? For godsake, he'd *died.* That's certainly being a victim. But of what? He hadn't been robbed. Despondency? There was certainly enough buzz going around ship that he'd killed himself because of his wife.

I added Virgilio to the victims column with a question mark. At the very least, he was the victim of malicious gossip.

Serena Bliss. Definitely a victim–although God knows she'd seemed to enjoy the experience. I shook my head. And, from what Serena had said, she'd been robbed of cash only. No jewels were taken for the first time.

New column. Crime settings.

Prom Princess: spa, probably. Although she claimed it was the sickbay, of course. I stabbed the point of my pencil at the woman's name a few times.

Mrs. Kravitz: her cabin. After she was taken to the sickbay.

Virgilio. I shivered. Hanging from the Sports Deck. Right near the putting green and the batting cages. Batting cages? Why did that ring a bell?

I took a swallow of my coffee and drummed the tabletop with the pencil. Hadn't the Men In Black asked Marie some crazy question about whether she liked baseball and if she used the batting cages? What was that all about?

And Serena Bliss: in the spa.

Okay, what next? I shook my head and felt guilt wash over me again. The information I'd made Marie find that night in the sickbay. The mini-stroke victims. And the other patients who had presented undiagnosed complaints of weakness after visits to the Mermaid Spa.

I couldn't remember all the names and, thanks to me, the list had been burned and flushed down the toilet. Whale food by now.

Along with the sock. Some spy. All I'd managed to accomplish was to further implicate my best friend.

The steward came to freshen my coffee and I thanked him. I'd switched to decaf, grudgingly, because all I needed now was to get my heart amped up with caffeine and give Scoutmaster Bernie another reason to fuss over me. I took one last sip, picked up the stack of napkins, and headed past the quartet. They were playing, "This Kiss." To remind me of how stupid I'd been.

I headed for the elevator and tucked the napkins into my purse. What about Luke? I hadn't said anything to Marie about the gun. Because, face it, I hadn't been able to figure it out in my own head, about why he'd need a gun. Why would a lawyer carry a gun? Disgruntled client, dangerous case? But he'd said he was on hiatus.

I jabbed the elevator button and the doors closed and then opened again as the dance hosts, Herb and Dan, stepped aboard. They smiled at me and I noticed for the first time that Dan had a toupee and that Herb's pants were shiny with wear.

I groaned inwardly and asked myself another question. The Big Question. The one kept at bay by moonlit kisses, lopsided grins, and the ever-tempting promise of champagne. By my own weakness. Why in hell would a lawyer work on board a cruise ship as a dance host? Answer: only if he were in trouble somehow and running away. Or stood to profit by it.

I opened the cabin door and felt an immediate wave of sadness. No lingerie sculpture. Now, no Marie. What was next? Iceberg?

I'd switched on the lava lamp and started tidying the cabin—rolling up a dozen pairs of Marie's socks—when there was a knock on the door. I opened it to the beaming face of a uniformed steward wearing a nametag with the logo of the Mermaid Spa. He was holding a gilded envelope.

"Mrs. Evanston?"

I stared at the envelope. "No, I think she's the next door down."

"Oh, I'm sorry, miss." The steward made a half-bow and backed away.

Before I'd closed the door, I heard the gush of excitement in the voice of the woman next door: "Oh, my goodness, Harold. It's true. I *am* a winner. Look, I've won a spa coupon! Can you believe it?"

I sat down next to a pile of Marie's clothes and pulled the napkins out of my purse. Goosebumps rose on my arms. I scanned down the columns I'd made. Victims. Crime settings. Mini-stroke patients. I'd forgotten something. Another column I should add: winners of spa coupons. The Prom Princess, Mrs. Thurston—the Queen Bee—and now the woman next door. How many more were there?

I crammed the napkins back into my purse and searched my dresser drawer until I found some bike shorts and a matching racer back tank. I held them up and smiled at my flash of genius. There were other ways to learn the information I needed to add to my list. For all the columns.

The phone rang just as I finished wriggling into the snug sapphire blue shorts. I answered and reached for my gym bag.

"How about dessert then?" Luke asked. "Chocolate mousse under the stars?"

"Thank you anyway," I said as I checked my watch. "But I'm late for my first ever yoga class."

SIXTEEN

"Just lie down and look dead, sweetie," Serena Bliss whispered.

I dropped my bag, grabbed a mat, and sank down to join the women lying on their backs on the gym's polished hardwood floor. I doubted, however, that the scathing look just directed at me by the instructor was conducive to spiritual harmony.

"For those who may be new or who have arrived *late* to our class," the nasal voice droned, "I am Gurani and this posture that we perform now is used at both the beginning and ending of our sessions."

I wondered for a moment if Grandma Rosaleen would benefit from something like this, the camaraderie of these women, the healthy stretch of body and mind, and . . . the risk of becoming a victim, too? What was I thinking? No, there would be no more victims. Not Marie or these women. Not if I could help it. I lifted my head from the floor and glanced around quickly, smiling. There were at least a dozen of the primary players here, with a monochromatic blend of graying hair, dressed in matching lavender leotards and breathing softly through their noses.

The instructor caught my eye and raised her brows, sending the red dot on her forehead due north. I dropped my head back onto the mat with a soft thunk. Yoga Nazi. A definitely tense woman.

"And as I was saying, in this posture not only should the body be motionless and at ease, but the mind as well should be quiet, like the surface of a still lake." The Yoga Nazi paused and took a sip of water. "It is called the Shava Asana, the Corpse Posture. You will hold it for ten minutes."

"Ten minutes?" I whispered after the instructor had padded barefoot toward the other end of the gym and begun a series of impossible contortions. She was posed with legs whipped over her back like an incensed scorpion. Yoga Nazi showboat.

"Yes," Serena whispered. "Ten minutes and sometimes longer, thank God. It's the best part. The rest of the time you actually have to move."

"Well, I applaud your, uh," I glanced at the lavender sausage casing masquerading as her leotard, "commitment to the mind-body connection." I smiled. "And I can only imagine how important this relaxation must be after that terrible trauma you suffered. You must feel so alone."

"Thank you," Serena whispered. "Health is important to me. But no, I hardly feel alone." She giggled. "We've got practically a sorority here. Of victims."

I squeezed my eyes shut and grinned. I was so good. "Really? I had no idea. Do you mean there have been several robberies?"

"Oh, dear girl. You can't imagine." Serena raised her head and glanced across the lavender corpses. "The security staff is keeping it all hush-hush of course, but in this room alone there are six of us."

I poked a fingertip against Serena's plump shoulder. "Get out . . . really?"

"Truly. Of course mine was the most traumatic, mind you. Because of the gun." Her body wriggled. "But yes, there's Loretta, Penny, Sarah, Gladys, and let's see . . . oh yes, Mimi. But Mimi was only missing some earrings from her pocket and she's so darned forgetful that I'm not sure I really believe her. Probably wants to feel like part of the group, you know?"

"And of course there was that poor Mrs. Kravitz. The heart attack victim?" I breathed slowly through my nose, reminding myself not to push too hard. Yeah, still surface of a lake.

"Oh, yes," Serena whispered. "But that's different. That's burglary, isn't it? At least that's what the security officers said."

"Burglary?"

"Because they took the stuff from her cabin. No personal confrontation."

"So, the others . . ." I tried to make my voice sound confused, "were actually confronted by a robber? That's so frightening, Serena." I patted the woman's moist forearm. "The robber just popped up in various places around the ship?" I held my breath.

"No. Ooh, shussh." Serena whispered out of the corner of her mouth. "Gurani's coming back."

"I have been informed," the Yoga Nazi whined, "that due to a scheduling mishap, we must move to the far end of the room and accommodate a strength-training group. Please pick up your mats quietly and we will resume in the new area."

I padded across the room and set my mat down next to the Prom Princess and then attempted to follow the directions for the next posture, the Hand-Foot-Big-Toe. I groaned as I reached for my toe, and heard the Prom Princess give a condescending snort before moving fluidly into the posture. I narrowed my eyes. Snoot. I'd like to see her try to run a 12K dressed like Mexican food.

The Prom Princess smiled with her lips firmly against her thigh, manicured fingers holding manicured toes. "It's a great relief," she murmured, "to see that your little roommate will finally be made accountable for her actions."

What in the—*the nerve of that bitch!* I exhaled through my nose and tried to stop the vision of holding the woman's head under the surface of a still lake. I stretched forward until my back screamed, grabbed my big toe, and forced a smile instead.

"Yes, it was such a shock," I said. "You think you know someone and . . ." I shook my head, breathing a silent apology to Marie. "I'd already asked for a cabin change; that woman was just too messy." I raised my brows. "So I guess the sickbay had turned into a continuous crime scene?"

"Actually, my robbery was apparently the only one that happened there. Or so I'm told." The Prom Princess took a firmer grip on her French manicured toe and smirked. "Miss Whitley was certainly versatile if not too bright."

I bit my lip and fought the irrational impulse to spit through my teeth. *Hold me back, Grandma.* My hands clenched into fists that had nothing to do with the Hand-Foot-Big-Toe Asana as I fought to control my voice. "Versatile?"

"I hear that she made most of her conquests in the Mermaid Spa."

"But didn't Serena say that she heard a *man's* voice? That she was, um, fondled?"

The Prom Princess snorted softly. "Women like Serena Bliss can only dream. And a man would have a pretty slim chance of sneaking into the spa. But, you've heard Miss Whitley's voice and seen the way she carries herself." She laughed. "Nothing feminine about that. Not to mention her particular . . . *persuasion.* Surely you knew?"

Shit. Enough was enough!

My elbow contacted Loretta Carruth's elegant ribs with a dull—and highly satisfying—thwack. "Oh, sorry. I'm so clumsy with this yoga stuff. Really, sorry."

A murmur rose from the women around us and I glanced up to see that a group of strength training participants had filed into the other end of the gym and had begun work with free weights. It was easy to see what caused the commotion among the Yoga Ladies. I felt the heat rise in my face. *Jeez.* Luke had removed his karate tunic and was raising a barbell, bare-chested. I had a sudden and all-consuming thirst for champagne. I exhaled through my nose. *Surface of a still lake.*

Gurani led us into the next pose—unbelievable, the Cow Face—and I sneaked another glimpse of Luke. He was standing next to that night nurse, Howie Carson, with his hands on his hips and grinning across the room at me. I raised my hand in a brief wave and then laughed as I caught sight of the Munchkin-size woman in a leopard-print leotard moving to stand closer to him—Edie Greenbaum hefting pink glitter dumbbells.

"Looks like Edie prefers strength training to yoga these days," a woman on the other side of me chuckled. She flicked a long salt and pepper gray braid from her shoulder and grinned. "Can't really blame her though, can we? I've heard rumors saying that man's body alone is responsible for the multitude of mini-strokes on board this ship. Hope Bernie's got her insured."

I laughed and tried to assume the Cow Face posture while talking out the side of my mouth. Not easy, believe me. "He's a hottie all right, but what do you mean about the mini-strokes? There have been a lot of them?"

"Hell, it's practically a plague," the woman whispered. "Maybe five of us in this room and a few more I've met at dinner seatings."

"Us? Meaning you, too?" My eyes widened. "Oh, I'm sorry to pry. I'm Darcy Cavanaugh, by the way." I moved my hand from its posed clasp behind my back and extended it. The woman reached her own forward, her green eyes warm against sun-tanned and freckled skin.

I felt a twinge of homesickness—put a "What Happens in Vegas Stays in Vegas" tee shirt on this friendly woman and she could be my mom.

"Sarah McNaughton," she said, introducing herself. "And no problem. I'm a retired practical nurse so medical questions don't embarrass me in the least. Ask away. And yes, I guess I did have a mini-stroke. Damnedest presentation though."

"How so?"

"Not the usual . . ." Sarah broke off, nodding her chin upward.

"Yes, please go on?" I prodded, not getting the message until I felt a fingernail poke against the top of my head. I looked up to see the Yoga Nazi glaring over me.

"Perhaps you are having some difficulty maintaining the vision of serenity?" Gurani hissed through a clenched teeth smile.

"Well, no, I . . ." I grimaced as the woman padded away.

I tried to follow suit as the group assembled on their backs and hiked a knee to their chests.

"What's this one called?" I asked turning my head toward Sarah. Before Sarah could answer, a sound like engine backfire erupted from the vicinity of the Prom Princess's mat. My mouth dropped open.

"Wind-Releasing Posture," Sarah choked, biting her lip with mirth. "And it couldn't have happened to a more deserving person."

Gurani instructed us in the Grasshopper and the Camel, and then told us to resume the Corpse Posture for the remainder of the class time. I stretched out on my back and tried not to think of the last corpse I'd seen. Virgilio. Of course, his would have been the Hanging Man Pose. Yes, he'd definitely been a victim somehow, and it sure as hell looked like the Nepalese weren't doing anything about it. Especially since they were so busy fabricating a case against Marie.

At least I was finally getting some information, and I wasn't about to quit now.

"I'd really like to know more about those mini-strokes," I whispered to Sarah. "Because my grandmother has had some peculiar symptoms and I'm kind of worried." I stopped talking as the Yoga Nazi padded between our mats.

"Be glad to help," Sarah whispered. "This group usually meets for a cocktail right after class. In the Lobster Disco. Want to join us?" She glanced across the room and frowned. "Damn, young Mr. Skywalker has disappeared into the galaxy. So much for the Menopausal Women in Lust Asana." She winked at me. "Do come have a drink, Darcy. Please."

I searched the pile of belongings on the table again and shook my head. Hadn't I dropped my gym bag there with the others when I came in? I'd been in such a hurry after seeing the look on that Yoga Nazi's face. But I thought I'd put it there. Where else?

"What's the matter, Cookie?" Serena asked, wrapping a peppermint-stripe pareo around her hips. "Lose something?"

"My bag. This is so weird. I thought I'd set it here."

"Oh my God, maybe you've been burgled!"

"No," I shook my head. "My purse is in it, but it's got nothing but a lipstick and my keycard. What could I have done with it?"

"Wait. Is it green with little glittery shamrocks?" Serena pointed. "I saw one over there next to the doorway."

I grabbed the bag and headed for the ladies room, still muttering to myself about my carelessness. And thinking about Luke. The Yoga Ladies met in the Lobster Disco, and that was dance host territory. But I was on a mission and there was absolutely no reason to worry that I couldn't carry on a conversation with a group of women without being distracted by Luke. I pulled a knit skirt and my jean jacket over my workout clothes, applied some lipgloss, and headed for the disco.

* * *

I arrived to find the table conversation very focused.

"So, good heavens, did you see that chest?"

I reached for a chair, watching a trickle of martini dribble from the corner of the woman's mouth. Her eyes gleamed with so much mischief that I wondered if she were doubling up on estrogen.

"Stop drooling, Ruthie." Edie Greenbaum laughed. "Of course I saw it; I was close enough to touch it, sweetheart. And believe me, I—" She blushed and cleared her throat as she glanced down the table and recognized me.

"Ah, there you are, Darcy." Sarah smiled at me and signaled for the waitress. "Sit down, please. You know everyone?"

I nodded at the familiar faces and ordered a glass of merlot as the waitress reached my elbow.

"This young lady had some questions for us," Sarah explained. "For those of us who had that interesting mini-stroke experience. Is that right, Darcy?"

"I . . . uh . . ." I stammered and watched Edie Greenbaum's brows rise toward her pink hairline. "I don't want to intrude on anyone's privacy, of course. It's only that I have a grandma with high blood pressure. And she's had some unusual symptoms, and . . ." My wine arrived and I took a huge sip and choked. "Sorry." I dabbed at my mouth with a lobster-logo napkin and reminded myself not to push this too fast.

"She's worried about her grandma," Sarah said, "and I personally find that very refreshing." She clucked her tongue. "I doubt that my grandkids worry about anything more than if their birthday checks arrive late." She patted my arm. "So what did you want to know, hon?"

"Symptoms? What I should watch for?"

Edie Greenbaum played with the lemon wedge in her soda water. "Couldn't you get better information from her doctor, or maybe the Internet?" She smiled indulgently. "You young people are all such computer whizzes."

"Oh, heavens, Edie," Serena slurred, plucking a cherry stem from between her lips, "just because you and I don't have anything to report doesn't mean the others don't want to help."

"Weak all over," the Prom Princess said, voice flat and playing with a stone on her diamond tennis bracelet. "Just suddenly and progressively weaker."

"So bad you couldn't lift your arms or even swallow very well," another woman chimed in.

"But no pain," a tiny lady with snow-white hair added, then giggled. "Of course, after so many mimosas who could feel anything?"

"Mimosas?" I asked.

"Champagne and orange juice, sweetie. Delicious."

"I think Darcy knows what a mimosa is," Sarah sighed and turned to me. "What Gladys meant was that she was in the Mermaid Spa when she had her mini-stroke. We all were."

Goosebumps rose on my arms. I was getting somewhere now. "Didn't you tell me that these symptoms were somehow not ordinary for a mini-stroke?"

"T.I.A." Sarah nodded. "That's short for transient ischemic attack. And yes, usually there's just one side of the body affected with weakness or maybe a problem with speech or vision. Our symptoms weren't that typical. But they cleared up very quickly afterward, fortunately."

"Not fast enough to fight off a robber," Serena said.

"It was a helpless feeling all right," Sarah agreed, "lying there in an herbal wrap and cucumber mask, while someone silently and methodically stripped the rings from my fingers and even unscrewed my diamond earrings. Believe me, I'd have fought like a beast if I could."

"You were lying there like that when you were robbed?" I saw the rest of the women nod.

"That's right," the Prom Princess agreed, "the mask and wrap are part of the Royal Spa Package." She narrowed her eyes at me. "But I was robbed in the sickbay, of course. Afterward. "

Edie stood and took one last sip of her drink. "Well, all I can say is that I'm grateful to have escaped all that nasty business. And now," she glanced at her watch, "I've got to run and meet Bernie if we're going to have time to dress for dinner. How about the rest of you?"

The other women checked their watches and there were murmurs of agreement as they drained their glasses and gathered up their belongings. In minutes I was alone at the table. I took a sip of my wine and shook my head. They'd all been in the spa.

I flinched when Luke put his hand on the back of my neck.

"Aren't you a little young for that group?" He smiled.

"Aren't you?"

The D.J. began the dance music in the distance.

"Touché. But how about a quick dance before I'm tackled by the first wave of Golden Girls?"

"I'm sorry," I said, rising from my chair and picking up my gym bag. "I've got some things I need to do."

I brushed off his protests and headed toward the elevator. I needed to get back to the privacy of the cabin and compile the information I'd learned. See if I could get a clearer picture. I'd order room service and pull an all-nighter like I was studying for finals. I tried to remember if macaroni and cheese was on the room service menu, and then groaned as I thought of Marie. What was she eating, bread and water?

I inserted the keycard and flipped on the cabin light. The shadow cast from overhead flickered across my peripheral vision and I jumped. What the hell? I immediately thought of Virgilio and knew that was impossible. It was a lingerie sculpture, a large one. Suspended from the ceiling by a coat hanger.

I stepped closer. It was made of several articles of my lingerie this time. Victoria's Secret bra joined cup-to-cup to form a head, a half-slip for a body, and panty hose for arms and legs. And what was that wrapped around at the top? The belt to my robe? Yes, coiled and knotted to form a—*Oh my God.* My stomach lurched. It was a sculpture of a hanging man.

SEVENTEEN

"So, you're saying that you didn't hang this thing from my ceiling?" I stood with my hands on my hips and watched the young steward's anxious face.

"No, miss." Alfonso reached up and nudged the sculpture with a fingertip. It swung toward him and his eyes grew wide. He jerked his hand away, blinking rapidly, and then touched his fingers to his forehead and chest in the sign of the cross. "I swear." He looked back at me and shook his head. "I did the others, the monkey and the swan . . . those were nice? But I only did them because Virgilio said that I must."

My brows furrowed. "You did them, not Virgilio?"

"Yes, miss. I do everything for your cabin."

I nodded. "You mean since Virgilio died."

"No. For many weeks now. Even for the passengers before you. Virgilio paid me. You won't tell? I'm strong and can do the extra work, no problem." He nodded his head quickly. "And now I am assigned to this cabin. Officially."

"But he introduced himself as our steward." I shook my head. "And he paid you? How could he afford to do that?" Marie had said that the cabin staff worked for minimal wages and that what tips they received came in a lump sum—at the end of the cruise.

Alfonso shrugged. "It wasn't only me. He paid three of us to do his cabin duties. Because he had business, miss. And he needed the time for that." He sighed. "He was going to buy a car, an American sports car, and let me drive it sometime."

I watched as Alfonso stepped up on a chair and snatched the sculpture by its head. He blushed furiously as his thumb dented the satin bra and then handed it to me quickly.

I clasped the sculpture behind my back and glanced around the cabin. There was a towel draped across a chair and the bed wasn't turned down; the room hadn't been made up for the night. I turned back to Alfonso. "But how could someone have gotten in here?"

"Only with your card, miss. I have the other. But I promise you again, I had nothing to do with this." He edged toward the door. "And now I must go turn down the beds for the passengers at dinner."

My mind raced. *Who . . . how?* I glanced over at my card on the bedside table. But I had my card. "Of course, Alfonso, thank you."

"I will turn your bed down later, miss. Two chocolates tonight?" He smiled tentatively.

I returned the smile. "No sculptures, though." I watched the door begin to close and looked down at the underwear effigy in my hands. The silky belt-noose dangled from my palm as I watched the door close. Virgilio had money and plans to buy a car? I stepped forward and called out. "Alfonso?"

His face appeared at the slit of the partially closed door.

"About Virgilio . . ." I tipped my head to watch his face, "he hanged himself because of his wife, right?"

Confusion flickered in the steward's eyes and then he paled. "No, miss. Virgilio wasn't married."

I sat down on the bed and picked up my keycard, blue plastic emblazoned with a digital photo of the ship. Universal card really. Cabin door key and identity card. Charge card for the bars, the ship's boutiques, the spa—for everything.

I smiled thinking of little Tweedle-Dee having hers denied in the casino. Edie had the mistake cleared up—with her usual bull-dog tact, no doubt—and I'd seen her back at her favorite machines a couple of times since. I poked my card against the lingerie sculpture on my lap. How else could anyone have gotten into my cabin? I'd had the card with me; used it to get in here after the gym. My fingers tightened on the card and my stomach lurched. Oh, no. My gym bag.

I inhaled sharply. The bag had been moved during the yoga class.

My mind raced and then I sighed, pushing the what-if's aside—like what if I'd had money in my purse, my credit cards, or important papers? I'd been lucky that I'd carried only a comb, my lipstick, the keycard, of course, and . . . *Oh God*. I grabbed the gym bag off the table and yanked my purse from it.

My hands shook as I opened the little suede hobo. *Please, Lord.* The napkins from the Java Café, my neat hand-written columns assigning names to victims, crime scenes, and patients . . . my fingers reached the bottom of the bag. Empty.

I looked back at the sculpture with the noose still coiled around its neck. This was no random prank. It was a warning.

I picked up the phone and set it down again. What was I going to do, call the security staff? I thought of Gombu's face the day he'd interrogated us. No way. And Luke? I knew how he affected me and the worst thing I could do right now was to lose my concentration. Not to mention, of course, the unexplained fact that he was packing a gun. I tried to banish the vision of Luke pressing the barrel of a gun against the fat rolls on Serena Bliss' neck.

I groaned aloud and wadded the lingerie sculpture into a ball, hurling it across the room at the lava lamp. Marie. Dammit, where was she when I needed her? In custody, because of me. Tears sprang to my eyes and I wiped them away angrily. No time for crybaby stuff. I'd started something and I was going to finish it. I could work without a list, no problem. Safer that way.

My stomach growled and I glanced at the bedside clock and then slowly smiled as the idea dawned. I could still make it to the dinner seating. What better opportunity to get a little more information?

I showered, slipped into my black cutout halter dress, and then stepped out into the hallway, pulling the door securely closed behind me. I stared down at the keycard in my palm for a moment before reaching toward the door handle once more. It took only a few moments to yank all my lingerie from the dresser drawer and shove it under my bed.

* * *

The Neptune's Bounty Dining Room was teeming with passengers and the white-coated waiters glided across lavender carpeting holding trays of silver dishes aloft. I smiled as the headwaiter nodded and waved me inside. This cruise was "Free-Style," without committed seating arrangements or even strict dining times, so it would be much easier to simply slip into a chair at any table I liked. And continue my investigation.

I paused beside a twelve-foot statue of a bearded and scantily clad King Neptune, complete with admiring fishes and a huge three-pronged spear. The king smiled broadly as vigorous jets of blue-tinted water spritzed his privates. I bit my lower lip and stifled a laugh. The moment begged for a crude remark. Jeez, I missed Marie.

The tables were set with ice-blue linens and centerpieces of pink and cream freesias tucked into golden conch shells. In the distance, a waiter inspired applause with a flaming entrée and a young harpist's slender arms stretched across gilded strings.

I scanned the tables and spotted a woman waving a napkin furiously. Perfect, Serena Bliss. Seated with the Greenbaums, Mrs. Evanston from the cabin next door, the Queen Bee, and several others. I waved back and headed toward the table with a satisfied grin. Too darned easy.

I'd just passed the table of the tight-lipped Yoga Nazi when a hand caught my elbow and made me stop.

"I thought you weren't coming to dinner." Luke stood up from the table he was sharing with the Prom Princess and looked down at me, his brows scrunched.

I sighed. "Got hungry?"

He shook his head and pressed his lips together. "I don't get it. Are you avoiding me for some reason, Darcy?"

I didn't have time for this, and I couldn't risk getting swept up in that inevitable confusion that rocked me every time I was with this man. The only important thing now was clearing Marie.

"It's just," I said, lowering my voice and looking into his eyes, "that I'm involved in something right now. Something I can't talk about yet." *Sound familiar?* "And," I added, "you'll have to trust me, okay?"

Bernie Greenbaum rose as I approached the table and smiled almost boyishly, gold tooth glinting. "We are honored, dear girl."

I re-introduced myself to Anna Evanston and her husband and observed the expressions on their faces, as well as several others, that clearly identified me as *Roommate of the FBI's Most Wanted.* Serena Bliss, at my left, pointed to the menu and sighed.

"The scallops with sherry sauce are to die for, and so are the Lamb Chops Français." She shivered. "I couldn't decide so I ordered both."

The wine steward and waiter arrived at my elbow within moments and I ordered a glass of chardonnay, producing my keycard and forcing myself not to stare down every damned suspect at the table. I ordered the fillet of halibut in lemon caper sauce and moved forward with my plan.

"I'm going to go to the Mermaid Spa after dinner," I said, reaching for my seashell embroidered linen napkin. "But I'm not sure what package I should order. Anyone have suggestions?"

Luke walked past our table on his way out and I somehow managed to stay focused on my tablemates. I could feel his eyes.

"Get the whole darned thing." Serena laughed, raising her glass to her lips. It was full of ice and pink liquid with cherries and a little plastic seahorse. "Massage and pedicure and herbal wrap and cucumber mask. The Royal Package." She grimaced and licked a drop of liquid from the seahorse's nose. "Only I won't do the vitamin shots, and of course I don't drink alcohol, so the mimosas are out, too." She giggled and pointed to her drink. "This is a virgin Pink Lady."

"You missed all the best parts," the Yoga Panther argued. "The mimosas give you enough of a buzz that you don't give a flying fig what color they paint your toes. And the vitamin shot? Hell, I figured since it was free, I'd take the whole shebang."

"Free?" I asked, leaning back so the waiter could set my wineglass down. "What do you mean?" I tried hard to keep the excitement out of my voice.

"I won a free spa coupon," she explained. "The Royal Package."

"You did?" The Queen Bee asked, raising her brows. "Me too, except I haven't used mine yet."

"Well that's a strange coincidence," Edie Greenbaum interjected, glancing up from her entrée and then using her napkin to dab at Bernie's chin.

"I won, too!" Serena Bliss and Anna Evanston spoke at the exact same moment and then collapsed into laughter.

"Well, my goodness," I purred, with perfect incredulous pitch. "This is amazing. If only I could be so lucky." My heart was pounding and I wanted to dance on the table.

Edie Greenbaum frowned, obviously indignant. "No one offered anything free to me. Had to pay my way as usual." She poked her finger into her husband's shoulder. "You'll check on this for me, Bernie. First thing in the morning."

"So," I said, pressing onward. "Should I go for the vitamins or not? I'm a little nervous about shots; how did they do that?"

Bernie's face blanched and he pushed his plate away. "Shots? You mean needles? Oh please, I'm not sure I want to hear about—"

"Sorry. Never mind." Jeez, if Bernie got sick it would derail this whole conversation. I tossed him a reassuring smile and then waited as a steward set my entrée down in front of me. "I guess I'll play it by ear when I go in," I said. "No problem. But I'm so curious—how did you folks win the coupon?"

"A drawing, I guess," Serena shrugged. "I didn't really ask. A steward delivered it to my cabin door and I gobbled it up."

"Me too," Mrs. Evanston agreed. "But I got the news first in the gym." She laughed. "You wouldn't ordinarily catch me there, but my bowels were so sluggish." She blushed and looked down at her plate. "Anyway, I was informed right over my earphones on the treadmill. It was thrilling."

I could hardly believe my ears. Not only Mrs. Thurston, but a second treadmill "winner" as well. I suspended my forkful of halibut in midair. "Really, the lucky treadmill. Maybe I should look for it. Do you remember which one—"

"Oh look!" Edie pointed excitedly toward the spiral staircase in the center of the dining room. "Baked Alaska. And the waiters are going to sing!"

The room darkened and the white-coated waiters resplendent in red-white-and-blue sashes paraded down the dining room aisles holding their sparkler-topped trays aloft and singing "America the Beautiful." Ooh's and ahh's erupted from the tables and people began to stand, holding their hands over their hearts. Bernie the Scout Master sang loudly and completely off-key, his chocolate eyes misting.

"Excuse me," I whispered to Serena, "I need to slip out to the ladies' room for a moment." The dining room guests were still cheering over the Baked Alaska as I hurried down the corridor and on toward the glass elevators.

*   *   *

172

Twenty minutes later, I padded barefoot to the polished cherry-wood reception desk of The Mermaid Spa and a smiling hostess offered me a mimosa. I watched as the young Malaysian woman topped the juice-filled crystal glass with French champagne and then raised her eyebrows.

"Have you decided which package you prefer, Miss Cavanaugh?" she asked, offering the glass.

I touched my lips to the rim, enjoying the tickle of the bubbles and the taste and aroma of the dry French champagne paired with sweet fresh-squeezed orange juice. I tucked my chin down into the white terry robe embroidered with the ship's logo and smiled. "I had some friends recommend the Royal Package. Lucky ladies, they won the package in your free promotion."

The hostess tilted her head slightly. "Free promotion?"

My heart quickened. "Yes. Those coupons delivered to the winners' rooms. And sometimes you notify the women over the earphones at the gym." I smiled and shook my head. "Clever marketing."

"I . . ." The young woman flipped through some papers on her desk. "I'm afraid you've misunderstood somehow."

"Misunderstood?" I held my breath.

The hostess swallowed and then attempted to re-phrase as if remembering that The Customer Is Always Right. "Oh, I'm sorry, Miss Cavanaugh. You must mean the gift certificates." She picked up a gold bound book. "Yes. Quite a lovely idea. And to surprise the lady is especially nice."

I set the mimosa down on the cherry wood and watched a moisture-ring bead up around its base. "You have no free promotion?" My skin prickled under the elegant terry robe.

"No, miss," the girl whispered.

I waited for the masseuse to prepare my cucumber mask and watched as other patrons dried their nails, sipping mimosas and giggling. The herbal wrap was one-size-fits-all, a thin terry moistened in warm spring water infused with twenty-seven different herbs. I lifted my swathed arm and waved in response to the Phantom Dancer as she nodded and headed for the exit. Whoa, I felt like a lump of dough after the mimosa and the massage. Still, it was pretty wonderful.

Strains of Debussy's *Claire de Lune* filtered through speakers overhead and I let my body melt into the warmed massage table. What was in this herbal thing again? Sea clay, bee pollen, bladder wrack . . . *bladder wrack*? I stifled a laugh and let myself pretend for a moment that it could be this simple—this promised detoxifying, revitalizing—and that there could also be some sort of cellular level fix for career uncertainty, relationship trauma, and family tragedy. I opened my eyes when the masseuse returned with the chilled mask.

"Do I get the vitamin shot with this package?" I watched the young woman's face.

"Shot?" Her beautifully sculpted brows wrinkled. "You mean the herb infusion? It's in the wrap, miss."

"No." I felt my stomach quiver. "The injection with a needle. Vitamins."

The masseuse shook her head and her silky black mane tumbled across her shoulders. "Maybe you mean the acupuncture? We did have that. But not for several months now." She smiled. "The woman who did that is on maternity leave. A baby boy—eight pounds six ounces."

My mouth was so dry that my words stuck to my tongue. "No shots?" *Oh God.* Who gave what to those women?

"No, miss." She fitted thin slices of cucumber over my eyes and topped them with an elastic strapped ice-mask. "No one here is qualified to do that. Perhaps if you ask at the sickbay."

The voices of the patrons grew fewer and were sprinkled with yawns as I tried to free my mind and relax in the herbal wrap, listening to classical music and the tick-tick of the little timer that was set for an hour. An hour to "revitalize and stimulate." I felt my skin flame and knew it wasn't the herbs. Revitalize and stimulate? Luke Skyler could do that in three minutes flat. And he couldn't be a criminal. Could he?

"Anyone there?" I raised my head from the table and listened. I couldn't hear voices anymore. Only a faint murmur from the hostess out in the far hallway. Wow, it was kind of like sensory deprivation. Or maybe more like sensory overload: warm tabletop, wet clingy terry wrap, frosty mask over the eyelids, champagne buzz, and the darkness whispering Vivaldi . . . wait a minute. What was that?

A breath by my ear and fingers on my shoulder. The masseuse? No. Grasping. Too hard. Squeezing into my skin, pinching, *bruising. Oh my God!* I tried to sit up but the hands gripped tighter, pinning me down. There was a scrape against my face—beard stubble? And then lips moved against my ear.

"Stop asking questions," a muffled voice whispered, "Or you'll be a very sorry girl."

EIGHTEEN

I squeezed my thumb to make the tiny wound start bleeding and when that didn't work, I popped it into my mouth and sucked on it. *Bleed for godsake.* Damned safety razors—you could count on them to make your legs bikini smooth, but what if you needed a bloody good excuse to get into the sickbay? When it finally welled up red enough and drippy enough to leave a ketchup-y blob on the sickbay door, I headed in.

Howie Carson wasn't there.

What the . . . "Where's Howie?" I asked after glancing around the all-too-familiar room. A pink and blue striped privacy curtain was pulled across a far stretcher. I stared in confusion at a gray-haired nurse. Her ID badge read "Miss Fallon." Hadn't Marie said Howie's shift went until eight AM? It was barely seven.

"Mr. Carson," the nurse explained, "is taking a couple of days off. Did you need some treatment?"

Off? Damn. I'd planned on grilling Howie, but maybe that wasn't necessary. What I needed was information. A source was simply a source and the means to an end. I would change tactics like any good spy.

"How do I go about getting this taken care of?" I asked, holding up the now dripping digit and trying my best to look squeamish.

After the bleeding was staunched, Miss Fallon applied liquid adhesive to my skin and a single narrow steri-strip to close the wound. Not a bad job, actually, for a woman wearing lenses as thick as the glass on Marie's lava lamp. She phoned the ship's doctor and obtained an order for the tetanus shot that I had requested in hope of prolonging my visit.

"Thank you," I said, not having to fake a wince as the achy vaccine cramped my shoulder muscle. "You've got everything here, don't you? Equipment and medications, almost like a real hospital."

Miss Fallon started to frown, caught herself halfway, and smiled instead. Her eyes blinked behind her lenses. "We like to think of ourselves as real, my dear. Real nurses, real doctor, and really here when you get a pesky little cut." She allowed herself a quick smirk. "As real as you're going to encounter short of a helicopter ride, that is."

"My sister is a nurse," I lied. "Emergency department. In a big hospital in L.A. Scary neighborhood, I guess. She said they've even had trouble with patients carrying weapons. And sometimes stealing drugs." I glanced toward the medicine cupboards, syringe boxes, and red metal crash cart. "At least you don't have to worry about things like that here." I wrinkled my nose. "Not much excitement at all, I would imagine. Just laxatives and seasick patches, and," I rubbed my shoulder, "a tetanus shot once in a while." *Go on, take the bait, woman. Rise up and defend the nursing sisterhood.* I arched my brows, waiting.

"Well," Miss Fallon lowered her voice. "Unless you think that one of our nurses being asked to cooperate with Federal agents isn't exciting?"

Bait snatched. I could reel her in now. "Oh Lord, that's what all the fuss was about." My voice dropped to a whisper. "Drugs?"

Miss Fallon glanced toward the other patient cubicle and lowered her voice. "Of course I couldn't say. But security has gone through everything in here. Drugs, too."

"Oooh. Something missing?" I murmured, leaning closer to the woman like we were two girlfriends sipping martinis and sharing dating disasters.

The nurse tore open a Band-Aid and sighed with obvious disappointment. "Not since maybe a couple of months ago. A question on the narcotic count, only a single vial. Probably a clerical error. And most of the other medications aren't even counted anyway, simply re-ordered when they outdate or run low. Howie does all that."

She stretched tall and smoothed her uniform, all business suddenly. "Medical protocols. You couldn't be expected to understand, of course." She handed me a packet of antibiotic ointment and a few extra Band-Aids. "That should do it for you. Now I have to go finish up with a medication." Miss Fallon nodded toward the drawn curtain in the distance. "It needs to be given before breakfast."

I took my food tray out onto the Lido Deck, sat on a chaise lounge, and watched the morning sun try to break through the clouds. It was having about as much luck as I was at figuring out this whole mess. Stolen jewels, mini-strokes, Virgilio hanging himself, fake spa coupons, and vitamin shots that didn't exist. Not to mention personal threats. What did it all mean?

I hadn't slept more than an hour last night. And for those sixty minutes I sat fully dressed in a chair wedged against the cabin door holding the heavy fluid-filled glass globe of the lava lamp. I shook my head and swallowed a swig of the decaf coffee and then held the ceramic mug close, letting the vapor steam my face. Marie would be proud of my choice of weapon. *"Get out—you were gonna nail 'em with my lamp?"*

But nail . . . *who*? That was the question, wasn't it? Just whom was I barricading from my room and fully prepared to knock senseless if push came to shove? Who got into my gym bag and took the napkin list, let himself into my cabin, and then followed me to the spa?

I shivered at the memory of the voice against my ear and the helpless sensation of darkness and claustrophobia beneath the mask and herbal wrap. *"Stop asking questions."* Who had overheard me asking the questions? Or worse, who didn't like being questioned? In all likelihood, the voice had been muffled on purpose. Because I'd recognize it?

"Penny for your thoughts?" Luke's lips moved against my ear and I lurched forward, sloshing my coffee onto the tray and table. The blood drained from my face and plummeted toward my stomach.

I whirled around and my hands balled into fists. If I'd had the lava lamp, I swear I would've whacked him.

"I scared you. I'm an idiot. Sorry." Luke watched my face and sank down into a lounge chair beside me, running his hand through his short hair. He smiled sheepishly and handed me the mug. "Drink the coffee; you look like you've seen a ghost."

It took a moment before I could pry my tongue off the roof of my mouth and speak and, when it came, my voice was a barely concealed hiss. Blood swept back into my head like high tide, thrumming in my ears. "Stop it. Stop following me! I mean it."

I leaned toward him and jutted out my chin. He was wearing the same leather jacket as that day at Montmorency Falls, and I tried not to think of what might be concealed beneath it. I wrestled with an image of him leaning down to whisper into my ear at the spa. I needed time to figure this thing out. And space. And Luke Skyler could not safely occupy one inch of that space.

"Are you hearing me?" I whispered. "Please *leave me alone.*"

I lowered my face onto my hands and waited until I heard him walk away. I'd been kidding myself about that man. It was time to face it. And also face the fact that there was really no one I could trust. Whatever happened, I was in this alone. At least until I could put the pieces together and feel safe again. I squeezed my eyes shut and sighed. At least until Marie came back. *If she ever does.*

*   *   *

The ship's PA system awakened me and I lifted the fringed wool plaid blanket from my face, trying to remember where I was.

"This is your captain." The speakers overhead crackled. "We will be conducting several more tests due to difficulties we have encountered with the public address system. We appreciate your patience." There was a pause and then a polite British chuckle. "Never fear, however, bingo times shall remain completely unaffected."

I stared down at my watch. Good Lord. Four thirty? In the afternoon? I'd slept all day? I attempted to rise from the chaise lounge and my back confirmed it. Ouch. I'd been lying there since breakfast but at least I'd gotten some sleep. Safely, even if—I shrugged as two Yoga Ladies smiled down at my makeshift bed—rather publicly. And I'd gotten some good thinking in before I fell asleep, formulated a suspect list. I knew everyone I questioned and I knew who heard me do it.

Back at my cabin, I inserted the keycard into the door and then opened it slowly, holding my breath. *What a sissy.* I glanced at the ceiling; no lingerie sculptures. My breath escaped with relief and then sucked back in sharply as the phone rang. I hurried to pick it up. The voice was ship-shape polite.

"This is First Mate Albright. I apologize for the intrusion but it appears that the PA system is still malfunctioning. I need to inform you that your cabin section is required to take part in a drill." The clipped British voice paused. "A special security drill. Please report to your assigned muster station in ten minutes, at five fifteen. This is mandatory and roll will be taken. Thank you for your cooperation."

Security drill? I stared at the phone receiver. What did that mean? We'd had a lifeboat drill, of course; the entire manifest of passengers dressed in salmon-egg orange life vests and lined up on the Promenade Deck half swacked on complementary rum and making sick Titanic jokes. *I'm not lining up until the band starts to play.* But a special security drill, and only for this cabin section? I forgot—did the First Mate say to bring a life vest?

I glanced at the travel clock. Nearly five. Almost time for the dinners to begin. Could the timing be worse? I grabbed my life jacket, puffy orange and complete with whistle and water-activated signal light, and headed for the door. I'd simply have to hurry back afterward and get dressed for dinner. Not that the food was my priority.

No. What I was going to do was to finally look my little lineup of suspects straight in the eye.

I took a shortcut through another cabin section and nodded as a man dressed for dinner and mouthing a fat cigar stared at me, his bushy brows raised.

"Life vest? Something you want to tell the rest of us, little darlin'?"

"Just a drill," I called back over my shoulder. "And only D-section, Aft. No big deal."

I felt like a fish swimming upstream as I waded in a zip-front sweater and jeans past a hundred people in sport coats and cocktail dresses headed in the opposite direction, all making a beeline for the dining rooms. My little cabin section was going to be pissed. Those seniors could really eat. Anna Evanston, for one, looked like a woman who made it a point to never be late for dinner. If the First Mate hadn't said they were taking roll, I wouldn't even be going myself. I could only hope that this untimely security drill was brief and to the point.

I got tired of explaining about the life vest, and reached for the door to a stairwell marked "Crew Only" to climb the last flights of steps to my lifeboat station. If someone questioned me, I'd say I was lost. Plausible. Most people on a cruise ship were anyway, heading fore instead of aft or on the completely wrong deck at any given moment. I pulled open the door and found myself face to face with Luke.

"Where . . . ?" Luke stared down at the life vest. "Why do you have *that*?"

I lowered my head and tried to squeeze by him but he caught the strap of the vest and stopped me short.

"What's going on Darcy?" His voice had that edgy quality again, authoritative, commanding. Junior high school vice principal checking the restroom for smokers.

"Drill," I said, not looking up. "And you're in the wrong stairwell, buddy."

"Life boat drill?" He asked, ignoring my jab.

"No. Special security drill." I looked back up and glared, then pulled the strap from his grasp. "My section. Not yours. And I'm going. *Now.*"

I found my lifeboat station without a problem, it would have been impossible not to; the corridors were dotted with diagrams like caveman hieroglyphics, doors stenciled with letters and the floors lined with tiny bulbs that lit up in the event of power failure. Muster Station D. *Right here.*

I opened the door to the Promenade Deck slowly, careful not to knock over dozens of other orange-vested passengers. Instead, the door opened onto darkness and fog and a stretch of empty deck. What? I looked fore and aft and glanced at my watch. Five twenty. Where was everybody?

I stepped out to the rail and looked down the deck once more and then up toward the Sports Deck above. I couldn't see much but the bottoms of the lifeboats—nothing like the life rafts in the Titanic movie—huge, enclosed orange and blue fiberglass boats with inboard engines and a seating capacity for 150. All suspended overhead on cables end to end.

I widened my stance as the ship dipped beneath my feet, then glanced at my watch again and frowned. Was I the only one who'd followed orders? I shook my head. I was sick of always coloring carefully inside the lines, walking with scissors pointy end down, and signaling before making turns; naively believing that Darcy

Cavanaugh's personal crusade for integrity would make any difference in anything at all. Bogus crock of shit, obviously.

I glared down at my watch. Five thirty. Nobody was here because they were all at dinner. Like I should be. I felt like a fool standing here with the ridiculous life vest. I'd give it three minutes more and that was it.

The boat rocked again and the lifeboats shifted on the cables overhead with a metallic groan. A clicking then whining sound, like something sliding, began very slowly. Like a boat was being lowered? I craned my neck and stared upward, trying to see. Why would they even use lifeboats for a security drill anyway? Did it make sense? Another noise. Behind me. Was that . . . the door opening?

I started to turn when a thunderous metallic scream, like the brakes of a runaway train, split the air overhead. In less than a second, the night sky was obliterated by a huge expanse of orange and blue fiberglass lurching and tilting and then hurtling downward . . . toward me? *Oh my God, the boat!*

Before I could move, a man's voice shouted my name and his body collided with mine. *Luke.* His tackle launched us both into the air and we slammed back down onto the deck, sliding on our bellies across the wet teak surface to crash into the rail wall beyond.

I screamed as my shoulder connected with the cold metal and then again as the huge lifeboat struck the deck behind us in a shattering explosion, shaking the surface beneath us like an earthquake. The next scream was muffled when my mouth squashed against the decking as Luke threw his body over mine. He ducked his head as a cloud of debris exploded outward and pelted us in sharp stings. The ship's horn split the air with blasts and searchlights lit the deck like an electrical storm.

I tried to lift my head and felt Luke's hand push me down again. I could taste the marine varnish on the deck. And the salty residue of blood. *I can't breathe.* My pulse pounded in my temples and pain knifed through my injured shoulder. "I can't breathe . . ."

"Quiet. Stay down." Luke's voice was a bark, his face close to mine. He groaned and moved his arm, fumbling with his jacket, and his elbow connected with my ribs.

The horns were deafening as I tried to shift my head to a position where I could see. I rolled my face side-to-side and winced at a stab of pain along my jaw. There, better. I could see bright lights shining on the lifeboat that hung over the splintered remains of a deck rail. Oh, God. My throat squeezed closed. *Right where I was standing.*

I felt my breathing ease as Luke stood and his body weight no longer pinned me to the deck. I raised my head a little and watched as he stood over me scanning the deck and the remaining row of lifeboats suspended overhead. What . . . ? I raised myself on one elbow and blinked my eyes.

He was standing with legs wide in a military stance and whispering into a hand-held radio. In his other hand, obscured slightly behind his pant leg, was the gun.

NINETEEN

"FBI AGENT? *F-B-I?*"

"Mmm-hmm," Luke murmured, his lips warm against my forehead.

"Not a lawyer?"

"Law school first, but not a dance host." He laughed softly. "Although you have to admit the cha-cha's pretty good. My sisters get credit for that, not the Bureau." Luke leaned away from me on the bed and smiled, lifting a strand of shower-damp hair away from my face. His eyes were gentle, concerned. "You're not trembling as much as you were. Feeling better?"

"I'm having some trouble . . ." I squeezed my eyes shut and hugged Luke's huge University of Virginia sweatshirt closer around me. "It's kind of hard to take this all in, you know?"

I opened my eyes and glanced around the large teak-paneled stateroom at the computer, stack of papers and CDs, hand-held radio, flak jacket, badge, and the shoulder holster draped across a chair. A framed photo was propped on the dresser; Luke in a scruffy beard and football jersey standing beside an older man with an identical smile and a woman with her arms around two blonde girls wearing riding boots and hugging a golden retriever.

"It happened so fast that I didn't know what to think." I shook my head. "You leap at me from out of nowhere on the deck, and then there were all those lights and sirens, and when I can finally catch my breath, I look up to see you holding a gun."

Luke nodded and touched a fingertip to my bruised lower lip. "I'm sorry it had to be so rough; couldn't really be helped."

I sighed. "And then Gombu whisks me here to your stateroom, and I'm wondering if I'm like . . . under arrest or something." I pointed toward the glass door to the balcony and laughed, my voice choking. "If he hadn't finally told me the truth, that he was *protecting* me at the order of 'Special Agent Skyler' and not holding me captive, I'd have knotted your fancy damned sheets together and lowered myself down to the next deck. Swear to God."

Luke nodded, chuckling. "I don't doubt that for a second, Wildcat." He plucked at the hem of the borrowed, baggy sweatpants and then tickled my polished toenail poking out from below them. "Didn't take you long to settle in after that though. Find my shower and shampoo and rifle through my closet?"

I produced a wad of rumpled gold papers from the pocket of the sweatshirt and smiled. "And I ate the chocolates from your pillow. I was starving." I started to laugh, and instead my eyes filled with tears until I was powerless to stop them from spilling over. My voice was a half-moan, half-whisper. "God, Luke, someone was trying to *kill* me?"

I wasn't sure if it was the brandy Luke poured into the black coffee or the way that he held me against his chest and rocked me, but when Gombu delivered the silver-topped tray about twenty minutes later, my tears had evolved into a healthy dose of indignation.

"Drop a freaking boat on me?" I growled and slid a cold spear of asparagus from its wrapping of ham and jabbed the air with it. "Sneaking into my cabin and scaring me with my lingerie and whispering in my ear in the spa is one thing, but *murder*? That's unimaginable. Could this person—these thieves—really be desperate enough to risk killing someone?" I sat cross-legged on the bed, holding the tray on my lap and waiting for Luke's answer.

He started to speak and then hesitated, sliding closer to me and covering one of my hands with his own. "They already have."

I set the asparagus down and watched his face.

"Virgilio didn't hang himself, Darcy." He squeezed my fingers. "That's what I was doing that night when I disappeared. I went in the chopper with Virgilio's body. Escorted it to the Bureau's medical examiner."

"And?" I swallowed hard.

"And Virgilio was hanged from that railing *after* he was murdered. His skull had been fractured. By a baseball bat probably."

Baseball bat? "That's weird. Gombu's staff was asking Marie about the batting cages up on the Sports Deck." My hand flew to my mouth. "Oh my God. Marie! You're not saying that she had anything to do with this?" I shoved the tray aside and struggled to stand, yanking at the sweatpants as they slid down my hips. "If you let them do anything to her, I swear, I'll—"

Luke grabbed my shoulders and pushed me gently back down. "Hey, are we back to stomping and biting? Stop." He laughed softly. "Marie had nothing to do with any of this. In fact, she's been invaluable in helping us to get as far as we have." He shook his head. "Of course, that damned cow sock had me going there for a minute." He lifted a strawberry to my lips and smiled as I gave in and took a bite.

"So then, forgive me?" He touched a fingertip to my nose.

"Depends. When's she coming back?"

"Soon, I promise."

"And," I licked the strawberry juice from my lower lip and winced as my tongue touched the injury, "are you going to tell me why someone would want to kill Virgilio?"

Luke took a slow breath and I watched a series of expressions pass over his face, hesitant, uncomfortable, and then all business again. He'd opened his mouth to speak when his cell phone rang. He raised his palm toward me and mouthed, *"just a second,"* and turned away to step into the stateroom's small foyer, speaking barely above a whisper into the phone.

I pushed a strawberry around on my plate and watched Luke from my vantage point on the bed. He'd pulled off his sweater and was dressed in faded blue jeans and a lavender-blue Henley shirt half tucked in at the waistband. His hair was tousled from the roll across the deck and a dime-size red abrasion dotted one cheekbone.

He used his hands when he spoke, making little gestures in the air and even extending his index finger and thumb at one point to mimic a gun like a small boy would do. Goosebumps rose on my forearms as I glanced back at his real weapon draped so casually across a chair. I buried my face in my hands. This was not a kid's game. It was Luke's world. And someone in that world wanted me dead.

I looked up to see Luke standing bare-chested in front of me, wadding his shirt into a ball to hurl it overhead in a slam-dunk toward the closet door. "I should probably take a shower; nothing like sliding across a ship deck." He touched his cheek and winced. "And maybe I'll clean this up a little, too."

My eyes dropped from the wound down to his chest and then to the vertical line of golden hairs just below his navel. My cheeks burned as I tried to think of something coherent to say. It was not possible with him standing there like that. "I, uh . . . hey, wait." I glanced away for a moment and feigned interest in the fruit plate. "You didn't answer me about Virgilio. Why would someone want him dead?"

Luke's smile faded and his lips pressed together in a tight line, the muscle at the angle of his jaw tensing. I remembered the look on his face just an hour earlier as he stood over me, scanning the perimeter and holding that gun. All business, with no soft underbelly of emotion. It was the same now.

"I can't talk to you about the case." He took a step backward and frowned, pressing his fingers to his forehead. "I really shouldn't have said anything at all."

"But I already know some things." I leaned forward on the bed, nodding rapidly. "You wouldn't be revealing anything if you simply confirmed what I already know."

I continued when he made no comment. "Like I knew Virgilio didn't commit suicide over a marital problem. Because he wasn't married. And I found out that he'd been paying the other stewards to do his work, to give him time for his other business. And that he was making a lot of money at that business." I jumped as Luke's hand shot out and closed over my wrist.

"*What*? You found out? What do you mean by that? How?"

I pulled my hand away, watching his face. "By asking, of course. Alfonso told me. Our new cabin steward. It was simple." My brows furrowed. "Hey, what's wrong? Why are you looking at me like that? I was trying to help Marie."

"By asking questions? Enough questions to inspire someone to drop a boat on you?" Luke shook his head and turned away, muttering under his breath.

"Yes, I asked questions. So what? It didn't look like anyone else was going to do anything."

Luke turned back sharply and scowled, his hands on his hips. He suddenly looked for the entire world like a brother who'd been bested in an arm-wrestling match. My heart did a strange little flip-flop that was in no way sisterly.

"Excuse me?" He bellowed, "I think we've just revealed the fact that this is my job. *My job?*"

I bit my lower lip in time to stifle a laugh. Oh Lord, I wasn't going to laugh. I didn't dare. But a snort erupted through my nose and my eyes filled with tears.

"I know that now," I said with as much seriousness as I could muster. "But from where I sat before, it looked like you were just a pretty face cha-cha-ing with a bunch of old ladies, and . . ." I snorted again and doubled over, my voice rising higher. "So, Lord knows the only way to solve this thing was to go one-on-one with a horrible Yoga Nazi. Upwind during the Wind-Releasing Posture, of course and—" I half-groaned, half-laughed. "I'm *so* sorry to be laughing like this, Luke." Tears streamed down my face and the laugh progressed into a belly-cramping howl as I stretched out across the bed, knocking the dinner tray aside and sending strawberries cascading to the floor. "I'm *really* so sorry, but it's been . . . an awfully tough couple of days."

My laugh softened to a giggle and ended in a sigh as Luke turned me onto my back and leaned over me, looking down into my face. He was smiling now, tenderly, and shaking his head very slightly back and forth. I could see the pulse pounding at the base of his neck and heard him clear his throat softly. His voice was husky, halting.

"What is it about you that gets me . . . so damned crazy?" He asked.

My face infused with warmth and I shrugged. Crazy—that's good, right? *I make him crazy?*

He shook his head again and his eyes searched my face. "I mean look at you, for crissake. You're beautiful, so beautiful it blinds me sometimes. And funny and feisty and smart, and . . ." Luke's voice dropped to a whisper. "And everything I've been looking for in a woman." He swallowed and then cleared his throat again.

I could hear my pulse thrumming in my ears as I held my breath.

Luke's brows scrunched together. "But you're a liability here, Cavanaugh, don't you see that? I've only got twelve hours to wrap this up before we dock in New York."

What? I narrowed my eyes and squirmed under him. *Liability?* That wasn't good, was it?

"A liability?" I glared at him. For godsake, Firefighter Sam and his football stats were more poetic than this. "Let me . . . *up* and I'll get out of your way, Special Agent Skyler." I growled under my breath. Damn him.

"Wait." Luke pinned my arms gently and laughed. "No biting. I think I said that all wrong." He sighed. "What I meant was that, yes, I have a job to do, but it's harder now because I've begun to . . ." he hesitated for a moment. "To care so much about you, Darcy. Think about you all the time. And worry about you, dammit." He frowned. "How the hell can I keep you safe if you—"

"Keep me safe?" I whispered. My head had started to swim and my heart was pounding like crazy. I didn't know if I wanted to laugh again or cry. *Begun to care so much?*

He lowered himself over me, smiling again before touching his lips to the corner of my mouth. Then he moved away. "Too sore?" He whispered. "Your lip, where it's bruised from the deck?"

The pounding of my heart was making me deaf. But I didn't want to listen anymore anyway; I just wanted to feel. "What bruise? Which deck?" I stretched my arms up and wrapped them around Luke's neck.

His lips parted and his mouth covered mine, kissing me softly at first and then more deeply, fingers weaving into my hair to cradle the back of my head. His mouth moved over mine, lips and then tongue warm and insistent, and I could feel him exhaling through his nose as he refused to move away even to breathe.

His back was warm under my fingers, the muscles stretching as he moved to draw me closer against him, and I felt my sweatshirt begin to ride up until his bare chest and belly met mine. Those incredible golden hairs brushed against my skin until I thought I was catching fire, and then one of his hands crept under the sweatshirt.

"You're sure?" Luke whispered.

"Sure?"

"Your mouth. I'm not hurting you?"

"Mmm." I smiled against his lips. "No. Never felt healthier. Don't stop."

"Actually," he murmured, his lips brushing mine again and then drifting to the hollow of my neck. "I was planning on starting with your lips and then . . ." His fingers traced across my bare breast and found my nipple.

"Good plan," I whispered somehow, and slid my hands from his back toward the buttons at the front at the front of his jeans. Best plan I ever heard, in fact.

Luke sat up and tugged the sweatshirt over my head, chuckling as I blushed and spread my fingers to modestly cover the tiny shamrock tattoo. The laugh faded and his brows furrowed as he brushed my hair aside and touched his fingertips to a purplish bruise on my left shoulder.

"God, I'm sorry, Darcy." He shook his head slowly, lips pressed together. "I can't—*I won't* let anything else happen to you."

I dropped my hands from my breasts then smiled at the look in his eyes and his immediate soft groan of pleasure. "I only know *one* thing that's going to happen, Skyler. Right here and right now." I stretched backward on the bed, reaching my arms up toward him, and he settled over me again, his mouth moving eagerly to—

A sharp rap on the stateroom door was followed by a rapid series of them. Then a squawk of a radio and Gombu's voice.

"Agent Skyler?"

Luke's mouth left my breast and he scowled before sitting upright and allowing his face to compose into the all-business expression I'd seen earlier.

"Yes?" he answered.

"The helicopter has landed, sir. They've all come through the private passageway and are here now. Right outside the door."

"Good. Just a moment." Luke handed me his sweatshirt, then traced a fingertip across my breast one last time before I pulled the fabric over my head.

"A helicopter?" I asked, pulling the ends of my hair free from the shirt's neckline. "What does he mean—*who's* here?"

"Reinforcements."

I leaned forward and brushed my lips across the hairs on his chest, giggling. "I don't think you need reinforcements. You were doing a damned fine job all by yourself."

Luke grinned and kissed me quickly before standing and stepping toward the door. "Oh yes," he said looking back over his shoulder. "There should be a little surprise out here for you, too."

He opened the door and Marie stepped inside wearing dark glasses and an FBI ball cap. The teats of the remaining cow sock protruded from the pocket of her denim shirt.

"So," she said with a grin, lifting her glasses and looking from Luke's bare chest to where I sat cross-legged on the bed and then down at the strawberries scattered across the carpet. "Looks like you were bored as hell without me."

TWENTY

"The FBI knows about Sam?" My mouth dropped open.

"Oh hell, they probably know my dog passed a kidney stone last summer." Marie finished unpacking her duffel bag and tossed a pair of Garfield boxer shorts into our closet.

I buried my head in my hands. The FBI. Luke. He knew about Sam? All of it? Could it get more humiliating? My breath escaped in a moan. "Oh my God."

Marie swatted at me with the FBI ball cap. "Get a grip. I was joking about Zella's kidneys."

I brushed the hair away from my eyes and peered up at Marie. "Luke knows about Sam?"

"Yeah, those guys are like ferrets." She winked. "Be glad your little shamrock's never been photographed or he'd know about that, too."

I folded my arms across my chest as my face flamed.

"*Ooh?*" Marie sank down onto the bed beside me. "That FBI gigolo's been tap dancing on your heart, huh?"

I moaned again and flopped backward. "All I know is that this whole mess is making me crazy." I raised my head. "Tell me again what we're supposed to do."

"'Act natural.'" Marie shook her head and sighed. "Which basically boils down to the fact that we act as if we know nothing. Luke is a dance host. I am a shipboard nurse. You are," Marie grinned, "the tattooed prey of an obsessive podiatrist."

I glared.

"Hey," Marie said, winking, "Dr. Foote isn't asking *me* to wear open-toed shoes in his office."

"I'm serious here, Marie." I rubbed a hand across my forehead. "Do you know how frustrating it is that Luke won't talk to me about any of this?"

"He can't."

"Dammit, you sound just like him."

Marie rubbed her fingers over the three embroidered letters on the ball cap. "Darcy, I spent twenty-fours hours with these guys. They're freaking serious. This investigation has been going on for months, tracking tens of thousands of dollars in stolen goods moving from this ship and others out across state lines. And now there's been a murder." She shook her head and grimaced. "Could have been two murders if that lifeboat had hit its target tonight." She squeezed my forearm gently. "The best thing we can do is step out of the way and let these men do what they need to do. While we pretend to know nothing."

I pulled the neckline of the hooded sweatshirt up around my chin and inhaled. It smelled like Luke. Marie was right; I'd be dead if it weren't for him.

"But the truth is that I do know things," I said slowly, sitting up and picking at a thread on the sweatshirt. "Apparently too many things. Do you think I'd be targeted like this if I hadn't been close enough to the truth to make someone pretty nervous?"

"C'mon, Darcy," Marie shook her head.

"No, seriously. I knew that Virgilio wasn't married and that the suicide story Edie Greenbaum and the Yoga Ladies were passing around was bogus. I found that out myself."

"Okay, but did you know his fingerprints were all over that heart attack victim's cabin, purse, and luggage, too? Lots of places a steward's hands shouldn't be." Marie watched my mouth drop open and smiled. "See? The Feds are down to the wire on this, so back off before you blow Luke's cover."

"Virgilio was in on the robberies and he was killed because . . ."

"I don't think the question is why, it's who. Who killed Virgilio? And that's what the Feds are narrowing in on now. Tonight."

I stood and yanked at the sweatpants as I headed for the closet. "C'mon, we haven't got much time."

"Wait." Marie followed me, catching my arm. "What are you up to now?"

I lifted the hanger of a deep V-neck silver gown and smiled. "Last Night at Sea Extravaganza? Dancing with the Captain, Diamond Dazzle Sale, Champagne Waterfall, and Death By Chocolate." I narrowed my eyes and my voice grew hoarse. "Way worse ways to die." I shook my head. "Can you even imagine how bad I feel for being wrong about Luke?" Tears stung my eyes and I wiped them away angrily. "I was so stupid. Marie, he saved my life. More than once. What if there is some way I can help him now, stop him from being—"

"*No*, Darc.'" Marie shook her head. "No you don't. I promised the agents that we would stay completely out of this."

"Well, I'm not going to stand by while Luke's at risk because of something I may have stirred up." I grabbed my silver mesh sling-backs and nudged Marie aside. I carried the shoes and gown toward the bed and smiled as I noticed the small drawstring velvet bag looped over the hanger. My grandmother's black pearl strand. Perfect. *Let's go get 'em, Grandma.*

"Shit." Marie sighed and opened her own side of the closet. "So what are we going to do? Provide back up for the FBI with a frigging lava lamp?" She grumbled and slid the hangers across the rack. "And what is the dress code for something like that?"

*   *   *

I watched the glass elevator doors close and stared at Marie again. "I can't get over it; never seen you in anything but pants." I patted the sleeve of the lavender silk tunic then stepped back, giving a low whistle as my gaze took in the side slit in her long, matching skirt. "Stunning, girlfriend."

"Oh, cut the crap." Marie's cheeks flushed. "I just figure we're gonna end up being helicoptered out to federal prison. And when Ma comes to visit, I don't want her poking her bony finger through the cell bars and whining, 'Do you always have to dress like a brick-layer, Marie Claire?'" She shrugged and pinched the fabric at her hip. "But don't worry—I've got my lucky Yankees boxers under here." She watched me push the floor button and sighed. "Okay, so what's the plan?"

We headed for the Sports Deck gym to have a look at the "lucky" treadmill, figuring it wouldn't be in use because of the end-of-cruise activities. Only a few fluorescent lights flickered in the weight room at the far end as we entered the deserted gym.

"Seems like months ago that I did that belly flop in here," I said as my heels echoed across the hardwood floor. "Here, it's that treadmill there, third one down."

Marie pulled her penlight out and shone it across the darkened control board; unlit indicators for incline, RPM, time, distance and calorie count. "Here's the radio jack; did you say it only had one station?" She touched a fingertip to the little box and it's tuning dial. "Looks like lots of choices here." She shone her light on the treadmills adjacent. "Same as the others."

"But I remember trying to turn away from the station and being frustrated 'cause there were no other choices. One arrow on the knob for one selection. Not even the TV channel. It was like—"

"Like it had been fixed that way on purpose," Marie whispered. "Look." She pointed the light's beam at the vertical bar of the treadmill. The wires leading into the audio box were frayed and the paint on the pole itself was covered in scratches—tool marks, maybe—and layered with remnants of black electrical tape. Marie shone the penlight back toward the other treadmills. "The rest of them look fine. This one's had the earphone box changed a lot of times."

The lights flipped on overhead and the room was suddenly daylight bright, making us squint.

"You need some assistance here?" The Yoga Nazi marched into the room carrying a basket of incense and candles, the red dot on her forehead rising to a menacing height. Her lips formed a small "O," tight as her thighs. "Yes?"

She had already whipped herself up into the Scorpion Posture before we could retrace our steps across the gym and escape into the corridor. I glanced back through the door toward the tread-mills.

"So," I said, tugging gently at my grandmother's pearls and trying to keep my thoughts organized, logical. "Let's think this through. We know that the goal was robbery and now we know that the victims weren't random and that they were pre-selected 'winners' of a spa coupon." I suppressed a shudder remembering the voice in my ear on the massage table. "A free coupon that didn't exist, for a spa treatment that included," I watched Marie's face, "a mysterious vitamin shot which doesn't exist either."

"What do you mean?" Marie lowered her voice as a small group of passengers filed by in tuxedoes and evening gowns from the direction of the Polynesian bar.

"I asked. The hostess at the Mermaid Spa said they have no promotional contest, only gift certificates that could be presented as an anonymous surprise."

"From a secret admirer who wants to jam a gun against your neck and steal your purse? Maybe scare you into a mini-stroke in the process?"

"No, maybe not a stroke at all." I paused and smiled, raising my hand to wave as Serena Bliss waddled by in an ostrich trimmed polka-dot gown. "Maybe just a vitamin shot that wasn't so very healthful after all." I took a slow breath and willed my voice to steady. "How well do you know Howie, the night nurse?"

Marie blinked rapidly and shook her head. "Howie? You think Howie has something to do with all of this?"

"I don't know for sure," I whispered. "I'm trying to retrace my steps, remember what I did or said and who I talked to before that boat almost dropped on me tonight."

"And?"

"And I went to the sickbay early this morning to talk to Howie about the vitamin shots. But he wasn't there. So I asked the nurse that was covering for him a lot of questions. About missing drugs."

"And you think she told Howie?"

"Exactly," I said softly.

Marie was quiet for a moment and then ran her fingers through her hair. "The Feds asked me about that, too. About drugs. And about Howie."

We joined the other passengers in the elevator and pushed the button. As the elevator descended, we could see down into the atrium where white-jacketed crew members were carrying and stacking dozens of silver trays topped with crystal glasses.

"What's that all about?" Marie asked.

"The Champagne Waterfall, dear," a voice behind us answered. I turned to smile at the Yoga Panther who was wearing a gold-sequined jumpsuit and a scary amount of lipstick. "At eleven PM. It's breathtaking, over a thousand vintage glasses in a huge pyramid. And a specially chosen person—Edie Greenbaum this time—climbs a ladder and starts pouring champagne into the top glass. Bottle after bottle, until it fills all the glasses and runs over like a giant bubbly waterfall. They dim the lights and it's . . ." she sighed, "very romantic."

"I'm sure it is." I smiled. *Champagne?* I felt my skin flush under the clingy gown. Would I ever taste that elusive champagne with Luke? And how on earth could I "act natural" around him now? Patriotic duty or not, it was a lot for the FBI to ask.

We exited the elevator just as the Greenbaums stepped forward to board. They were both dressed in shades of pink—Edie in an embroidered-rose silk gown and Bernie in a tuxedo with a ruffled shirt, mauve paisley vest, and burgundy tie. He puffed out his chest when he saw me and blushed as pink as his boutonniere.

Edie nodded at Marie approvingly. "You look wonderful, dear. Feminine and, well, kind of free. Is that how it feels?"

The elevator door closed before Marie could think of a reply, but I grumbled, "Irritating little woman. Bernie's a saint to put up with that. Where do you think they're headed just now?"

"Down to the theater," Marie said. "The last night's performance is a talent show for the passengers and crew. I was going to enter." She frowned and then tried to erase it with a smile. "Not that I wouldn't rather help you on this mission, of course."

I put my hands over my eyes and peeked between my fingers at Marie. "Talent show? I'm afraid to ask, but what were you going to do?"

Marie grinned and cupped a palm underneath her elegant silk sleeve. "Armpit Aria. Still could, if we—"

I wasted no time in propelling her down the corridor, past the casino and the twinkle-lighted Shopper's Row. We had to weave through a crowd of women outside the jewelry store. The roar of voices was deafening.

"What's going on there?" Marie shouted.

"Diamond sale. Last night aboard. Fifty percent off anything that remains unsold. Man, it looks like one of my Dad's termite nests." I shook my head at the swarming crowd of sequined and fur-draped passengers holding their shipboard charge cards aloft. "And look, it's the Queen Bee right out in front."

Marie stopped me before I could open the door to the Lobster Disco. "Game plan? What are we going to be doing in here? Please God, nothing that gets us into that federal prison."

I smiled and reached for the door handle. "Stop being such worrier. We're here to *act natural.*" I bit my lower lip and grinned. "And to figure out who in the hell tried to squash me with a boat."

The disco had been transformed into a glitter-dome; veil-thin layers of silver fabric wafted overhead and fiber optic beams lit the ceiling like lightning inside a cloudburst of diamonds. Each table was draped in silver satin and topped with an oversize champagne glass heaped high with chocolate truffles. A digital message display over the stage chased itself over and over, announcing the events: "Death by Chocolate . . . Diamond Dazzle . . . Champagne Waterfall . . ."

I scanned the faces at the tables and nudged Marie, whispering, "Perfect. Pretty much my whole list is here." I nodded toward the chairs pulled up near the dance floor. The Evanstons from the cabin next door, Serena Bliss, Sarah McNaughton, the retired nurse from the yoga class, the Prom Princess, and the Yoga Panther. My eyes did a double take toward the corner of the room. Gombu, out of uniform, was sitting with the hostess from the spa. I glanced at the patrons at the adjacent table, the off-duty stewards including Alfonso and—amazing—even the Yoga Nazi, wearing a silver-thread Sari. How'd she get here so fast?

Marie nudged me and nodded back toward the entrance. Howie Carson, wearing a dark tuxedo and balancing a glass of champagne, had just walked in. All my ducks in a row.

I startled as a hand closed over my bare shoulder from behind and a voice whispered close to my ear, "Well, hello there."

I turned and looked up into Luke's face, feeling an immediate flutter in my stomach. Act natural? How?

"Dance, Miss Cavanaugh?"

I glanced quickly around the room, unsure.

Luke chuckled. "It would be more suspicious if I didn't dance with you, Darcy. We've been seen together a lot."

He held me away from him as we danced, much more formally than before, and I was surprised at how badly I wanted to close that gap. I traced my fingers over the shoulder of his tuxedo, stiffer than usual, and realized with a little shock that he was wearing the flak jacket I'd seen in his stateroom. Bulletproof vest. Bullets. I glanced over his shoulder at the faces beyond, my rogues' gallery of victims and suspects. And I wondered, with a little chill, which of them was watching me as well. *Who?*

Luke leaned forward and whispered close to my ear. The warmth of his breath made my skin tingle. "Excuse yourself to the restroom?"

"What? No, I don't need to go, thanks." I looked up at him, wrinkling my brows with confusion.

Luke smiled, the corners of his eyes crinkling. "That little dark alcove in the outside hall, just past the potted palms. Handicapped restroom. Nobody ever remembers it's there." His hand caressed the small of my back, one fingertip slipping under the plunging drape of fabric. My breath caught. He drew a slow circle and I swear I could feel it way down between—

"Well, Mr. Skyler," I said quickly. "Please excuse me, but I need to use the ladies' room."

I whispered to Marie on my way to the door and then walked casually outside and toward a narrow corridor beyond. A palm frond snagged my hair as I stepped into the darkened alcove. I glanced around. Luke was right, no one was even near and the lighted lock on the unisex restroom door read "Vacant." What was he up to? Warning me about something? And I'd thought the ER was tense. Luke's brand of intrigue was completely unnerving.

He joined me in less than three minutes and was kissing me only seconds later, pressing me into the alcove wall with the length of his body and taking my breath away. His fingers kneaded the silvery fabric over my bottom and his lips moved to my neck, down to the swell of my breasts, and then back up to cover my mouth once more. After a long moment he stepped away and smiled, his voice husky and soft.

"I thought I was going to go completely crazy if I couldn't do that," he whispered.

I caught my breath and tapped my fingertips against his shirt-front, feeling the rigid flak jacket beneath. I frowned. "And I'm going crazy worrying about you." I raised my hand to his cheek, gingerly touching the abrasion. My heart squeezed. "Why won't you let me do something to help?"

Luke lifted my hand away and kissed the palm. "You just did." He glanced at his watch. "We're pretty close to wrapping this thing up now. Just waiting for a fax confirmation of a few details."

"Before you arrest someone? Who?"

Luke shook his head and squeezed my fingers. "I'll tell you that afterward." He cupped my face in his hands. "Right before I pop the cork on that champagne I promised you."

I closed my eyes as his mouth covered mine once more; lips and tongue warm, promising so much more than bubbly wine . . . *What was that?* A buzzing sensation tickled the front of my dress. There it was again. I stepped away and glanced downward. "Your pants are buzzing?"

Luke pulled me close again and chuckled, his lips at the corner of my mouth. "I'm not surprised. My whole body buzzes every time I think about that little shamrock."

"No, really. Is it your cell phone?"

He pulled the tiny phone from his pocket and listened for a moment, his face transforming back to his somber business mask. He turned away, murmured a few words, and then turned back to me again.

"Got to run," he said, snapping the phone closed. "It's going down right now." He took hold of my chin and looked down into my eyes. "You and Marie stay put in that disco. Promise me? No matter what."

I watched him disappear out into the brightly lit corridor and then I headed back to the disco, my mind racing. I reached for the door handle and saw that my hands were shaking.

Was it really almost over? If they were moving to arrest someone, then . . . I held my breath and stepped inside, letting my eyes adjust to the darkness once more. I walked toward the table where Marie waited and I scanned the room. Arrest someone. My rogues' gallery—who was missing?

TWENTY-ONE

"YOUR LIPSTICK IS SMEARED down to your chin." Marie shook her head as I sat down opposite her. "And seriously, as a taxpayer, I really have to question the need for that man's strong-arm tactics." She watched my face for a moment and sighed, then handed me a cocktail napkin. "Never mind, the need is pretty obvious."

I gave my chin a half-hearted swipe and then glanced around the room, fighting a rising anxiety. I needed to figure this out. It was more crowded now, with different faces at different tables mingling and blending together. Impossible to sort through. Damn. I scanned the room again and groaned. "I can't tell if . . ."

"If what? Who are you looking for?"

I turned and leaned across the table, whispering, my voice as panicky as I felt. "Help me here. Who left the room while I was gone? You know, from the group I was watching. Think, quick, it's important." Because Luke was out there somewhere. And maybe one of those people had a gun.

Marie turned and swept her head side to side. "I didn't know I was supposed to keep tabs." She turned back to me and raised her brows. "What's going on?"

I glanced toward the exit and felt my stomach lurch, remembering the feel of Luke's bulletproof vest under my fingers. "Luke got a call a few minutes ago. They were setting things in motion to . . . to make an arrest." My hands begin to tremble. "God, Marie, what if—" I fought the images of gunshot victims I'd seen wheeled into the ER. Blood and powder burns. Faces as lifeless as Virgilio's. *Luke.* No.

Marie turned toward the dance floor and slid her chair back to get a view of the tables. "I don't think anyone's gone. If anything, more people are arriving." She picked at the edge of her nicotine patch. "The activities director is supposed to announce the winner of the free cruise any time now." She handed me a canapé. "Here, eat something. You look pale as a fish belly."

Marie nodded her head toward the dance floor. "Yes, three more arrivals, Edie Greenbaum and Herb and Dan—you know, the dance hosts." She chuckled. "No, wait, four. I forgot. The Phantom Dancer was dancing by herself in the corner a minute ago. Not sure if she's still there, but she's wearing lace stockings and fluttering one of those vampy old Spanish fans. Gotta love that broad."

I tipped my head to peer around the table in front of us. "And Howie?" I bit into the canapé.

"Howie's still there. Although he comes and goes. Hopefully, just answering sickbay pages. He does seem kind of fidgety."

"I don't get it." I rubbed the bruise on my shoulder. "The person who was following me around, who warned me about asking questions, *has* to be one of these people." I lowered my voice to a whisper. "And if Luke and the other agents think they're closing in on the killer, then it doesn't make sense for that person to still be here, unless . . ."

"Unless there's more than one person involved?" Marie suggested.

"Well, we know Virgilio was, at least for a while. But for one person to do all of those things, rig the treadmill, sneak into the spa, and steal the jewelry . . ."

"Jewelry." Marie flicked her fingernail against her glass. "Can you even imagine what some of these ladies are carrying around in their purses after that diamond sale tonight?"

I felt the blood drain from my face like someone had pulled a vital cork at the base of my neck. *Oh my God.* I dropped the canapé and reached over to grab Marie's hand. "The Queen Bee. Think! Have you seen her since we passed her at the Diamond Dazzle?"

Marie turned her head toward the dance floor and back. "Yeah, I did see her earlier, sitting with Serena and wearing a feather arm sling. But I don't see her now. Hey, Darc', where are you going?"

I leaped from my chair and headed toward the tables nearest the dance floor. I could finally see into the far corner where Gombu and the spa hostess had been sitting. Had been. Gone now. Where? And there was Edie Greenbaum dancing with Herb; and over there the table with Sarah McNaughton. Yes. And Serena Bliss. I waved, made my way to the table and knelt down next to Serena's chair, flashing a casual smile. Serena grinned and gushed.

"Darcy, you look beautiful. All silver and shiny like the sparklers on top of the Grand Mousse in the Death by Chocolate brochure." Serena licked her lips. "You're going, aren't you? It's in the Neptune Dining Room, right after Edie pours the Champagne Waterfall."

"Serena," I said, glancing down the length of the table, "I thought I'd seen the Qu—I mean Mrs. Thurston—sitting with you earlier and now she's gone. Not sick or anything, I hope?"

"Oh, no." Serena patted my arm. "You're so sweet to worry about us, but she had an appointment. Waited until the last night to do it, until the worry about the robberies had died down. And then she was all a-twitter, poor thing, trying to fit it between the Diamond Dazzle and the wonderful chocolate."

My throat squeezed. "Appointment?"

"At the Mermaid Spa. She was a winner, remember?"

I looked down at my watch and fought to keep my voice calm. "But it's almost eleven. Isn't that kind of late?"

"Ordinarily, yes." Serena smiled. "But they made an exception for her."

I knocked over a glass as I sprang upright, then apologized and bolted back toward our table as fast as I could go. I had to get to the spa before something bad happened. Warn the Queen Bee to get out of there. This thief had killed before, and what if he figured it was easier that way now? He'd brandished a gun at Serena, hadn't he?

I spotted Marie and wove through the tables, my mind racing faster than my feet. Luke said to stay here, but how could I? Maybe Luke was already at the spa. Maybe I'd get there and he'd already have taken care of it all. *Please, God.* But what if he hadn't? What if I was right and there was more than one thief, and Leona Thurston was alone? Waiting to become a victim of a killer.

My voice escaped in a gasp as I reached the table. "I'm going . . . to the spa. Give me . . . ten minutes." I sucked in a mouthful of air. "If I'm not back, call security. And then come after me, okay? I've got to check on the Queen Bee." I turned toward the door and Marie grabbed my arm.

"Are you crazy?" Marie tightened her grip. "There's no way I'm going to let you run off alone down there. *No way.*" She stood up. "I'm coming with you."

I wrestled away from Marie's grasp and rose on tiptoe to see over the crowd and back toward the dance floor. "Howie's up and moving around again, dammit." I shook my head. "No, *listen.* You've got to stay here and watch him. Keep him talking or something." I rubbed my hand across my eyes. "I don't want him or anybody else to leave here until I warn that woman. Please, give me ten minutes?" I squeezed Marie's shoulder. "I swear I won't do anything crazy. I'll pick up the phone down there myself and call security if I have to. Ten minutes."

*   *   *

I glanced back over my shoulder a half-dozen times as I covered the short distance down the carpeted corridor from the disco to the spa entrance. I tried to slow my breathing. *Calm down, this is probably nothing.* The Queen Bee could be somewhere else, maybe at the show. Maybe she even had some talent. Sure, a simpering duet with Bernie Greenbaum. The thought—no matter how comical—did nothing to ease my anxiety and I quickened my pace at the sight of the bejeweled double doors of the spa. I needed to make sure, that's all. I jumped back and almost stumbled as the door opened outward against me.

"Oh, excuse me, I didn't see you there." The dark-haired hostess, the one I'd seen with Gombu, looked up and smiled at me over a fistful of keys.

I glanced past her and tried to see inside the soft-lit entry. "You're closing? Nobody's still in there?"

"What? Oh, no. The masseuse is already gone and the last patron wanted to let herself out the back entrance." She smiled. "Mrs. Thurston wanted to fix her makeup before she went back to the party. I'm sorry, but there won't be any more appointments this cruise."

Back entrance? Where Marie and I had peeked in before? My stomach plummeted. In the herbal wrap room where the killer threatened me.

"Wait." I thrust my hand toward the door before the hostess could turn the lock. "I think I left my cosmetic bag in there. Let me run in and check. Just for a minute?"

The hostess glanced at her watch, suppressed a sigh, and then nodded. "Of course. But I doubt it's there; we always check for patrons' belongings pretty carefully. And there was nothing in the lost-and-found box today. Do you want me to help you?"

"No, I'll only be a minute." I was being an idiot, but I couldn't shake this feeling. This really awful feeling. "Be right back, thanks."

I hesitated at the desk, my eyes adjusting to the low light, and tried to remember which way the massage and wrap rooms were. Yes, down there. I hurried down the carpeted hallway to a door at the far end: *Sauna, Wraps.* I opened the door and my fingers searched the wood-paneled wall inside. Where was the light switch?

The recessed lighting clicked on and I jumped as overhead speakers immediately began to play classical music. I held my breath and glanced around the cherry-paneled room. Empty, as far as I could see. The private entrance and exit was straight ahead on the opposite wall. The Queen Bee had probably left that way safe and sound. One more peek and I'd be out of here.

The doors to the individual cedar-lined saunas were open, with fresh towels stacked and ready on the benches. A warmer for the herbal wraps stood in the corner, its heater light glowing softly next to a closet marked *Linen*. On the wall above it was a first aid box. New, and not a bad idea, considering.

My eyes moved to the three wrap tables, with orchid motif curtains for privacy. One curtain was still drawn closed. The hairs stood up on my arms. No, couldn't be. I took a deep breath and stepped forward, sliding the curtain aside. *Oh dear God.*

TWENTY-TWO

I shouted for help and knew it was futile.

The Queen Bee's face was gray, one glazed eye covered by a dangling cucumber mask. Her lips were blue and saliva pooled at the corners of her mouth. Her uncasted arm hung free from the herbal wrap and over edge of the table. She was as still as death.

Do something. My vision narrowed like I was peering through the wrong end of a telescope, filtering the horror to see only what I needed to see. That's the way it always was—sometimes the only way I could do what I needed to do. My mind snapped into autopilot—algorithms, possible outcomes, and life-support skills ticked through my brain by rote. A-B-C. *Start with A: Get the airway open.*

I yanked the mask off of the woman's face, lifted her lower jaw with two fingers and then checked for air exchange. Look, listen, feel—*none.* Not breathing. God, for how long? Four minutes without oxygen and a brain begins to die. *Doesn't matter, I've got to try.*

I pinched her nose, took a deep breath, covered her mouth with my own and exhaled. The Queen Bee's chest rose under the herbal wrap. Another breath. Another rise. I pulled my mouth away and suppressed a gag, tasting lavender-scented massage oil and slimy cucumber. *Check for a pulse. Oh please, God, let this woman live.* I forced the image of the dead patient in the ER hallway from my mind as I slid my fingers along the side Mrs. Thurston's neck. Her carotid artery bounded beneath my fingertips. Thank God. Heartbeat present, a little erratic but strong.

"I'm right here, Leona," I whispered down at her still face, "and I'm not going let you die. Count on that." My own heart drummed in my ears as I frantically scanned the room for a phone. No phone. And the music was so loud. Could the receptionist even hear me if I—

"Help!" I shouted over my shoulder for all I was worth. "In here. I need help!"

Countless cycles of CPR and long minutes later, I was finally able to take a moment to scan the faces of the people who had arrived in addition to Marie. *Marie.* Thank God, she'd come. There was also the spa hostess and Howie, who'd arrived with the resuscitation bag. *Howie?* And two security officers and the doctor.

Marie checked the Queen Bee's heart rate and raised her eyebrows as I continued to squeeze the bag-valve-mask device over our patient's face. Oxygen hissed from a green metal tank. I knew that each squeeze of the football-size bag would enrich Leona's blood oxygen, protecting her brain and other vital organs.

"Why won't she breathe on her own?" Marie whispered. "She's pink as a baby's butt and her heart's pumping like mad."

She looked back over her shoulder to where the doctor was directing the incoming stretcher. "She's floppy as Jell-O. Like—"

"Like she's paralyzed from a massive stroke?" I nodded my head as Marie lifted the Queen Bee's flaccid arm. "Exactly," I said, "and did you get a look at that? Her finger? Her *ring* finger?"

Marie looked from the bruised and bleeding finger back to my face, her gray eyes huge. "It looks like an open fracture."

I raised my head to check Howie's whereabouts and then whispered hoarsely, "Yes, like someone ripped the diamond rings off her finger." Before Marie could respond, a series of bursts split the air overhead—staccato blasts from the ship's PA system.

One of the security staff lifted his radio to his ear and then shouted to the other officer. "Let's go. They need us in the lobby atrium. Crowd control. Some woman's fallen off the ladder into the Champagne Waterfall."

We loaded the Queen Bee onto the stretcher and Marie took over with the breathing bag for the transport to the sickbay. I checked the portable monitor, reassured as the heart's electrical tracing moved steadily across the screen. No rhythm disturbances now. I nudged Marie as our patient's face began to twitch in tiny jerks, hiking up the skin around her eyes and mouth. Her lips pursed in an attempt to puff the saliva away. Within seconds her battered fingers were twitching and then beginning to move as she struggled to stretch her leg up beneath the stretcher's safety straps. The Queen Bee's eyes blinked and she took a shuddering breath. Her voice was raspy and unintelligible under the resuscitation mask as she tried to speak. *"C-C-Car-mn-n."*

"Don't try to talk, Mrs. Thurston," I patted her arm as the staff began to carry the stretcher from the massage room.

I shook my head. The Queen Bee was waking up and breathing now, thank God. What happened? Not a stroke. She wouldn't be moving her arms and legs if that were true. And a mini-stroke?

Way too dramatic for that. She'd completely stopped breathing. Alcohol? Drugs? But she'd seemed almost *paralyzed*, like . . . *Oh my God*. I fought a wave of nausea.

I looked up at the team and shook my head. "No, go on. I'll only be a minute. Need to check something. Meet you in sickbay." I nodded my head at Marie. "Really, I'm right behind you."

I closed the door behind the crew and the room was silent once more. The discarded cucumber mask lay on the floor along with the wet towels from the herbal wrap. A small red stain, wicking into the damp fabric, decorated one of them like some macabre monogram. Blood. From when someone had wrenched the jewelry from the Queen Bee's fingers. I whirled around to scan the room. And probably stole her purse, too, while she lay helpless and paralyzed. I squeezed my eyes shut. I only knew one way a person could appear paralyzed without stroke or trauma. Chemically. Drug-induced, by a paralyzing agent.

I'd used it in the ER countless times, in preparation for breathing tubes and before procedures that required profound muscle relaxation. Short term and in small doses and safely monitored. And I'd seen the typical display of symptoms as the drug wore off, the twitching and salivation prior to muscle recovery. Yes, a paralytic drug like succinylcholine. My mouth went dry. The vials I saw in the sickbay. But someone would need syringes and . . .

I scanned the room and grabbed the small wastebasket, scattering the contents to the floor, sifting frantically and then spreading them across the polished parquet floor with trembling hands. Pieces of cucumber, a nail file, paper towels, and—I jerked my head upward as a door, the linen closet door, creaked open behind me. *Who?* Before I could turn, there was the sound of a baseball bat slicing the air. My head exploded in pain as everything went inky black.

* * *

I opened my eyes and then closed them again quickly as the pain in the back of my head launched a wave of nausea. *Oh God, what . . . ?* A warm, wet trickle escaped from the hairline at the back of my neck and I opened my eyes once more. My lids blinked against the light as my eyes slowly focused. *Who is that?*

Black lace dress. A face with blonde hair, heavy makeup, and toothy over-bite. Familiar and smiling down at me. Speaking to me now. "Yes, dear, it's Carmen."

Carmen? Oh yes. I felt a merciful flood of relief. *Thank God, the Phantom Dancer.* I started to smile but my face wouldn't move. *What the . . . ?* My face, the skin itself, was impossibly heavy and pooling like wax from a burned down candle. My nose felt strange, wooden—hard to breathe through it. *Why?*

I tried to raise my hand to wipe at my nostrils but my arm was too weak. It twitched and flopped back down along my side. My heart began to hammer, sending shock waves through my head with every beat. *Thank God this woman had found me,* because something was terribly wrong. I tried to speak and my lips wouldn't move. "Don't bother. Your arm won't work," the Phantom Dancer said softly, brushing the hair away from my face. "Pretty little girl, such a shame."

What? I tried to blink, to see the woman's face better and to understand what was going on. But I couldn't even manage to close my eyelids now. My eyeballs were stinging and drying out. What was going on?

"I tried to warn you," the voice was cooing. "Tried to get you to butt out, but you wouldn't do that, would you, pretty girl?" The Phantom Dancer shook her head and the blonde hair swirled. "Snoopy girl. So I had no choice, did I?"

I tried to clear my throat, swallow, but the effort was ineffective. Saliva pooled inside my mouth. *I'm choking.* My head began to swim, float.

"But I gave you a sedative too, sweetie. More humane that way. Not only the paralyzing drug, like the others. Oh, excuse me, I meant the 'free vitamin shots.' Stupid cows, way too easy. Not like you." She petted my hair again and then grimaced as her upper denture loosened and slipped downward, exposing a gold tooth that gleamed in the pale light.

Oh my God. My moan died in my chest and the room grew foggy as I struggled to understand. *Bernie Greenbaum?*

Bernie yanked the false teeth out and glanced back over his shoulder as another series of alarms sounded overhead. He grinned and ran his tongue over the gold tooth. "Edie's little swan dive into the champagne glasses is working like a dream. The perfect diversion. No one will be back here for a long time."

He reached up and peeled a strip of lashes from his upper eyelid. "Gives me plenty of time to clean all this makeup off. Edie does a pretty damned good job don't you think? Couldn't have gotten my foot inside the door of this little gold mine without her talent. Thirty years with Warner Brothers is nothing to bat an eye at." He peeled the other strip of lashes and waved it in my face, chuckling. "Get it? Bat an eye?"

I felt saliva trickle from the corner of my mouth as Bernie continued to chuckle and began to trace the curly edge of the false eyelash across my face, down my throat, and over the pearls that lay against my chest. He gave a little sigh and touched a fingertip to one of my breasts.

"Yes, we learned a lot in those years with the studio, Edie and I." Bernie's voice dropped to a growl. "Too bad we learned more about foundation makeup and voice-overs and less about retirement investments." He yanked the blonde wig from his head and his scalp glistened with sweat. "Lost every damned dollar in those energy stocks; bunch of crooks." He grinned again. "I guess that's what people would be calling me, too, isn't it? But we had it going pretty slick for a while, lifting a little jewelry from a few old biddies. Hell, they were probably ripping their insurance companies off for more than we ever got. We never *hurt* anybody."

He grimaced. "Not until that greedy little Virgilio figured fencing the jewels wasn't good enough and decided to do a job on his own. Sloppy son of a bitch. Would've led the cops right to me." Bernie sighed and shrugged. "And then of course there was you, a pretty little fly in the ointment. I was going to let it go until Edie heard you this morning in the sickbay. Snooping, asking about drugs. Pretty and smart." His tongue swept across his painted lips. "Sexy, too."

He leaned over me and a small bead of sweat dropped from his forehead onto my face before he pressed his lips to mine. I could smell his armpits, his breath, and feel the oily makeup and beard stubble as his mouth and tongue lapped at my face. Please, *no*. My mind screamed as my body lay uncooperative and motionless. A wave of nausea rose and I willed it away. *Don't vomit; you'll choke to death.* It was almost impossible to get a deep enough breath now. Oh dear God, why was rape suddenly the less horrifying fate? *I can't breathe.*

"Well, I don't want to rile the wife. She can be a real bitch, believe me." Bernie moved back and then gave a little laugh. "Besides, honey, I really prefer a woman who at least wriggles under me. Necrophilia is not my thing." He shook his head. "Oh, sorry. That was blunt, wasn't it?"

Bernie gathered the eyelashes and the wig and shoved them into a gym bag and then began to unzip the black lace dress. "Now, if you'll excuse me, I'm going to wash the makeup off my face and get out of here." He glanced at his watch. "You ought to be nodding off pretty soon, doll. And when they come back and find you . . . ?" He clucked and shook his head. "It'll make for plenty of breakfast conversation in the morning, 'Poor girl, so young. But she had that worrisome heart condition, remember?'" He walked toward the dressing room. "Edie's fully prepared to weep openly on your behalf. Rest assured." He rolled his eyes and then grinned. The gold tooth glinted. "No. That would be *rest in peace*, wouldn't it?"

Bernie disappeared from view and my mind slowed almost as if he'd tucked my focus into that gym bag along with the false eyelashes. My body was grounded, but somehow I swam. Through dark molasses, thick and sweet. No hurry. It was a relief really, to rest for a moment. Maybe for a few minutes, until I could think of a new plan. Sure. I'd float and plan and . . .

There probably was a plan. Wasn't there? Someone would help me. *Marie, Luke* . . . I tried to take a breath and my chest wouldn't rise. I tried again and no air would come. *I'm not breathing.* The room turned foggy gray and then lights-out black. So quiet. Only my heartbeat in my ears. *Grandma, help me hang on!*

TWENTY-THREE

WHAT IS THAT? HISSING sound, acrid scent of plastic, and . . . cherry cigar smoke?

I blinked and my lids moved over my eyes, scratching like broken glass while every muscle in my body cramped. I ran my tongue across my lips and felt a teardrop slide down my face. *I'm crying, I'm breathing. I'm alive.*

I pushed the oxygen mask away and raised my head from the sickbay stretcher. Marie was asleep in a chair next to me with a smoldering cheroot wedged between her fingers, its ash an inch long. She jerked upright as I cleared my throat.

"Well . . . for . . . godsake." My voice was a hoarse whisper, and my throat splintery painful. "Are you trying to blow me up here? Cigars and oxygen?" I watched Marie's face break into a smile and felt more tears slide from the corners of my eyes. Warm, wet, wonderful tears. Thank you, God. I'm alive.

"That's damn picky." Marie grinned and stubbed her cigar against a ship logo coffee mug. "For someone who required mouth-to-mouth resuscitation."

She rolled her eyes and grimaced. "And the next time you try to be a murder victim—could you please wear a little less makeup? There was lipstick from one side of your face to the other and mascara streaks . . ." She pointed to a beside table with a crumpled washcloth and comb and a toothbrush. Bless her butt—she'd tidied me up. I smiled, starting to remember all that now. The effects of the sedative must be wearing off. I was about to make a crack about mother hens when Marie flung herself over the stretcher rail and hugged me hard.

"Damn, you scared the hell out of me, babe," she said, leaning away again, her gray eyes shiny. "How's the head?"

"It's okay," I said, touching my fingers to the lump on my scalp and wincing a little. "But where are . . . ?" I glanced toward the door to the corridor.

"Don't worry," Marie said, handing me a glass of water and a straw. "The Feds got Bernie and Edie. And that little rat Alfonso. Or at least they're questioning him. That's where Luke is now."

"And Howie?"

"No. Howie's innocent. Just sloppy. Leaving that door unlocked to the sickbay, not counting the drug inventory carefully enough. Turns out there were a few vials of paralytic unaccounted for over the last few months." She shook her head. "Still can't believe all this. The Greenbaums of all people. Shit. Bernie seemed like such a wuss."

I nodded, took a sip of water and then puckered my lips—Marie had spiked it with lemon. "He said something about losing all their retirement money in an investment scam. They worked for Warner Brothers for years, I guess. Edie did makeup. That's how she made Bernie into Carmen." I suddenly remembered the smell of the greasepaint makeup; the rough stubble of beard beneath it and the disgusting feel of Bernie's mouth against mine. I shivered. I'd have to get Marie drunk before I explained that half the lipstick she'd scrubbed away wasn't mine.

Marie shook her head. "Sounds like old Edie did a lot of things for the studio. Even stunt work." She nodded. "Like diving into a pyramid of champagne glasses?"

"The diversion, that's what Bernie called it. Guess it almost worked. How did the agents figure things out?"

"They'd already narrowed it down to Bernie, investigated his background in voice-overs—that was him doing Elizabeth Taylor on the treadmill station—his financial problems and his relationship with Virgilio. Not to mention more than a few other scrapes with the law; those two were not just innocent victims of a retirement fiasco, kiddo. They were hardcore scammers." Marie nodded. "The agents were looking for Bernie at the talent show but had no idea he was masquerading as the Phantom Dancer. Makes sense in hindsight of course; a lot easier to get into the spa dressed as a woman." She rolled her eyes. "He actually bragged to the agents about doing it on a couple of other ships, too. Said he has a wardrobe . . . 'to die for.'"

I gave a weak smile. "So how did they make the connection?"

"The Queen Bee. She'd pulled the edge of the cucumber mask up before her arms were paralyzed, enough to get a peek at 'Carmen.'"

"And the gun? Bernie didn't try to defend himself when they arrested him?"

Marie grinned. "Stage prop from *Annie Get Your Gun*. Remember? He only used that because Serena Bliss doesn't drink and refused the 'vitamin' shot. He was desperate for cash that time, since he'd lost Virgilio as a fence for the jewelry. And he hadn't set Alfonso up yet. And of course, Edie was spending money like crazy in the casino."

I shivered and pulled the blanket up around my shoulders, feeling it catch on the wires to the cardiac monitor. I glanced at the screen, watching the rhythm of my heartbeat march across in a glowing green line. For the second time in a week.

"You're fine." Marie smiled. "That wacky little ticker is totally behaving itself. Drugs are all worn off. Lungs clear, even though you bubbled like a salted snail for a while. Pretty gross." She shook her head. "Small cut on the back of your head, decent lump. We put in a few stitches, but your neurological checks have been fine. You've been answering questions like a champ between snore sessions. No evidence of concussion at all. The doc's basically cut you loose. No restrictions. You just have to come back for one more check before we disembark today." She grinned. "He told me you could leave here as soon as the sedative wore off and you woke up and got sassy."

I pried the monitoring electrodes off my skin and then raised my fingers to the back of my scalp. "Yeah, I remember the stitches. What time is it anyway?"

"Nearly four. We've been watching you for maybe four and half hours. I pulled your IV line out about half an hour ago. Just me here now. Howie went with Mrs. Thurston in the helicopter."

"She's okay?" I squeezed my eyes shut, remembering the horrible moment that I pulled the spa curtain aside. What if I hadn't been there?

"Basically okay. She'd been on some medications that complicated her recovery from the paralytic but they think she'll do fine." Marie smiled slowly. "You saved her life, Darc' . . ." she hesitated, "Probably couldn't have done that with orthotics."

I felt my eyes fill again. I was turning into a big crybaby. "It felt good, Marie. You know what I mean? Being there for that woman and knowing exactly what to do. That felt so good."

I sniffled and a tear escaped down my cheek. I wiped at it for a moment before my fingers dropped to the pearls nestled under the neckline of the hospital gown. Cool, smooth, and familiar as a rosary. My grandmother's pearls. My grandmother, the nurse. Maybe what she'd always said was true. Maybe one person could make a difference. "It's important, isn't it? *Being there?*"

I watched as Marie nodded and then I saw her pick up the little cherry cheroot.

"Wait," I said, narrowing my eyes, "what's with those cigars? And I don't see your nicotine patch."

Marie switched off the oxygen, rummaged around in her fanny pack, and produced the Volkswagen lighter. The flame rose after two flicks and she grinned at me after taking a drag. "I've been thinking," she said. "You remember when we were laughing about old Bernie Greenbaum? How he insisted on doing those lousy Elvis impersonations?"

"Mmm-hmm." I took another little sip of the lemony water.

"You asked me why he would do that. And I said, 'Whatever floats your boat.'"

"Yes?" I shook my head and waited, watching my best friend's face and secretly enjoying the little whiff of cherry smoke.

"Well, maybe that's the point. We do what we do. We are who we are." Marie raised her brows and grinned. "I smoke cigars and wear pants. With cow socks." She exhaled, the smoke swirling around her head. Her expression was as wise as Yoda. "And you, babe, are a nurse. A damned fine one. Don't fight that."

Marie turned as the door opened behind her. "Looks like you've got company, so I'm gonna run, okay?"

"Wait, Marie." My voice choked over the sudden lump in my throat. "Thank you for . . ." I struggled for words and then stopped as she held up her hand.

"No big deal. You'd do the same for me." She winked and then stepped away to give Luke a quick hug, before leaving and closing the door behind her.

"Well hello, Sleeping Beauty." Luke smiled and reached for my hand. His voice was husky-soft and his eyes watched my face like he was afraid I might disappear. "The last couple of times I stopped by, you were sound asleep." He pressed his lips to my fingers. "You want Bernie Greenbaum's gold tooth to wear on a chain around your neck? I can arrange that."

My eyes threatened tears again and I tried to laugh them away. Oh God. He looked so good. Tired, but good. Golden beard stubble showing, hair tousled, and the abrasion on his cheek a little swollen now. He'd shed the tuxedo jacket and wore the tuck-front white shirt open at the collar, bow tie hanging loose. The leather shoulder holster was snugly in place under his left arm and creaked as he stooped to hold me. I inhaled and sighed. "You smell like cherry cigars and chocolate."

"Bonding with Marie," Luke murmured, his lips against my neck. "And Serena. She saved us a plate from Death by Chocolate." He leaned away and looked into my face, blue eyes soft and suddenly serious. "You're really okay? I feel like hell about all of this. Thought we had it all figured out about Bernie. And then we got thrown that curve with the dual identity, and missed the incident with Leona Thurston in the spa. And with you . . . *dammit*." He squeezed his eyes shut.

I raised my palm to his cheek and smiled when he opened his eyes. "I'm fine." I nodded my head and smiled again. "Fine, okay? And *we got them*."

"We?" He grinned and then nodded his head. "Yes, we did. Although taking that man alive was not exactly what I wanted."

"Sh-shhh. You know what *I* want?" I traced my thumb across his lower lip and let my fingers trail down to the golden hairs at the open front of his shirt.

"What?"

"I want you to kiss me. And then I want you to figure out how we can do that a thousand more times without helicopters and dead bodies and," I sighed, "damned burning cow socks interrupting us."

Luke leaned toward me, brushed his lips against mine, and then pulled back. "Oh," he said, smiling. "I took care of it, by the way."

"Took care of what?"

"Marie's cow sock. The government's going to replace it. The whole pair, in fact. Requisition's already been submitted."

I raised my brows. "You're joking."

"Not joking," he whispered, brushing my hair away from my face and kissing first my forehead, then my cheek, my nose, and finally my lips. "She was a citizen inconvenienced by a government investigation and it's only right that she be compensated."

He kissed me again and I wound my arms around his neck, parting my lips and yielding to the warm pressure of his mouth. "But of course, it's far more complicated with you," Luke murmured, his lips leaving mine briefly.

"Complicated?" Silly man. It all felt pretty simple to me right now.

He pressed his lips to my throat. "You will require de-briefing, of course. Fairly extensive. The Bureau's made arrangements with your employer for a week's leave, effective immediately."

I leaned back and narrowed my eyes, biting my lower lip to keep from laughing. "De-briefing?"

"I've volunteered for the assignment myself," Luke said, tracing a fingertip down the front of my hospital gown and stopping to draw a little circle over my left breast. "There, right?" He whispered. "The shamrock?" He pressed his lips to the spot.

"You have incredible aim." I felt my heart hammer beneath the thin fabric as heat flooded into my face and then headed south. Way south.

"Job requirement," Luke said. "And anyway, it's all arranged. We fly out at 0900 today. Nice spot the Bureau has in Bermuda for R&R. Secluded. Pink painted cottage on a private beach, thatch roof." His lips curved against my breast in a smile. "Skylight over the bed to watch the stars. Jogs down the beach, and piña coladas? No interruptions. What do you say?"

I sat upright, slid my legs over the side of the stretcher, and then hopped down to stand with my hands on my hips. I shook my head at Luke. "Don't just stand there. Help me find my dress so I can get out of here."

"Wait," he said, laughing and catching my hand. "Where are you going now?"

"*O-nine hundred?*" I raised my brows. "That's nine AM."

"Yes?"

I stepped toward him and rose up on tiptoe, lacing my hands behind his neck. "I figure we've got maybe four hours until we have to sit on a plane with our hands in our laps. Making nice and behaving ourselves?" I frowned. "Well, I don't intend to spend them

230

lying around here." I pressed my lips to his throat, nestled my hips against his, and heard his breath escape in a soft groan. His arms closed around me.

"You don't?" He smiled as my lips found the corner of his mouth. "So where would you rather be, Wildcat?" The ship rolled under our feet and Luke tightened his grip to steady me. To keep me safe—the guy was big on that sort of thing.

I smiled. Okay, my track record with men was pathetic and I knew that. But then, there was something about this Special Agent. And I'd just decided to give my career a second chance, hadn't I? That called for a celebration and any decent celebration calls for . . .

I traced the tip of my tongue gently across his lower lip and whispered before closing my eyes. "In your stateroom—tasting that champagne."

He nodded and I heard a soft chuckle before his mouth covered mine and made me forget everything else. Damned great vacation.

ABOUT THE AUTHOR

CANDY CALVERT is a registered nurse who blames her quirky sense of humor on "survival tactics learned in the trenches of the ER." Born in Northern California and the mother of two, she now lives with her husband in the beautiful Hill Country of Texas. Grueling cruise research for the Darcy Cavanaugh Mystery Series has found Candy singing with a Newfoundland country band, roaming the ruins of Pompeii, doing the limbo atop a jet-powered catamaran, and swimming with stingrays. Visit her website at: www.candycalvert.com.